A DAISY BLOSSOMS

Daisies can blossom in barren soil

The story of a girl who begins life as watercress
seller in Victorian London

Cecilia Pyke

A DAISY BLOSSOMS

Chapter 1

Daisy froze as something soft and furry snaked around her bare legs. Wide-eyed with horror she gasped and caught her breath. Was it a rat? There were plenty roaming the streets of London and she'd heard they ate children. She couldn't scream in case it became frightened and ran up her leg, so stood still, not daring to move. Then she heard a soft purring sound and realised her stupidity. It was a lonely cat, looking for affection and she smiled with relief as she bent to stroke its sleek fur.

Standing up, she pulled her tattered shawl closely round her shoulders, and continued to trudge through the streets in her bare feet. It was a December morning in 1851 and the cold penetrated her fragile bones as she made her way to Covent Garden to buy watercress. It was a long walk from her home in Mile End and she must reach the market early in order to get the decent leftovers. Shopkeepers and lodging houses took the prime cress, and Daisy needed the best of what remained to sell to workmen for their sandwiches. If she was late, they'd have gone to their jobs and she'd lose their custom. She shivered and tried to quicken her pace, even though the cobbled streets were hard on her feet. She'd discarded her old boots the previous week when their fragmented soles finally left the uppers.

Fog lay thick on the ground and figures appeared through the gloom, but they took no notice of five-year old Daisy. They were too deeply immersed in their own quest for survival. Life for the likes of them was hard, with inadequate shelter and little opportunity for employment.

When she smelled coffee, Daisy breathed a sigh of relief, knowing her destination was near. She stumbled towards the bustle of Covent Garden where her friend, Blackie — an African — ran the coffee stall. He was thickset and more than six feet tall and as he greeted her genially, his jet black skin emphasised his beautiful white teeth.

"Good morning, little missie, come and warm your hands."

Daisy had no money for food but Blackie, ever aware of her wan little face, handed her a half eaten sausage roll cast aside by some frolicking theatregoer. She accepted the food gratefully, warming her hands over his stove as she looked longingly at the sheep's trotters, baked potatoes and thick pea soup.

"Thanks Blackie, it ain't half cold today." She picked up a used coffee mug and drank the dregs as she called her thanks again and made her way to Sparrow, who supplied her with watercress.

"Watcher, Sparrer. Got anything any good left today?"

"Saved you some, darlin'. Cop this." He threw a bundle of cress to her, which she took to the tap at the side of the square. She flicked it to and fro under the running water to ensure it was as clean as possible for her customers, before drying her cold fingers on her tattered apron.

Daisy had been a cress seller for a year now and had come to tolerate her red, swollen fingers and freezing feet with their blackened toenails. She had to do it. There were mouths to feed at home. Dad toiled for the blacksmith from six in the morning until seven at night, and his wages barely covered the rent. Mum took in mending from one of the big houses, but was able to provide only meagre meals with the little money she received in return. The few coppers Daisy earned from cress selling were spent on fuel for the stove. There were three more children at home, Maudie who was four, Billie now two and Lily, the baby.

Daisy frowned as she recalled her parents' conversation last evening when they thought she was asleep.

"This one's going to a waifs and strays home and that's a fact," came her mother's angry cry.

"No, you can't do that, Em! *We* can't do that. We'll manage somehow," her father had pleaded. But her mother was adamant.

"We can't feed the mouths we've got and with another one on the way, we'll be done for. If you lose yer job, it'll be the work'ouse for the lot of us. You said yerself that old Bolton was thinking of laying you off."

"I do me best, Em," came her father's plaintiff wail.

Daisy could hear her mother cluttering around the room angrily.

"You'll have to sleep with the kids in future. Look at me, I'm worn out with all this birthing." A casual observer would have thought her mother to be nearer forty than twenty-four, but her father sobbed pitifully.

"Don't do this to me, Emmie, you're the only bit of comfort I got."

It was true. Her father needed his comforts, although Daisy wasn't sure what they were. She worried about this as she started on her journey through London, stopping now and again to blow on her icy hands. On and on she walked, through The Strand, up the Haymarket, along Piccadilly and into Mayfair, with the occasional housemaid stopping to buy watercress from Daisy's tray. As the fog began to lift, the figures of other street sellers became visible. There were flower girls, milkmaids, pie men, bakers, Indian toffee men, to name but a few.

They, along with travelling musicians, were all walking the streets to earn enough money for food. With a few pence jingling in her pocket, Daisy looked longingly in shop windows.

She'd never known anything but poverty so accepted it as her way of life. She neither asked for much nor expected it, but as the eldest, felt she should be able to provide more for the little ones. Tomorrow was Christmas Day and in the past, Dad had brought home a chicken and some potatoes from the market, but there were never any toys, so a brightly lit toyshop in a narrow thoroughfare caught her attention.

She stood on tiptoe and peered through the window at the miscellany of playthings crowding the display area. Teddy bears and dolls nestled among clockwork models, china tea sets and other things to delight a child. Books and games were piled around the perimeter, all having been festooned with silvery garlands. Daisy gazed in wonder but without envy; such luxuries were unattainable and of no more than a passing interest.

The growl of wheels caught her attention and a coach emblazoned with a coat of arms pulled up beside her. Startled, she scuttled into a nearby doorway and watched with interest as a tall woman stepped out of the coach and entered the toyshop. Daisy waited for her to come out again and after some time, she reappeared with her arms full of packages.

With the help of the shopkeeper she handed them to the coachman before noticing Daisy who was about to come out of her hiding place. The woman crossed the narrow road and bought some cress, sniffing disdainfully as she handed Daisy the payment. As the coach slowly rumbled off, Daisy noticed a parcel in the street and ran to pick it up before darting back into the doorway.

Pulling the wrapping apart she discovered a box and when she carefully lifted the lid found a doll wrapped in layers of soft tissue paper. The doll's body was made of leather and its porcelain face was beautifully painted. The china legs and arms could be moved and it was smartly dressed in minute, but perfectly sewn clothes. It had obviously been bought for some rich child. Maudie would love it, Daisy thought, and was tempted to take it home but remembered the significance of the following day.

Although tomorrow was Christmas Day, it was also *her* birthday. Her mother had told her that because she and Jesus shared the same birthday, she was special. She knew she'd betray the trust of Jesus if she kept the doll, so went into the shop to ask the address of the owner.

"That woman what just come in the coach, where does she live?" she asked, as she wiped her nose on the sleeve of her dress. The shopkeeper coughed as he noted the child's ragged appearance and reacted with suspicion. "I beg your pardon. Why do you want to know?"

"I've got something for 'er."

"She won't thank you for pestering her and I'm not at liberty to disclose her address." He cleared his throat pompously and waved her away.

"Right," said Daisy defiantly, "I'll find out some other way, and let 'er know you wouldn't tell me."

"In that case, it's Bloomsbury; second turning past the square. Number 88, next to where the judge lives," growled the man. "I don't suppose they'll have any truck with you. Now be off!"

"Thanks, Sir."

She ran down the steps and into the street. At least Bloomsbury wasn't far off her route home and she might sell the rest of the cress on the way. The streets were becoming busier now and she made her way through alleys where street urchins lurked to pick the pockets of inattentive shoppers. "*Stop thief,*" was a familiar cry. She passed areas where tiny children played in garbage thrown from windows, seemingly oblivious of their near nakedness. Their parents congregated in groups, smoking and drinking gin, their speech a cacophony of various languages and dialects, interspersed with shrieks of laughter and wails of despair.

Daisy hurried on and when she found the house, it looked very grand. It was terraced and arranged over five floors. The outside walls had been newly painted in cream, and its windows gleamed against black, shiny frames. Surely one family didn't occupy the whole house? Daisy knocked on the polished brass knocker moulded in the shape of a lion's head. She stepped back smartly, thinking for a moment it might bite her. A man dressed in striped trousers and a black coat answered her rap and snorted disdainfully at the figure before him, before glowering from mistrustful eyes. "What do you want? We don't answer to beggars."

"I want to see the woman what dropped a parcel."

"If you have business, go to the back of the house." The door was slammed in her face so Daisy went down the area steps and tapped on the glass panelled door. Her knock was answered by a maid, who viewed Daisy's ragged appearance with distaste, raising her eyebrows imperiously before enquiring,

"Can I help you?"

Daisy held up the parcel. "I found this. It fell out of your mistress's coach."

The maid stepped back into the passage. "Cook!" she called out. "There's a small person here what says she's found something

5

belonging to Mrs Withers. Remember she went shopping in the coach this morning?"

The cook came to the door and sniffed at Daisy, but suggested she follow her through the dark passage leading to the basement rooms and into the kitchen.

Daisy had never been in such a large room and was overcome by the delicious smells that wafted up her nose. She handed over the parcel and prompted by Cook told how she had found it. "I was waiting to look in the shop winder again, see, and when the coach went off I seen it must 'ave dropped something. I got this address from the shopkeeper and thought I could sell me cresses on the way. No trouble really."

Cook gave her a pitying glance, taking note of the worn clothes and blue fingers. "I'll get you some nice hot soup, love?" She shouted to a girl who was peeling vegetables. "Becky! Get a bowl of soup."

The girl put down her knife and went to the large pot that was simmering on the range. Daisy watched as she ladled thick soup into a basin and on Cook's instructions, added bread, and a large chunk of ham and pickles.

Daisy ate ravenously and was wiping her plate clean with a thick slice of freshly made bread, when she recognised the tall figure entering the room.

"Is this the girl?" the housekeeper enquired of Cook.

"Yes, Mrs Withers." Cook flicked her eyes in Daisy's direction and the woman continued,

"Ah yes — there she is."

She nodded to Cook and added by way of explanation. "I bought some cress from her today."

She turned to Daisy. "I hear you have the doll I bought this morning. I'm impressed with your honesty. Here." She dropped a few coins into the girl's grubby hand, a frown creasing her forehead as she addressed the cook again.

"She needs some warm clothes. There must be something outgrown in the attic wardrobes. Send Amy up to ask Nanny, and give the girl some food for the family. Perhaps a plum pudding would be appropriate."

She swept out, with keys rattling on the long silver chain she wore around her waist. A maid scuttled up the backstairs to fetch the clothes from Nanny and while she was waiting, Daisy looked around the kitchen. Pots and pans gleamed in the glow from the fire, above which hung a side of beef being slowly roasted on a spit. As the fat missed the pan beneath, it fell spitting and hissing into the coals.

Pine dressers were laden with carefully labelled preserves of all kinds, and shelves held matching crockery and bowls of fruit. Cook continued to roll out pastry, slicing and placing it on baking dishes, before coating it with milk in light, deft movements. Smells of spice and roasting beef fused, and to Daisy, this was some kind of heaven.

"Any jobs going 'ere?" she enquired, swinging her thin legs under the table.

"Not for you, missie, you're too small. We don't take 'em until they're eleven at least, when they've got some muscles. You need strong arms to lug the water for bathing upstairs, not forgetting coal for fires."

"What about when I'm eleven then?"

Cook nodded as she trimmed the edges of a pie. "You can always come and see us then. I expect your Mum needs you just now and if you worked here, you'd have to live in."

She was right. Daisy was needed at home and as soon as she was kitted out with boots, a warm dress and a shawl, she picked up the bundle of food and started her journey back to Mile End.

As she plodded towards home her spirits lightened, thinking how she could entertain the family with the tale of her adventure. Mum and Dad would be pleased with the food and she could tell them all about that lovely kitchen and the wonderful smells. She almost skipped up the rickety stairs with her bundle and was surprised to find the door to their rooms unlatched.

She pushed it open carefully and gasped when she found the place deserted. It had all gone, wobbly furniture, her mother, kids, everything. She ran around the empty rooms looking for some sign of her family, but there was nothing to give her a clue as to where they might be. Panicking, she ran to the woman who lived opposite and banged on her door crying, "Polly, Polly, where's me Mum and Dad, and the kids?"

When the woman answered the door, she took Daisy's arm and led her into the parlour.

"There's no easy way to say this, Dais. They've gone to the work'ouse. Your dad was put off when he went to work this morning."

"But why didn't they wait for me?"

Polly patted her bright orange hair and licked her recently rouged lips before plunging on. "Your mum left a message. She said you're a big girl now and must look after yourself as best you can."

"But what will I do on me own? What's the work'ouse like? Will they be all right?"

Polly averted her eyes. "They ain't bad places, Cocker. Not bad. It's a roof over their heads, ain't it?" She inspected her nails and added, "I expect you'll hear from them soon."

Daisy wasn't so sure. If it was all right in the workhouse, why did people dread going there? She'd heard them talking about it on the streets. 'I'd rather die than go in one of them places,' she'd heard someone say. She felt so alone. Her family had gone and with it, her home. She looked up at Polly.

"Can I stay with you?"

Polly looked askance. "Of course not. It ain't right."

"Why not?"

"Your mum must have told you. I have gentleman callers."

"I won't get in the way. I'll disappear into the bedroom when they visit."

Polly was firm and shook her hennaed curls. "I need my bed for my callers. You're too young to understand." She continued to study her nails as Daisy countered, "I could help. I could run errands, peel potatoes. I could do all sorts of things."

But Polly was emphatic. "No, Daisy. I've never had no kids of my own and I ain't about to take on nobody else's. You can leave your things with me until you get settled. I shan't be going nowhere."

"All I've got is what I stand up in. I've got some food though." Daisy looked up at Polly hopefully, but she was adamant.

"I'm not short of food. You'll have to go now, I'm expecting someone any minute." She shoved the girl out of the door and closed it smartly.

Daisy slept on the bare floorboards in her old home that night. She'd have to be out in the morning. Mr. Tranter, the landlord, would have no difficulty in moving another wretched family into the rooms.

After an uncomfortable nights sleep, she washed her face under the cold tap in the yard and looked in the bag where she found a plum pudding and a bottle of sarsaparilla. Realising how hungry she was, she ate half the pudding and drank some of the cordial then put the rest away for later, before she ventured out into the cold streets.

Everywhere was quiet but when she heard music coming from the church, she remembered it was Christmas Day. Pushing the huge door open just widely enough to squeeze through, she sat on the back pew, gazing in wonder at the beautiful stained glass windows. The inside of the church smelled of incense and polish, and candles flickered on the altar. Mesmerised, Daisy watched the grease fall on to the starched linen altar cloth. Drip, drip, drip. As it settled on the cloth she felt her eyes close but was woken when the door closed with a bang, bringing a sharp gust of wind into the back of the church. The vicar was speaking and although she liked his voice, she didn't understand the sermon, but was sure it was beautiful. She listened attentively as the choir sang, with voices trilling upwards to reverberate through the rafters of the beautiful old building. She'd never been in such a wonderful place and wanted to stay in its warmth, but when the congregation rose, she slunk through the half-closed doors and began walking through the streets once more.

Chapter 2

There were few people about, only beggars and other street children, so Daisy sat in a corner of Trafalgar Square. She watched the pigeons as they fluttered and hobbled around the statues looking for food, their feathers a diffusion of patterns of white, black, grey and brown but like her, intent on survival. She was wondering where to go next when a voice broke into her thoughts.

"Wocher! What's your name?"

She looked up to see a boy of about ten years old. "Daisy," she said, "and I'm five. No. I've just remembered, I'm six, today."

He squatted beside her. "Wot? born on Christmas Day — I'm not sure if that's good or bad. Nice name —Daisy.

"Me mum said I reminded 'er of a flower when I was new born. She said what she wished for me was that I'd blossom into a beau'iful daisy."

"Nice thought, that. You waitin' for someone?"

"No. I'm looking for work."

"Bit young for this lark ain't you?"

Daisy was puzzled. "What lark?"

"You know. Living on the streets. No family?"

She shook her head. "Me dad lost his job. They're in the work'ouse. What's your name?"

"Tom."

"Tom what?"

The boy stood up and tucked his fingers in the lapels of his frayed jacket and looked at her proudly as he rocked on his heels. "Thomas Ebenezer Albert Watkins. That's me."

"Coo! That's a long name. Want some plum pudding?"

"Don't mind if I do. How d'you make a living?" Tom got down on his hunkers and Daisy noticed his clothes weren't much cleaner than hers. His body was just as thin, but he had a cheerful way with him and she was happy to have somebody to talk to.

"I bin selling cress," she replied as she rummaged in her parcel and broke off a piece of pudding that she handed to Tom.

He snatched it and suggested, "Why don't you join up with me. I do the crossings?"

"Crossings — what's that?"

"I uses me broom and sweeps a clean path in front of the toffs, so they don't get their finery dirty."

"I haven't got a broom."

"We can get one easy enough. Two heads is better than one you know. Especially since you're so young. You need looking out for."

"Where d'you sleep?" asked Daisy, as she assessed him curiously.

Tom ran his hands through his matted hair.

"Ma Biggin's place. She sleeps about nine of us to a room. Puts a couple of old mattresses on the floor and we make do. It's better'n the streets though. We stuffs the broken winders up with paper and rags, and sleeps close together."

"What, everybody together?" she asked dubiously.

"Course. We keeps our clothes on so it don't matter."

Daisy considered his offer, realising she had to get some money for food. "How much does she charge?"

"Not much. I'll stake you for your first night. We can go to Ma's after we've bin to the soup kitchen. You ever been to one?"

"No. Me Dad said he was too proud. Even when we was 'ungry he said he didn't want charity." Daisy's face was glum as she rested her chin on her hands. "Now they're in the work'ouse."

"The food's not bad in the soup kitchens. You come along of me tonight. We'll go to old Cosby tomorrer and get you a broom. I'll learn you what to do."

"Thanks, Tom."

Daisy was pleased to have found a friend and chatting to Tom was better than thinking about her family all the time. She was disappointed later to find Ma Biggin's hovel was worse than she had imagined. The stench of stale bodies and dried urine stung her nostrils as she entered the front door.

Ma had only about three brown teeth left in her mouth, and spat when she spoke. "I hope you're not on the run my girl?" she queried, spraying Daisy with saliva.

"Course not," was the prompt reply. "I'm going to do the crossings, with Tom."

"I don't want no trouble. That's what I'm saying."

That night, Daisy slept on the filthy bedding beside Tom and got closer to him as the night grew colder. Sour vomit and excrement was embedded in the floorboards, and it was difficult not to retch. Drunks and tramps lay in various positions on the filthy mattresses, all too far gone to take any notice of Daisy. Tom woke her early.

"Come on, let's be having yer. Time for work."

Daisy yawned and started scratching her arms and legs.

"Here, there's bugs in these mattresses!"

"Stop moaning. All these places 'ave got bugs. Wouldn't be the

11

same without 'em."

"Is it still Christmas?"

"Sort of. Boxing Day. There won't be many toffs about but we can't stay here all day. Ma don't allow it. Tell you what, we'll look up some of me friends." Tom and Daisy sat outside the lodging house and finished off the plum pie and sarsaparilla, then trudged off to meet Tom's pals.

"Where do they live?" asked Daisy.

"Up 'Beffnal Green."

She showed Tom her blue fingers. "Will we be indoors, I'm cold."

"Gawd Blimey, you've got shoes on yer feet and a shawl. Who d'you think you are, a gentry?"

"Course not but there's a fair old wind today."

"You're right," he replied, rubbing his hands together. "Me friends live in an old stable. The 'orse died a long while ago so they just lines the place with straw and sleeps there. Nobody's cottoned on to them yet."

"How do they make money?"

"Any way they can. Jake's lucky. He works for a fruit and veg man in the markets. He keeps the boys going with food, really. The others, Sam and Lennie, they go into the country in spring and catch birds and pinch their eggs."

"What! Wild birds?" asked Daisy as she struggled to keep up with him.

Tom threw her an impatient look. "Course. What else would they be."

"My dad told me about that. He said it was wicked."

"I don't agree with it meself. That's why I don't go with 'em. I seen some of them poor critters when they's caged. Ain't natural but then it ain't none of my business and don't you say nothing to 'em or they won't let you in."

Daisy decided it was best to acquiesce. "All right."

Tom's friends were a lively crowd and Daisy warmed to them as she listened to their banter. The stables were a bit smelly but it was quite cosy and she kept nodding off to sleep while the boys played cards. Something was cooking in a large rusted utensil on the top of an old spirit stove. Every now and then Jake, who seemed to be in charge, gave the pot a stir.

"What's in there, Jake?" asked Daisy, nodding in the direction of the stove.

"A chicken and some carrots, taters, onions and parsnips."

"It smells good. D'you do all the cooking?"

"Mostly I does. Used to watch me mum when I lived at 'ome, like. I'm lucky. Me boss let's me have any leftovers of an evening. We don't get much meat but sometimes the boys net a couple of pigeons and we put them in the pot. Plenty of veg though. Fruit sometimes too."

Daisy sighed at the thought of fruit. "My family's in the work'ouse."

"That's bad, gel, bad. They don't often come out of there," replied Jake, as he tasted the food. He sat down on the straw and looked at her thoughtfully "What are you doing with Tom?"

"He found me yesterday," she replied. "In Trafalgar Square. We're going to do the crossings together."

Jake should his head knowingly. "Take you to that old doss house, did he?"

Daisy nodded. "Ma Biggins? Yeh."

"That ain't no place for you. I'll ask around. Me sister, Lou might know of something. She and some other girls kip in a cellar up Holborn. You'd be better off there."

Daisy hesitated, "Tom might not like it, but you could ask yer sister I suppose. Thanks, Jake."

"We're going ratting this afternoon. You coming along?"

"Ain't that where they set live rats on each other?" said Daisy, turning up her nose.

"Yeh, it's a good laugh. Many a time we've skinned a rat and made a stew of it."

Daisy shuddered. "Ugh. That's 'orrible. Don't like the sound of it. I'm scared of rats. They used to run up the stairs where we lived. A big brown one bit one of the kids once. P'raps I could stay here and sleep on the straw?"

"Don't see why not. It's quiet today, being Christmas still. I'll ask the others. We've got this deal, see. We all have to agree before any decisions is made."

None of the boys minded Daisy staying in the warm and soon after they left, she fell into a fitful sleep. She dreamed rats were biting at the baby's feet in the workhouse and that her dad hit them on the head with a piece of wood.

She woke when it was getting dusk and wondered if the boys would invite her and Tom to share the meal. Picking up the rusty ladle she dipped it in the stew. It was hot so she blew on it a few times before tasting it. The boys seemed to eat well. Daisy was used to not eating and the familiar rumble in her stomach didn't affect her much but at last the boys returned to the stable, laughing and shouting. Daisy realised they'd been to the alehouse. They regaled her with stories about rats while she sat in the corner recoiling with horror.

"Time we ate," called out Lennie as Jake looked around for some old tin bowls.

"Ladies first," he nodded gallantly, as he handed her a bowl, brimful of hot pungent soup. Daisy sniffed before she lifted the bowl to her lips and sipped. She savoured the taste as it trickled down her throat. The bantering continued while they feasted, and too soon Tom said it was time they were on their way.

"We must get back to the Strand so we can book our place at Ma's."

The following morning they rose early and called into the ironmongers to buy Daisy a stout broom.

"Now what you do Dais, is when you see a lady or a gent, get in front of them. But don't get so close as to trip 'em up, of course.

"Go to about three yards away, like this." He measured the distance with his feet. "Then start sweeping a pathway so they don't get their skirts wet. Or their trousis, as the case may be."

Daisy found the broom heavy but was determined to do her best. By the end of the day she'd only earned a few coppers but had at least found that by giving the gentlemen the benefit of a smile, she was more likely to be thrown some money. She made a pathetic picture, with her blue hands and dirty face. The ladies weren't so sympathetic, in fact most were downright rude, telling her not to get under their feet.

The second day was easier and Jake swapped his broom with hers, as his was lighter. They walked to Bond Street where there were fine shops and with their combined earnings were able to buy a pie from the cook shop, which they shared with great relish. Later, a visit to the soup kitchen staved off hunger pains during the night and by the end of the week Daisy's arms were used to the constant movement of the broom.

She learned to nod ingratiatingly to the women as she tried to dance around their feet, but she was often so hungry that she didn't have the strength to do more than drag one foot in front of the other. Had it not been for the soup kitchens, she and Tom would never have been able to work their brooms. One day, she offered to hold the lead of a lady's dog while she made her purchases, but the woman waved her away, saying, "Trust you with my dog? You'd sell it within five minutes of my back being turned."

"Course I wouldn't," Daisy replied, near to tears. "I'm honest, I am."

Within a few weeks she and Tom were scratching all over.

"We'll have to move," said Tom. Ma's letting her beds to all sorts now and next week the races are on. The Irish'll be swarming in and she charges more for race weeks."

"Can't we rent our own place? I'm earning more than I did. My boots need mending too."

"You're a cool one. A room'll cost two bob a week and we 'ave to eat."

"P'raps we could share with some other kids?"

Tom shook his head. "I'll have a think, but it'll cost too much. If we leave Ma's we'll have to kip in a cellar or under the arches."

That evening, Daisy sat outside the alehouse while Tom popped in for a quick one. When he came out again, he was leading a dark haired girl by the hand.

"Daisy, this is Blanche. She's got her own streets already, just up by The Dilly. She's going to join us. It's better of we stick in a group."

Blanche smiled. "How do?"

"How old are you?" asked Daisy as she eyed the girl curiously.

Blanche looked Daisy up and down in return. "Nine, you?"

"Only six. You look much bigger'n me."

Blanche, who towered over Daisy, smiled. "Me Mum was a big woman, before she died, that was."

"What did she die of?"

"Fever, when she had another baby. Went into the lying-in home. They all get the fever in there." Daisy was surprised that Blanche could speak so easily about the terrible thing that had happened to her mother.

"What about your Dad?" she asked.

"Took to the drink, he did. Then got up one morning and said he was taking all the other kids to his mother out in Essex — just like that. I don't like the countryside so I ran away."

The three of them spent the night at Ma's, with Blanche complaining about the awful smells.

The next day the girls swept the crossings while Tom went to look for somewhere to sleep. Daisy was just about to finish for the night when he re-appeared.

"Got somewhere!" he called across the street, a grin spreading across his face. "There's an old ware'ouse down by the river. Lots of kids like us sleep there and the Bobbies don't interfere. The kids get driftwood from the water so there's a bit of fire of a night. We'll have to watch our backs but it should work out."

"How much?"

"Nothing, so we can spend what we earn on food. Might even get a second-hand mattress down Petticoat Lane."

He took them to the market the next morning. The streets were littered with rubbish and teeming with people, many of whom who spoke in foreign tongues as they picked over the vast selection of merchandise on offer. The filthy side streets were desolate save for some broken barrows and drunks swaying from one side of the alley, to the other. The main area was lined with second-hand goods of every description, from clothes, bed linen, towels, furniture, toys, boots and shoes. Anything could be bought from an eager vendor for the price of a few coppers.

"Look at this," Blanche laughed as she held up an odd shoe. "A shoe for a one legged man."

They each bought a bun from a food stall and bartered with an old Jew for a grimy mattress. Having struck the deal, they struggled along the Thames embankment with it, before setting it against the wall at the back of the warehouse.

"Won't it get nicked?" asked Daisy.

"No. I'm paying the cripple man to keep his eye on it," replied Tom.

For the next few nights the trio spent their evenings round a puny fire before sleeping on their very own mattress. Sometimes, during the evening, Daisy watched mudlarks as they swam at the edge of the river. They searched through the mud in the rags they called clothing. If they were lucky, they found a few items of little value, and there was usually some driftwood they could sell. Although Daisy felt sorry for them as they slipped and slithered through the detritus, she knew only too well that if she didn't keep her wits about her, she might end up as a mudlark too.

She loved sitting on the bank, watching life on the Thames pass by. Sometimes lighter-men waved as they passed, wiping their necks on rags as they came up from the holds of their barges. Daisy would wave back, but more often she felt as grey as the river looked when she stared into its murky depths, wondering about her family. Would she ever stop missing them? Had Mum had the new baby yet? Were they still in the workhouse? Did they think about her? She had an endless number of questions and Tom promised make enquiries but held out little hope. Once in there, people were rarely heard of again.

Tears came to her eyes when she thought about her brother and sisters, hoping they had enough to eat and were warm.

By the time summer came, Daisy was a little happier. She had Blanche for company when Tom went to the alehouse. One evening they were chatting idly on the old mattress when Blanche asked, "Here, how much money d'you make, Daisy?"

"I'm not sure. Can't count very well. Can't do my letters neither. I just give all my money to Tom and 'e takes care of everything. Why?"

"Just wondered 'ow Tom can spend so much time in the beer shop. Looks to me as if he's spending the money you earn, as well as 'is own."

"I don't think so Blanche. He's really good to me. He got my boots mended last week and I get a whole hot pie every day. What about you? How much do you make?"

"Bit more than you 'cos I'm stronger. I can afford to buy more food than you 'cos I don't give my money to Tom. Crossings ain't no good. I'd like to get some other work but I don't know what."

"Let's ask Tom when he comes in. He knows lots of people."

With a yawn, Daisy fell asleep and Blanche followed suit shortly after.

As they scuttled through the streets the next day, they mentioned their idea to Tom, who replied, "At least with the crossings you can work for as long as you please. If you went back to cresses, well, once they're sold, that's you done for the day. No cresses, no income. I'd like to give up the crossings meself. I asked Jake once to put in a word with his boss for me. The markets are good — you've always got something to eat, even if you have to sleep rough. We'll go and see 'im at the weekend."

Chapter 3

However, it was Jake who came to see them early the following Sunday — he had good news for Daisy.

"I asked after you at Ma's and she said you'd gorn. My sister says she'll fit you in at her place. She's with five other gels and they all look out for each other."

"What would I work at Jake?"

"Selling fruit and stuff I think. One of the other girls is expecting and is going back to her family in Suffolk, so you can take her place. You'll go to Covent Garden about five in the morning, get your stuff and flog it during the day. They'll show you the ropes."

Daisy turned to Tom, who shuffled his feet sullenly.

"D'you mind if I go?" she asked. "You know I'm not really strong enough for the crossings and you've got Blanche now."

He didn't look very pleased at the suggestion, so she added by way of an apology, "I'll always remember 'ow you looked after me."

Tom gave in with bad grace and Blanche whispered, "He's got the 'ump 'cos he won't 'ave your money now, so it's less beer for him of an evening. He knows I won't give over mine. We'll get by. You go and good luck to you."

A couple of hours later, Jake took Daisy to Holborn to meet his sister. Coaches threw up dirt and dust as they snaked through the back streets, before disappearing drunkenly round corners. Access to the cellar was through a disused alley where the dwellings were uninhabitable. Front doors gaped open and windows were falling off their hinges. These hovels, with their crumbling floorboards, gave occasional refuge to drunks and tramps, who soon moved on when they realised the structures were unsafe. The whole area was infested with rats as evidenced by the smell of their urine, adding to the stench of decay.

The cellar was approached through a ramshackle lobby from where stone steps led down to the underground room. A flickering candle cast an eerie light on its occupants. The area was quite large with two mattresses propped up on one side. A couple of broken chairs were arranged round a three-legged table that was supported by some discarded masonry and a chunk of wood. A glimmer of light came through a small, grimy window that looked on to the bottom of the area steps.

Jake's sister proved to be a cheerful soul, with the same shrewd brown eyes as her brother. She smiled at Daisy who took a liking to her immediately.

"Me name's Lou, short for Louisa, come and meet the other girls." She stood aside as Daisy looked at Lou's companions, who were of varying heights and ages, and cautious in their welcome. Some of them had been on the streets for years and learned not to trust strangers.

"Bit young ain't she?" asked a thin girl named Lizzie. She was very pretty and stared at Daisy from large cornflower blue eyes.

"I'm six," interrupted up Daisy, indignantly.

"Blimey. Quite an old woman ain't yer. I'm Lizzie and I'm ten. I've got one foot in the grave, me."

Another girl rose awkwardly from one of the mattresses. "Can she work?" she asked as she limped over to inspect Daisy.

"Yeh. She'll be working with me. She's Vicky," replied Lou, pointing her finger at the girl as she continued, "I'm taking her along to Sammie's. I'll show 'er the ropes. She'll learn to pay 'er way."

Lou turned to Daisy protectively. "You stay by me. I'll look after you. You remind me of one of my sisters — our Ethel. She died of TB when she was only three. Lovely little thing she was."

"Where's yer family?" snapped a mousy looking girl as she eyed Daisy up and down.

"Her people are in the work'ouse," replied Lou, nodding in Daisy's direction. "And I'm taking care of her. Understood?"

"How do we know we can trust her?" asked another girl who was called Alice.

"Cause I said so. She's only been on the streets for a few months." There was a hint of menace in her voice and the other girls turned their attention to each other. "You just do as I say and they'll give you no trouble," Lou whispered to Daisy. "Be careful not to upset Rose. She's got a bit of a temper. Just 'cos I work the markets, it doesn't mean they all do."

"What do they do then?"

"All sorts. A couple do bits on the markets, or go with men when they can but it's best not to ask. We stay together 'cos there's safety in numbers. We don't let nobody know where we live and we don't ask no questions. That way we can't give nothing away. Understand?"

"Yes Lou. I'll do anything you say."

"Good girl. I'll tell you more about 'em tomorrow when we go up the market."

That night Daisy slept at the bottom of a mattress and turned towards the wall when the smell of unwashed feet became too strong to bear. At least Mum had seen they all had a good wash now and again.

As they plodded towards Covent Garden just before dawn, Daisy asked, "Which one is having the baby?"

"Florrie. She's the dark girl with curly hair. She's been keeping company with a docker's boy. Thought she was on to a good thing but he's ditched her now she's in the family way."

"Is she old enough to have a baby?"

"Must be, but she says she don't know 'ow it happened."

"D'you think she kissed him?"

Lou tossed her head. "How should I know? Keep well away from anything in trousers is my motto. That's what me mum used to say."

"My dad kept giving my mum babies," replied Daisy. "Said it was his pleasure."

"So did mine. He used to grunt like an old pig. I could hear 'im puffing and blowing — don't know why my mum let him, but she did."

"I hope I'm not having a baby."

Lou looked at her curiously, then replied, "I shouldn't think so. Just don't get near a man. Don't kiss him, or shake his hand, or anything like that. You'll be all right then."

"What about Rose? What's she like?"

"She's quick tempered that one. Always reminds me of a mouse, sniffing and scuttling around in the dark. If she had whiskers she'd be tweaking 'em. Don't know much about her. She was up before the Beak a couple of months ago, for nicking. She reckons some people paid him to get her off, otherwise she'd be locked up."

"And that other one. Vicky?"

"Vickie's not much older than you. Usual story. Her people couldn't afford to look after her, so she left to make a new life for herself." Lou sighed and shook her head, "Some life living in a cellar with us. She helps Alice sew on buttons and gets a bit of food in return. I only hope she doesn't get into bad ways with Rose. She's not been with us long. Found her crying up Endel Street one night."

They completed their journey in companionable silence and as they entered the market, Daisy was overjoyed to see Blackie. He beamed as she ran over to warm her hands at his fire.

"Hello there, little 'un. Where you bin?"

"Oh, 'ere and there. But I'm back now with me friend, Lou. I'm selling fruit from today, I think — she's learning me." She darted off, calling over her shoulder, "I'd best go."

Lou was busy bartering with a jovial man who was selling vegetables from a horse and cart.

"All fresh this morning!" he shouted at the top of his voice. Daisy saw Lou hand over some coins, hesitate, then part with some more money for a tray of violets. She beckoned and Daisy ran over to her.

"Did you bring that string with you?" she asked.

Daisy rummaged in her pocket and handed over the string for Lou to pull through holes in the box and then round Daisy's neck.

"There you are! Now, you walk about four paces behind me, and do some selling like you did with the cresses. I bought them violets for a farthing a bunch, so you ask for three farthings. Hold on — ask for a penny, if they look rich. Okay?"

Daisy nodded as she adjusted the string and Lou looked on approvingly. "We'll get going early and have a rest when we can't stand up no longer. We'll go up the Strand and make for Piccadilly where the money is. I got some reg'lars up there."

The weight of the box began to make Daisy's neck ache but she knew better than to complain. She trotted stoically along behind Lou calling, "Violets, three farthing a bunch. Fresh this morning," and served two customers along the Strand. One housemaid recognised her,

"Here, ain't you the cress gel?"

"Yes," replied Daisy, pleased to have been remembered, "I'm doing violets now."

"Here we are then. Let's be having a bunch. How much?"

"Are you paying?"

"No. They're for the missus's parlour so comes out of the 'ouse-keeping purse."

"That's a penny then." Daisy was learning fast that there's no friendship in business. They passed a couple of dandies near Burlington Arcade and she called over to them cheekily, "Come on, Gents. Buy yer ladies some violets —all fresh today."

The men swayed across the road while Lou watched what was going on, from a respectable distance. "And who do we have here? You're a pretty one, if somewhat grubby."

"Me name's Daisy." She smiled, sorry that a front tooth had fallen out that morning. However, it served only to add to her charm.

"And what would you do for me, if I bought, say, two bunches of violets?"

"Do for you, Sir?"

She heard Lou's impatient voice. "Come on, Daisy. We're late."

With the string of the basket cutting into her neck, Daisy ran towards Lou who admonished her. "We don't need customers like that. There's some nasty men in this world. You sell flowers — they pay you. Never make any promises or go off with 'em. There's evil people about. Anyway, I think it's about time we had a stop."

They walked into Green Park where Lou dropped her basket on to the grass.

"Take yer tray off and I'll get some bread and soup off that stall over there."

Daisy released the tray and put in on the grass beside her before she lay back in the sunshine. She watched as the sun shone through the green leaves, changing their colour to pale yellow. Some fluttered to the ground where they waited to be tossed by the breeze. Lost in wonder, she fell fast asleep and was woken by Lou's angry voice.

"Christ Almighty, you can't fall asleep round 'ere. Where's me basket and the violets?" She stamped her foot and glared at Daisy. "You bloody little fool, someone's nicked 'em. I ought to dump you, here and now."

Daisy's response was to wail loudly, frightened by the tone in Lou's voice.

"Don't throw me out, Lou. I was worn out. I didn't mean to fall asleep. What can we do?"

"Nothing at all. Just have another go tomorrow. How much did you sell?"

"Four bunches."

"So you've got three pence and a farthing?"

"Yes. Here you are — take it." Daisy thrust the coppers at Lou, whose face softened when she recognised Daisy's real distress.

"Never mind, gel," she replied, kindly. "It was a bad place to stop anyway. Full of foreigners, up here. It's okay if you keep to the main streets but it's easy to get robbed in the parks."

"Sorry, Lou."

"Forget it. Let's have our grub and go over to the lake in Buckingham Palace Gardens. We may as well enjoy the rest of the day. We can watch the ducks on the water. It'll be the first time I've been there in ages. I usually go to Hyde Park when I get the time. It's lovely by the Serpentine but they've got the Exhibition on now and there's people swarming all over the place."

"What's an exp..ition?"

"It's where people show off what they can do and all the things they've made and that. You know, for other people to buy. They reckon it's wonderful, full of the most lovely fings. It's all made of glass and so big they had to build it round the trees. The Queen's always there. Prince Albert 'elped to design it, so they say."

"You ever seen the Queen?"

"No. I saw Prince Albert go by in his coach once though. Handsome man, he is. He's got lovely moustaches, so I can see why she loves him."

"Have you been inside the ex...pe-ition thing? I wouldn't mind seeing it meself."

"It's not for the likes of us, Dais. It finishes in October. Supposed to be going to Sydenham, so I'm told. Don't care much."

The soup was hot and spicy and when they were refreshed, Lou and Daisy strolled on to Buckingham Palace Gardens, where they sat on the grass. Nannies pushing baby carriages, swept past haughtily, as if the wealth they represented was their own.

"Don't they look daft in them funny 'ats!" giggled Lou as they watched one nanny running after a small charge. The child seemed determined to jump into the water and nearly dragged his nurse in with him. Laughing, the girls spent the rest of the afternoon in the park, until the sun began to drop behind the trees.

"We'll have to make do with bread and dripping tonight," commented Lou as they walked back to the cellar.

"Sorry," whimpered Daisy once again.

"Forget about it. We'll make it up. You've got things to learn."

"Nothing never 'appened to me when I was selling cress."

"You was just unlucky today."

"You were going to tell me about the other girls."

"Oh yeh. Well, you know about Florrie — she's waiting for a letter to say she can go home. Then there's Alice, she's the girl with the limp. Alice does some market work but sews on buttons and things for a dressmaker as well. She's a lovely little stitcher, is Alice.

"She's got beautiful hair, ain't she?"

"Yes. Get's it from her Irish dad she says. Lots of the Irish is red. Your 'airs a lovely colour red too — are you Irish"

"Don't fink so. What about Lizzie?"

Lou grimaced as she thought about Lizzie. "A miserable cow, she is. Her people are Maltese. Catholic they are, and her mother has a baby every year. She let's 'em stay at home until they're six, then tips 'em out of the nest. I think Lizzie goes to see her now and again."

"How does she live? poor thing."

"Poor thing? She's no worse off than you and she's ten. She buys and sells. Just leave it at that."

As they neared home they passed a vendor with a tray of bread on his head.

"How much?" asked Lou and laughed when he named his price.

"But it's almost stale by this time of day," she retorted. "You know it's only fit for pigeons." She tossed him a farthing and he handed over a loaf to which they added a small wedge of cheese when they passed a dairy.

They ate their bread and cheese in the cellar. Only Florrie was at home.

"Heard from your Gran yet, Florrie?" asked Lou speaking with a mouth full of food.

Florrie shook her head. "No. I should've heard by now." She moved awkwardly as she tried to get up and although she was thin, her swollen belly impeded her. Daisy and Lou watched as she held on to the brickwork for support. Lou hadn't realised how tired the pregnant girl was.

"You worried?" she asked. "You look it. It seems a long time since you sent word to them."

"To tell the truth, I am in a bit of a state. They may have moved or something. Never was reliable."

Lou looked at the girl sympathetically. "When d'you think you're due?"

"Not sure. Ain't seen no doctor. Went to old Kate last week and she said not too long now."

"Christ! hope you don't have it in here."

"So do I," came the retort. "I don't know what I'd do with it."

"How d'you think it got in yer stommick?" interrupted Daisy, who'd been listening to the conversation with interest. Florrie wasn't offended at the question and answered indifferently.

"It was the docker's boy. He did it to me."

Daisy chewed thoughtfully before she nodded knowingly. "He grunted on you then?"

Florrie didn't have time to reply before Rose came through the cellar door. As she slammed it shut with her foot she called out nastily as she nodded in Florrie's direction, "Still here then? Beware young Daisy. That's what you get for eels and mash of a Friday night."

"You cow!" yelled Florrie. "You're only jealous because nobody takes any notice of you."

"Notice, my arse! Look at the state of you. He wasn't interested in you my girl. As far as I'm concerned, you only got what you asked for."

"I'm not asking you, so shut your mouth."

"Now, now girls," called out Lou in an effort to diffuse the situation. "Come and sit over here with us, Florrie." She broke her off a piece of bread and tossed it in her direction. "Cop this."

"You won't tell them about when I fell asleep, will you?" whispered Daisy.

"Not on your life, young'n."

The following day was better for Daisy. She sold six bunches of bronze-coloured chrysanthemums and handed the money to Lou, who counted out some coins and gave the rest back to her.

"I don't want your money," Lou shoved Daisy's hand away. "You earned it."

"But I've never kept me money. First me Dad took it and then Tom."

"Things are different now. You've got to grow up and look after yourself. All you need money for is clothes and food. You put away what you can afford every day and then you can use it for stock. P'raps you can do fruit next year. Oranges are a good seller." Daisy felt very grown-up as her collection of coins grew bigger. She hid them behind a loose brick when the others weren't around. It was easy to find hiding places in the dark crevices of the crumbling cellar.

A couple of nights later she was awoken by a familiar sound. She sat bolt upright and peered through the gloom. Florrie was rolling around on the mattress with Lou and Lizzie wiping her forehead. Rose woke suddenly too, and realised what was happening.

"Bleeding hell!" she shrieked." She's giving birth — in 'ere. Tell her to clear off. We don't want no screaming kids yellin' their 'eads off. Someone'll hear and give the game away."

"Shut your mouth," commanded Lou. "She can't go nowhere. We'll have to take care of her."

"I could help," offered Daisy. "I used to help with Mum."

"No. You stay out of the way. Get some rags from that bag and lie down until we need you. You can take care of the baby."

Florrie screamed and moaned all night and just as dawn broken over London, her baby boy was born. Lou handed it to Daisy, saying, "Wrap it up and cuddle it to keep it warm."

Chapter 4

Daisy took the scrawny little body and bound it in rags as she'd seen her mother do. She held it close to her chest as it snuffled and tried to stretch it's limbs. The girls made Florrie comfortable and after she fell asleep, exhausted from her labours, they huddled together trying to decide what to do with mother and baby.

"Well, I've got to work," they cried in unison, looking at Daisy expectantly.

"So have I," she countered as she met their sullen expressions. "I'm trying to earn my stock money."

"We'll have to sort this out, here and now," cried Rose. "I think we should leave the two youngest with Florrie, and we'll buy their food for a few days. She should be up and around by then."

It was agreed. Daisy held the new baby close to her and watched the older girls leave for work. The tiny infant began to struggle, it's face red with exertion.

"It's hungry," suggested Vicky. "It needs feeding. What can we give it?"

"It needs it's mother's titty. Wake Florrie up and I'll give him back to her."

She was right. The tiny infant clung to Florrie's breast and the girls watched, fascinated, as it sucked.

"What are you going to do with it?" Vicky asked, as she chewed her matted hair.

"I don't want it," sobbed Florrie as tears began to trickle down her face. "I wonder why my Gran didn't write to me. She'd 'ave known what to do."

"Don't you love it?" queried Daisy.

"No! Scrawny little bugger. Looks like him. I've a mind to leave it on his doorstep, except I don't know where he lives. It's not fair."

Three days later, Florrie was back to normal health and needed to work so the girls held another council of war. "I've heard as how some mothers give their babies a mixture to make them sleep. You could leave it all day if you doped it, and it wouldn't cry," suggested Rose.

"It couldn't go all day without food," protested Lou.

"I don't like it crying all night. Keeps me awake. I think Florrie should take her chances and get the 'orse and cart home," Rose continued. Her remarks brought more tears from the new mother.

"I 'aven't 'eard from 'em."

Then Lizzie suggested, "How about dumping it outside the workhouse gates. That's what I've heard people do."

Florrie brightened at this idea. "It'd be looked after in there."

"I'm not sure it's such a good idea," said Rose. "Suppose someone catches us doing it? They might pull us in."

"We could do it in the middle of the night?"

After some discussion the girls decided the workhouse was the best idea. "Where's the nearest one?" asked Florrie.

It was Lizzie who replied, "There's one up near St Pancras. I've passed it lots of times."

It was decided. Two girls would accompany Florrie, so that should they be stopped by the police, they could scatter in different directions. The small posse, with Rose holding the baby, stealthily crept through the streets at three o'clock in the morning. A thin mist made their journey more eerie and the silence was broken once or twice by drunken laughter.

They stopped abruptly and hid behind a wall as they heard footsteps growing nearer. A couple passed them, and a gas lamp revealed a woman with a powdered face and brightly rouged cheeks. The lamp threw a golden haze around bleached hair that hung in wisps on her neck. She struggled with her keys as she unlocked a door under the archway. Her companion began pulling up her skirts as they lurched through the door, both of them screeching with laughter. When the girls heard the door being kicked shut, they continued their journey. The baby had been fed so he slept throughout.

It was Florrie who placed him outside the workhouse gates, hoping he wouldn't cry until they were well clear of the building.

"Thank Christ that's over," was the relieved mother's comment as they scuttled back to the cellar where they were greeted in hushed tones by the other girls. None of them were unaffected by the past week's events.

"You all right, Florrie?" asked Lou. She watched as the girl began to sob, dabbing at her eyes with a dirty fist.

"Poor little sod. I never even give 'im a name." The tears fell as Florrie realised the enormity of what she'd done. Although overcome with relief she still experienced the loss of the child that had grown inside her.

"Never mind, mate," soothed Lou, "It's all for the best. Just watch you don't get caught out again, and keep your legs crossed."

It was nearing Christmas again and the atmosphere in London was beginning to change. The markets came alive with ribbons, balloons and spicy smells. Christmas puddings went on sale, as did sugared fruits and dates. Families with a father in work, drifted through the streets selecting food and small gifts. Daisy began to sell nuts as well as violets and hid her meagre profit behind the brick, well aware that January would bring hardship in the form of an empty stomach.

Florrie, still recovering from the trauma surrounding the birth of her baby, decided to go to Suffolk in an effort to find her mother, and Rose took the early mail coach to Colchester to visit a cousin. The rest of the girls pooled their money for a chicken and some gin, with Lou scavenging around the markets at close of day for discarded vegetables. Daisy decided to buy sweets as another treat. She'd seen some blocks of coconut candy in the market, as well as chocolate-covered honeycomb.

They rarely ate anything sweet and she'd never had money before, so wanted to do something nice for the girls who'd so willingly taken her in. As soon as she was able she went to her hiding place in the wall. She felt behind the brick and was sickened to find nothing there. Panicking, she stretched her fingers, digging into the crumbling mortar but to her dismay there was nothing but dust.

"Oh no," she wailed, "Me money's gone." In despair, she sat on the soiled mattress and cried. The endless days of trudging round the streets, the haughty stares and the icy winds, what had it all been for?

Lou found her some time later and made it clear whom she blamed.

"It's that's that bleeding Rose. Never could keep her 'ands to herself. We won't see the likes of her again but you mark my words, if I catch up with her she'll know all about it." Lou put her arms round Daisy causing her to sob even louder.

"Never mind, love," she soothed, as they rocked to and fro. "It's life and that's for sure. Life for the likes of us, anyway. Pull yourself up and there's always something or somebody waiting to knock you down again."

Christmas day came and the girls rested, pleased to have a day free from work. Instead of putting the mattresses against the wall, they left them on the floor in order to rest as they bickered and shared jokes.

In the afternoon they ate chicken stew washed down with sarsaparilla and gin as they played cards. It was evening before Daisy remembered it was her seventh birthday and when she told the girls, they protested.

"You should've said," declared Lou. "We'd of got something extra for tea. Fancy having a birthday on Christmas Day!"

"Same as Jesus," rejoined Daisy. "Me mum said that made me

special. I wonder if she's thinking about me today?"

"I bet she is, young'n and I reckon she misses you no end. You was her first-born. She couldn't forget you, specially on Christmas Day."

Lou put her arm round Daisy and poured some ale. "Here, drink this. It'll take all your cares away."

Alice limped over to the girls and offered, "I could sew you a money bag for your birthday, Daisy — if you'd like me to that is."

Daisy looked at Alice's earnest face as she waited for an answer. The girl's eyes were shadowed with violet, which together with sunken cheeks, gave her a look beyond her years. It didn't dawn on Daisy that they probably all looked the same so she smiled determinedly and replied, "Thanks Alice, that'd be lovely."

"It's a good idea," confirmed Lou. "We all wear them round our middles. It's the only way to hang on to your money, I should have thought when I told you to save."

When the girls left the cellar the next morning, they were surprised to see the streets clothed in white. It had snowed during the night and there was an eerie quietness about the streets.

"I'm not going out in that," declared Lizzie and promptly ducked back under the cellar door. Lou lay back on the mattress and suddenly brightened.

"We could go and see Jake and his mates," she said. "There's always plenty of grub over there. If they're in, that is. D'you fancy it, Dais?"

"Course."

"Do your shoes let in water?"

"Don't think so. They need going to the cobblers though."

Gathering their torn and filthy shawls around them, they ventured out into the snow. Fine snowflakes fell steadily and began to settle on the rooftops by the time the girls reached the stable. Fortunately Jake was there and he and his friends stopped playing black-jack to make the girls some hot, sweet tea.

"Here," said Jake offering them each an old tin mug. "This'll warm the cockles of your 'earts.

They found a space in the bedding that hadn't been soiled by the scraggy old dog that now lived with the boys. Sinking into the warmth of the straw they stretched luxuriously and later drank some ale and munched hungrily on the pies proffered by the boys. The afternoon passed pleasantly and Daisy realised that, for the first time ever, she really felt happy. She and Lou sang as they plodded home through the snow.

They were not so happy to find that Rose had returned to the cellar while they were away.

"What are you doing back?" demanded Lou.

Rose's expression was petulant. "Live 'ere, don't I?"

"If you think you're coming back 'ere you can give Daisy back her money."

"What money?" challenged Rose as she spun round to face her accuser but Lou wasn't going to be intimidated.

"Don't pretend you don't know, Lady, the money you nicked off her."

"I didn't take no money," replied Rose indignantly. "I had plenty of me own."

Lou hesitated. "Who took it then?"

"Look here, Lou, if I'd had took it, would I have come back? I'm not the only one what lives here."

"You're the only girl that left for Christmas."

"Oh yeh. What about Florrie?"

Daisy spoke up indignantly, "Florrie wouldn't take my money, not when I helped her with the baby and everything."

Rose placed her hands on her hips and smirked. "Oh my, ain't you the innocent one," she sneered. "Her sort don't know no loyalty. She didn't work for a week and the fare to Ipswich don't come easy. Last we seen of her, bet your life."

The other girls waited for Lou's approval, while Rose glared at them defiantly.

"Well?" Lou asked her eyes glaring, "What about the rest of yer. Do we let 'her back, or not?"

They put their heads down and began to whisper and mumble between them, then nodded. Lou replied for them.

"All right. Rose," she said between gritted teeth. "You can stay but mind yer Ps and Qs or you're out. Understood?"

It was about two weeks later when Rose sidled up to Daisy. The cellar was empty as Lou had gone to the butcher to scrounge for scraps, giving Rose the opportunity to speak to Daisy alone. "I feel real sorry about your money, little 'un."

"Thanks Rose, but I'm over it now and I've saved up a few more farthings." Daisy was surprised that Rose was being nice to her as it didn't happen often.

"It's like this," Rose continued, as she watched the door furtively for Lou's reappearance, "I might be able to do you some good. Sometimes I need errands run and I could pay you to do it."

Daisy's eyes shone. "That's good of you Rose. I'll ask Lou."

"No!" said Rose abruptly, her lips tightening. "She won't let you. It's between you and me. You could get your stock money back. Be independent like. What d'you think?"

"Where would I have to go?"

"Not far. Just round the back and up Drury Lane. I'll tell you where it is. It'll only be a couple of times a week. I'll give you stuff to take to my friend. He's a dealer and he'll give you money for what I send you with."

"I'd like to help Rose but I'm always with Lou. It'd be hard not to let her know about it."

"She's not yer mother — you don't have to tell 'er everything. I'll leave the stuff in the old cupboard outside the cellar. Nobody ever goes in there because it's full of old rubble and I told the girls I've seen a rat's nest in there." Her brow creased in thought. "I could ask you to go to the shops for things. Lou wouldn't know no different. She'd think I was being nice to you."

Daisy nodded and beamed at Rose. "But you are being good to me ain't yer. So that's all right."

"Good girl. I'll tip you the wink when I've got something to go, but meantime I'll tell you exactly where the place it is. And keep your mouth shut."

At that moment Lou came through the door and eyed Rose suspiciously. "What you up to?"

"Nothing," replied Rose innocently. "Just chatting to Daisy about her family. Shame she's never heard nothing of them ain't it."

Lou ruffled Daisy's hair as she smiled at her affectionately. "They'll turn up one day, as sure as night follows day."

A few days later, they were all huddled under blankets to keep warm when Rose began wailing.

"I haven't half got a pain in me leg. Must be rheumatism or something from the dank weather. Couldn't go out and get me some liniment, could yer, Dais?"

"I don't mind, Rose. Give us the money."

On the way out Daisy opened the cupboard door and groped around until she found an old cloth bag with something heavy inside. She crept up the cellar steps and made her way through the back alleys into Drury Lane. Scanning the shop fronts, she found the one she thought was correct, stared in the window at the jars of sweets. *Henry Tibbet — Proprietor,* was painted in large letters over the window, not that it meant much to Daisy, who was unable to read. Deciding this was the correct place, she pushed the door open and as she did so a bell jingled above her head, startling her.

"Well, Miss?" enquired a large be-whiskered man. He stood behind the counter and looked down at her from behind his spectacles. "What is it, lemon sherbets, marshmallow, toffee?" He seemed quite kindly but she must have interrupted his dinner because the remains of his meal were running down his waistcoat.

"I've come from Rose. She said to tell you she's a friend of Jack."

Mr Tibbet bent to inspect Daisy more closely. "You 'er new runner?"

"I've come from Rose," she repeated, not understanding.

"I know. Like I said are you 'er new runner?"

Daisy nodded eagerly, "I'm doing 'er errands, yes." She handed the bag to him and he took out two silver candlesticks, humming thoughtfully as he held them up to the light to inspect the engraving on the bottom. "I'll give yer two shillin" he said.

Mr Tibbet pulled aside a curtain that led into a side room and Daisy stood on tip-toe trying to see what he was doing. He rummaged under a blanket and brought out a tin box from which he withdrew some money. Articles of all kinds were strewn around the room but at least there was a fire in the grate. A large cat was curled up in front of the flames. It hissed at the old man when he kicked it out of the way so he could put the candlesticks in a corner.

"Here's the money and tell her I'll take anything she can get hold of. Just don't you lead anybody to me, you understand?"

Daisy didn't really understand, but nodded in assent. "It's me and Rose's secret."

"Good gel. Here, 'ave an 'umbug." He took a jar of sweets off the shelf and handed one to Daisy with his filthy fingers.

"Ta very much." She popped the sweet into her mouth as she pushed the door open with her foot. Once out in the street again she ran to the apothecary where she bought the liniment.

"You've bin a long time?" queried Lou when she returned to the cellar.

"Yeh. There was lots of people waiting to be served." She felt bad about lying to Lou but knew that when she told her she'd be able to buy her own violets, Lou would be very pleased.

Instead she asked suspiciously, "What you been eating? I can smell something sweet on yer breath."

Daisy thought quickly. "Some posh woman in the chemists gave me an 'umbug. Said it was cold outside."

"That was nice of 'er." Lou seemed satisfied with the answer.

When the girls were walking to Covent Garden the next day Daisy asked Lou, "If Rose's always got money for gin, why does she live in a cellar?"

"I don't know, what makes you ask?"

"When I was with Tom he said he could get a room for a couple of bob a week and Rose is always half drunk of an evening so she must have money to spend. I just wondered that's all."

"She'd probably be lonely on her own. Although nobody talks to her much, we're still around in the evening and at night. It's nice just to 'ave somebody 'there. You get used to living like we do. It'd be funny for me, living in an 'ouse again."

"What happened to your mum and dad, Lou?"

"Neither of 'em was any good. Me mum was no better'n she ought to be. Always off with some bloke or another, and me and Jake had to do the best we could. Me dad was a thief and he got transported three years ago. Mum took to drink when he went. Gawd knows why she missed 'im. He clouted her often enough. She used to bring men 'ome to get the rent money and in the end she brought home some 'orrible bloke who stayed and filled her belly once again. She thought he was wonderful 'cos he used to get drunk with 'er."

Lou stared at the cellar wall as she continued softly, "Me and Jake had enough and ran off one morning. He did all right for himself. He got work right away with the barrow man. It's easier for boys. Lots of things happened to me but in the end I found this cellar. There was just Florrie 'ere then, by herself. Jake got me the job selling fruit and veg for Sammie and gradually the other girls moved in."

"I saw inside one of them big 'ouses in Bloomsbury once," observed Daisy, changing the subject.

"How come?"

"I found something that belonged to someone there. You should have seen their kitchen, Lou. It smelt like 'eaven. There was all this meat and things being cooked over the fire and the cook was making pies. I asked if I could 'ave a job but they said to go back when I was bigger. D'you think I'm bigger now, Lou?"

"Bigger 'n what?"

"Than I was?"

Lou laughed. "I 'spect so, nipper.

Chapter 5

A couple of weeks later Lou was laid low with a heavy cold so Daisy sold violets on her own. Rose lost no time in making the most of the situation and asked Daisy to run another errand. This time there were two pocket watches in the bag, and Mr Tibbet gave her a shilling for them.

"I've been bested," grumbled Rose turning the coins over in her hand when Daisy returned. "Old Tibbet'll make a fine old profit on them watches."

"He said something about there being lots of them on the market," explained Daisy, as she took the penny Rose handed to her. With her friend being ill, she had to provide food for both of them beside medicine for Lou, so the extra money came in handy.

One evening having not long returned from the streets, Rose whispered to her, "there's more stuff in the bag, when you're ready."

On the pretext of going to the apothecary Daisy wearily mounted the steps once again. She lifted the heavy bag onto her shoulder and made her way through the back streets to Drury Lane. Once or twice she thought she heard footsteps behind her as she neared the sweetshop but when she looked round, there was nobody to be seen.

Mr Tibbet greeted her warmly and the old cat, being used to her by now, arched his back as he came over to be stroked. His master spread the haul onto the counter and the silence was broken only by the loud ticking of grandfather clock which hung above the entrance to the back room.

"More bleeding candlesticks," muttered Mr Tibbet, shoving them aside to pick up and inspect a string of pearls. He peered through his eyeglass and made appreciative little sounds when he held it up to the light. A gold ring, a cameo brooch set in jet and some pocket handkerchiefs completed the array of stolen goods.

Suddenly the door burst open and two policemen thrust their way in the shop, truncheons at the ready. Their presence filled the tiny space and Daisy looked at them in awe. One put his tall helmet on the counter and grabbed Daisy, while the other took hold of a startled Mr Tibbet. The biggest policeman rocked on his heels, jutting out his chin as he thrust his face into Mr Tibbet's.

"At it again, are you, Tibbet?"

The shopkeeper looked to the floor and began blubbering, since there was no denying what he was doing.

"You're coming with us. We've been watching the premises for days and now we've caught you red handed once again. Her too." He pointed a finger in Daisy's direction. "We've seen her coming and going. You'll get a long term this time Tibbet. You sit there while we have a good search of the building."

The shopkeeper narrowed his eyes and protested. "I buy and sell. You know that. I help people out when they're feeling the pinch by lending 'em money. I wasn't to know the girl was bringing me stuff she'd stolen."

"A likely story," was the dismissive reply.

They handcuffed Mr Tibbet to a chair and a frightened Daisy to the brass rail which was fixed to the counter. The jars of brandy balls and sherbet lemons rattled as the policemen made her fast.

The first one scowled at her. "You stay there, Miss. I'm not letting you out of my sight. I know your sort, thieving little cow!"

"I'm not a thief," protested Daisy, "I was helping Rose out."

"And I'm a Dutchman's arse," grunted the policeman.

When they'd finished their search, Daisy and Mr Tibbet were frog-marched from the shop and taken away in a wagon.

"What'll happen to the cat?" whispered Daisy, as the police wagon rocked to and fro over the cobbled streets.

"Mrs Tibbet'll look after 'him," muttered the shopkeeper. "She lives upstairs. Fine mess you've got us into."

"Me? I ain't done nothing! What will they do with us?"

"I'll be sent down — and I dare say you will be too. They ain't got no mercy these beaks." He sighed. "My wife is used to me being in the nick."

Daisy digested what he was saying and replied, "The nick? I'm scared Mr Tibbet. What was I doing that was wrong?"

Mr Tibbet tried to explain. "Those things you got from your friend, let me see, what was 'er name — Rose? Yes. Well Rose is a thief but she ain't got the guts to do 'er dirty work herself, so she sends you to run her errands for 'er."

They were interrupted when it became apparent they were holding a conversation.

"Stop that talking, you two," commanded the burly policeman.

"But I ain't done no thieving," insisted Daisy, whispering into Tibbet's furry ear.

"You're guilty by the law nevertheless. They'll probably send you to jail," warned Mr Tibbet.

Daisy was trembling by the time they reached the police station, where they were both charged. That was the last time she was to see the hapless shopkeeper.

She was taken to the cells, which were already filled to the brim with prostitutes and thieves. Some were crying, most were drunk but all were dirty and ragged. Sitting silently on a bench amid the babble of coarse voices, Daisy concentrated her thoughts on her parents and the kids. The cells began to fill with more ladies of the night who were happily tipsy and sang raucous songs, while the rest of the motley mob shouted obscenities to all and sundry.

At last it was morning and exhausted from lack of sleep, Daisy was taken up some wooden stairs, to what she was later to find out was the dock. Three men were seated on a bench behind a table. The one in the middle looked very important in his fine clothes.

"What have you to say for yourself, Miss?" asked a red nosed man as he adjusted his spectacles.

"Nothin'."

"You will address me as 'Sir', Miss."

"Yes, Sir."

"Who did you steal the goods from?"

"I didn't steal them, Sir. It was Rose as asked me to deliver them for 'er."

The magistrates whispered to themselves and Red Nose said, "Yes, yes. We know all about that, but when the police found the cellar you spoke of, there was nobody there. Isn't that so?" He nodded to the policeman who replied pompously, "Yes, Sir. The rats 'ad deserted the sinking ship, so to speak."

"What age?"

"I'm seven, Sir."

There was more whispering. "What is your surname, girl?"

"Don't have no other name, Sir. Me name's Daisy."

"Very well, Daisy. We'll call you Smith. I think a spell in the prison might do you some good. Teach you not to steal again and not to tell lies." His eyes hardened as he squinted at her. "One year. Take her away!"

He rapped on the bench with his gavel and Daisy was removed from the dock. She almost fell down the steps leading to the cells again where she was given a piece of stale bread. Sitting on the cold floor she tried to ignore the stench and screams of drunks and prostitutes. She chewed the bread and wondered where on earth Lou could have gone, and why nobody had come to rescue her? Was Rose really a thief like they said? She'd been warned about Rose, and let Lou down. Tears of self pity began to trickle down her cheeks, making rivulets between the dirt.

Where would she be sent? She'd heard about prison and the things that could happen, but exhausted by recent events, it didn't take long for Daisy to slip down the wall and fall into a deep sleep.

She was woken by heavy footsteps and the rattle of chains as the key was turned in the lock.

"Out here, Smith," shouted the turnkey.

Struggling to her feet, she approached the half-open door where an elderly man looked her up and down. "Small, ain't she?" he sneered.

"All these pauper kids is small, Sir."

"What's her name?"

The turnkey looked at his list. "Smith. Daisy Smith. Says she's seven years old." He studied Daisy with a practised eye. "But small, as you say, Sir."

"I'll take her. One year, you say. Hum hum." He rocked on his heels then addressed Daisy. "You'll come with me. I'm Mr Grimley. You'll work in the laundry under Mrs Greenwood. The hours are long and arduous as befits a thief. You'll speak when you're spoken to and we'll only keep you, if you obey our rules. If you cause trouble, you'll return to be re-sentenced and sent to a place far worse than ours. Understand?"

Daisy's felt as if her heart would drop but she bobbed as a sign of respect.

"Yes, Sir. I'll do me best, Sir."

"Right — collect your belongings."

"I don't have no belongings, Sir. Only what I've got on."

She was led up the spiralling stone steps and along a dark corridor. They mounted more steps and at last she could see daylight through the small windows. Mr Grimley signed a release paper and instructed the jailer to open the heavy oak door. Holding Daisy by the scruff of the neck Mr Grimley shoved her into the back of a waiting cab and gave the driver an address. He was silent as they drove through the prison gates and the old cab rolled along the streets, with Daisy wondering what awaited her. It wasn't long before they arrived and she looked up at the grim, grey walls where she was to spend the next year.

Mr.Grimley took hold of her hand.

"Come along, girl, I'll take you to Mrs Peckerton."

They hurried though passages and down stairs until they arrived at the laundry. Daisy could hardly see through the mist as the vapour from huge cauldrons swirled around the great stone hall. Boys and girls appeared through a mist as they went about their labours. Their faces were grey as they toiled over the great vats, scrubbing and rubbing, and banging and hanging.

A woman loomed out of the gloom, looking down at Daisy from what seemed a great height. She had a long, thin nose with a red bump on the end. "That you, Grimley? Got another one for me I see?"

She looked Daisy up and down, exclaiming, "A bit puny, ain't she?"

"She's strong," replied Mr Grimley.

"What age?"

"Seven, so she says."

Mrs Peckerton sniffed. "What's 'er crime?"

"She's a thief. T H I E F. Make sure she pays for her sins."

"I will, Grimley. I will."

Mrs Peckerton took hold of Daisy by the ear and led her to a platform which housed both a washing vat and a vacant mangle. "Used a mangle before?" she asked.

"No."

"No, Madam, when you speak to me."

"Sorry. No, Madam," replied Daisy, as she looked around the laundry with her eyes open wide. Mrs Peckerton turned on her heel and addressed the boy at the next vat. "Brown! Come down 'ere."

The boy climbed down from the wooden steps and stared at Daisy.

"Look at me when I'm speaking, you impudent lout." Mrs Peckerton cuffed him round the head and he winced.

"Show the girl how to use the mangle."

"Yes, Madam," he muttered in reply. "Come here girl and I'll show you what to do." He moved to one side of the steps to make way for Daisy. She mounted the steps and stared into the huge washtub with dismay. On the other side two girls repeatedly moved the clothes around with a big wooden pole held in their red, swollen hands.

When they thought the washing had been rotated for long enough, they pushed them towards the boy who hooked them out ready for mangling.

"What's yer name," he whispered.

"Daisy. What's yours?"

"Barney Brown. Don't let 'er see your lips move, or she'll clip you one."

He showed Daisy how to hook out the clothes and put them through the huge wooden rollers.

"What you in 'ere for?"

Daisy looked round furtively before replying, "They said I'm a thief but I didn't do it. What about you?"

"Same thing. But I did do it. Took some bread from a baker 'cos I was starving."

"What's it like in 'ere?" asked Daisy, trying not to move her lips.

"Bad. Old Peckerton or Pecker as we call 'er is a cow. Smarms all over Grimley but 'e don't know what she's like behind his back. We don't get proper food 'cos it all goes in her stomick. Still, it could be worse. We could have been sent for transportation, like they do with lots of us kids. I wouldn't fancy being in the hulls of them old ships with the rats. At least you know where you is with cockroaches."

He looked furtively over to where Mrs Peckerton was harassing some laundrymen. She looked up and saw his glance. "Brown? Get on with it and makes sure the girl earns her supper."

Barney bent his head to the mangle and whispered, "Best not to talk. We could get put on the oakum – don't want that."

"What d'you mean, put on the oakum?"

"It's picking old ropes to pieces. Don't 'arf make your 'ands sore."

Daisy and Barney worked throughout the rest of the day, mangling and stacking the clothes ready to be taken away to another part of the washhouse where they would be hung to dry. Supper consisted of a bowl of thin soup and a slice of stale bread.

"We get the dregs of everything in 'ere. Stale bread, rotten veg, stinking meat," complained Barney. "We all sleep together in what they calls the dormitory and on top of that, we 'ave to wash in the mornings." He yawned as the warders hustled them all to bed.

Bed proved to be a brick shelf that was shared by about twenty other men, women, boys and girls, all huddled together for warmth. Daisy found a space and stretched her weary body as she drifted into a dreamless sleep.

The next morning she was given a mug of water, then porridge, before beginning another arduous day and thus began the longest year of Daisy's life. She made no friends, save Barney. The population of the prison was suspicious and unfriendly, so she deemed it wise to keep her thoughts and opinions to herself. There was no conception of time within the environs of the gloomy, dusty building.

Days passed in a haze of toil and hunger with Daisy spending her eighth birthday thinking about her family again. She knew it was her birthday when she saw Christmas Day ringed in red on the calendar Pecker kept on the laundry wall. Sometimes the inmates were visited by the clergy, who spuriously asked after their health before talking about God and his mercy. But Daisy no longer believed in mercy and human kindness.

It was a spring day in April 1853 when Daisy left prison. She was given a few coppers and told to clear off by the gatekeeper.

"See you don't come back again!" were his words of encouragement and farewell. She was eight years old and knew nothing, but what it was to feel cold and hungry.

Her boots had long since been outgrown and although she was pitifully thin, she'd grown taller. She held her red, dry hands up to the light and for the first time in her life felt frightened. She didn't know what was going to happen to her — she had no money, nowhere to go and nothing to eat. The fresh air wasn't bracing, it frightened her because it made her head feel light and feathery, so in a daze, she walked the streets and eventually found herself asking directions to Mile End, vaguely wondering if Polly was still in the old house. Even if Polly had gone, she'd feel more comfortable in her old surroundings.

When she arrived at the familiar street she felt a pang of emotion. Wouldn't it be wonderful if the family were back in the old house? She stumbled up the steps and banged on the entrance to their old rooms. An elderly woman answered the door, but Daisy couldn't understand her broad Irish brogue, so feeling tearful, she turned away without bothering to ask after the family.

Faint with hunger she knocked on Polly's door and whimpered.

"Polly, Polly, it's me, Daisy. Please be in and open the door for me." She heard footsteps and the sound of a bolt being drawn back. She held her breath and was overjoyed to see Polly's bright red hair.

"What d'you want. Who are you?" her old friend demanded, not recognising the pathetic waif who stood before her.

"It's me Poll, me from opposite. Daisy. Remember?"

Polly peered at the desolate figure, then recognition shone from her face. "You're not little Daisy? You've grown! Where've you bin?"

Daisy began to cry. "Oh Poll, terrible things 'ave 'appened to me. Let me in, please."

"You're an 'orrible sight, I can see that. Come in, Gel, and tell me all about it."

Warming her hands with a hot cup of tea, Daisy told Polly her story. "Can I stay the night Poll? I won't be in the way I promise."

Polly frowned. "Just for one night and before you sleep on my couch you can have a good wash. Hope you haven't got nits?"

"What are they?"

"Nasty little crawly things that make yer head itch. You been scratching?"

"No. Don't think so."

"Come 'ere. I'll bet you have." Polly washed Daisy's hair and combed it through for lice. "Look at the little buggers," she said as she popped them with her fingers. When she was satisfied Daisy's head was clean she wrapped her in a blanket and Daisy spent a disturbed night on Polly's sofa. She woke to find her slicing a loaf of bread. The smell was delicious.

"Here you are, you look like you could do with something in your stomach." Polly nodded towards the table.

Daisy took a piece of bread and spread it liberally with butter. "What shall I do?" she asked as she chewed ravenously, and frowned at the thought of tramping the streets again.

"You can stay for a few days and we'll see how it goes. It's against my better judgement, but I'll see what I can come up with."

"Thanks, Poll. I'll make meself useful. I'll run errands and keep the place clean. It'll just be until I get on me feet and used to being out in the daylight again."

Polly looked at her speculatively. "I've been thinking. I could get you a black dress made and a white apron and cap then you could answer the door to my gentlemen. I'm doing well enough and it'd be quite a novelty that, an eight year old maid. I'll think about it. You can start by making me a nice cup of tea."

"Thank you. Me Mum said you was a good sort. I never believed it when me Dad said you were a bad'n. You never seemed bad to me."

Polly absorbed what had been said. "He evidently thought I was," she snapped. "Must have had experience of the likes of me, I reckon. Now you shove off and make that tea."

"Okay, Poll. I won't let you down," said Daisy as she skipped out of the room.

"You'd better not."

Polly was surprised that the girl had retained her innocence despite years of rough living. She had just two gentleman callers that afternoon, and she and Daisy spent the rest of the day talking. Polly frowned in sympathy when Daisy recounted some of her experiences in prison, and her reason for being incarcerated.

"It's easy to get duped, Dais. It wasn't your fault, but it's best you put it behind you now. And don't let nobody know you've done time. You get a good nights' rest and we'll see how things go."

Even Polly's lumpy sofa was more comfortable than the sleeping arrangements in prison. It was upholstered in deep red velvet and had seen better days, no doubt purchased second-hand from one of the dealers in the market. Polly had done her best to make the parlour attractive by hanging net curtains at the windows, which were framed by red damask drapes with gold tassels. An aspidistra stood on the window-sill in a cracked ceramic pot, and a cheap rug covered uneven floorboards. It was far grander than anything Daisy had ever known and she appreciated her new surroundings.

Chapter 6

Daisy spent her first couple of days scrubbing the rooms and polishing furniture, as Polly had made it clear she'd have to work. Her bright red curls shook as she pointed a finger at Daisy.

"I don't want you to think you'll be leading no lady's life because you won't. Like I told you before, I've got no kids of my own and don't plan on bringing up anybody else's for free. So get stuck in."

Daisy's chilblained fingers ached as her hands were immersed in cold water but she scrubbed and polished and was grateful for a place to sleep, even if it was the sofa. When the cleaning was done, she fetched food from the shops and gin from the pub, becoming adept at dodging the outstretched arms of drunken men who loitered in the streets.

It took the dressmaker just two days to complete Daisy's outfit. She made a black cotton dress and produced two white cotton aprons trimmed with lace. A small cap completed the outfits and Polly bought her black stockings and boots. For the first time in her young life Daisy owned a pair of real leather boots that fitted perfectly, so she sat on a chair swinging her legs as she admired them.

"Thanks, Poll. They look really nice, don't they?"

"Lovely. I must say you look better after a scrub," admitted Polly. "Didn't realise your hair was that pretty, until we'd got rid of the tangles — and the nits." She tied the titian-hair in a bun but soft tendrils escaped to frame Daisy's face.

"I spend a fortune on henna for my hair and end up looking like me barnet's on fire. Wish it was natural, like yours. You'll be a looker when you've grown up some, that's no mistake."

Daisy smiled; delighted with the compliment and on the third day she started her duties as a maid. Polly was popular with her men, most of who visited regularly. She had a cheerful disposition and her ready wit was appreciated. There would be a knock on the door and Daisy would open it, bobbing a curtsey and chanting the prescribed words, "Good day, Sir, my mistress is expecting you. Please come in."

As they handed their hats to her, the men would duck under the low doorway and enter the small but now gleaming parlour. Polly would pour them a drink and after ten minutes or so lead them into her bedroom.

Daisy waited patiently, listening to the giggling and moaning, and wondering exactly went on, but the men were always smiling when they left so she supposed Polly must have shared some good jokes with them. Some tipped Daisy a farthing, or even a halfpenny, if they were particularly happy.

Polly knew about the tips and advised Daisy to put them in a tin. "People like us never know when fate will deal 'em another blow and if you ain't got money, you're done for. Like your mum and dad."

"Can't I keep some for sweets? I've never had no sweets. Only an 'umbug once."

Humbugs brought back the memory of Mr. Tibbet and Daisy wondered if he was still in prison. She hoped Mrs Tibbet was kind to the cat.

"All right, but only a farthing a week. They ruin your teeth anyway. Come on now, I'm starving, let's have some of that pork pie and pickle you got from old Harris."

Daisy was able to work out money for food but had never been to school, so couldn't do real sums. She told Polly she'd like to learn to read and suggested using some of the pennies she earned, to go to the school round the corner.

"What's the use of that," Polly mumbled sullenly. "I pay you to act as me maid and now you want to go to school. Is that all the thanks I get for saving you from the gutter. You're getting ideas above your station, Miss!"

"Sorry. I wasn't thinking. I know you've been good to me. It's just that when you're in the bedroom, I get fed up sitting here and if I could read a bit, I'd be more useful. Can you read?"

"Course not, you silly little bugger. Not properly any way. I got along all right without no learning; don't need it for my trade." She thought for a while then spoke again.

"Might be an idea though. If you could do reading and writing, you could read me out some of them penny novelettes I've heard about, while we're waiting for clients." She brightened visibly. "Tell you what, find out where there's a Sunday school. You know I don't work on Sundays and you could start after Christmas."

"Thanks. I will. You're really good to me. I'm a quick learner and you'll see, I'll be reading to you in no time."

"It'll give me a bit of peace too, you being out of the way."

Polly gave Daisy the money for a chicken and a plum pie for Christmas Day. She bought ale and gin from the beer shop for herself, and lemonade for Daisy. Her men would be at home playing happy families, she commented somewhat caustically, so she and Daisy spent the day quietly celebrating Christmas and Daisy's birthday.

The New Year brought Daisy her first steps towards an elementary education. She began attending Sunday school with other children whose lives made it necessary for them to work all week. She struggled to learn the alphabet and sums but enjoyed the scripture lessons more. She loved hearing about Jesus and his good deeds and her belief in God was gradually restored.

She still thought about her mother, father and the kids and wished Jesus would perform one of his miracles for them. She was sure if they were out of the workhouse they'd be seeking her out, and this was one of the many reasons she was glad she was with Polly. The local shopkeepers knew everybody's business and had promised to tell her, should they learn anything of her family's whereabouts.

She carefully hoarded her few coppers in the hope of the family being reunited. When she looked back on the days she sold cress and her life in the cellar with the girls, she shuddered. Although she and Polly hardly lived in style, there was warmth, food and comfort and she felt an overwhelming gratitude towards her rescuer. Daisy's frail frame had now filled out and her eyes shone with health. She was hardly recognisable as the demoralised waif who'd knocked on Polly's door nearly a year ago.

Although Polly had no maternal instincts at all, she had taken the place of a mother in Daisy's eyes and Polly in turn, had grown fond of Daisy. They staunchly defended each other in times of strife. On one occasion Daisy hit one of Polly's punters with a toasting fork when he refused to pay, and became abusive. She battered his back with little effect but it made Polly realise that for once, somebody cared for her.

Within time Daisy was able to read passages from Reynold's News. She'd stumble over the longer words but built the syllables up as she'd been shown in Sunday school, with Polly shrieking with delight at the radical views of that inspired gentleman. As Daisy grew they talked of moving to better rooms so Daisy could have her own bedroom but in the end, thought better of it.

They managed with the back room, parlour and bedroom. The lavatory in the rear yard was shared with six other families and nobody cleaned it, prompting Daisy to hold her nose when she emptied the chamber pot each morning.

By the time she was ten, Daisy could read and write and bought a daily newspaper to read out loud in the evening. Polly listened carefully to the hesitant words, her eyes wide with wonder as she learned of the latest scandals between the likes of actresses and the aristocracy. London was abounding with gossip. Daisy kept careful account of their income and expenditure and realised Polly made quite a good living. Daisy suspected that while she was at Sunday school, her old friend spent the day drinking gin but since she never became abusive like some mistresses, the girl reckoned she deserved some recreation.

She bought their food mainly from the markets where it was cheaper than in nearby shops. She loved wandering along the Mile End road swinging a basket on her hip with her purse tucked safely in the deep pocket of her dress. Ready cooked food could be purchased in abundance, from sheep's-trotters, meat puddings and eel pies, to tarts of every description. They came in all varieties, such as rhubarb, gooseberry, apple, cherry and damson, as well as cakes, muffins and crumpets. The stallholders got to know Daisy's cheerful face and offered her the best vegetables and meat. The fact that she rarely quibbled over the price, made her even more popular. Sometimes she'd buy a glass of sarsaparilla, and sample jellied eels or cockles from the fish stall, enjoying the hustle and bustle of the market and the cheery voices of the East-enders. She'd buy ribbons and combs for Polly's hair, always making sure she was home before the first punter arrived.

Due to the regular availability of good food, her eleventh birthday brought an adult body, with Polly's customers commenting on Daisy's rounded figure. Polly was not amused and Daisy had to carefully sidestep some of the men when they visited. They took to patting her small behind and trying to fondle her in more intimate places and while Daisy learned to accept these annoyances she admitted to herself the full implication of their calls.

As she grew more attractive, poor Polly became more unattractive, the years taking their toll, and one evening Daisy found her groaning and clutching her stomach. Daisy was frightened despite Polly's claims she would be all right. She begged to be allowed to run for the doctor.

"Not on your life," said Polly, wincing as the pains grew stronger. "Doctors die, don't they. What do they know?"

But Daisy remembered the night Florrie's baby was born.

"You're not having a baby, are you?"

"Course not, you silly little bugger. I don't like doctors. They know nothing," came the firm reply, but by midnight Polly was worse and Daisy insisted on getting help. The doctor remained silent as he examined the patient and when Daisy saw him to the door, his face was grave.

"She might recover for a while but what she has in incurable. It's the disease of her profession." He snapped back the lock on his medical bag as Daisy carefully counted coins to pay his fee. He took the money, adding, "She's paying for her sins."

Daisy nursed Polly for the next couple of months. In the first few days of Polly's sickness, her callers continued to knock on the door, but word soon got round that Polly was 'indisposed', and she and Daisy were left on their own.

The doctor prescribed more medicine and Daisy mopped Polly's brow when the pain got bad, but there was nothing to be done and they knew it.

Another Christmas came and went, with Polly telling Daisy to take some of her precious hoard of money to buy something for her birthday. Daisy came back from the bakers with an iced cake and tried to tempt Polly to eat, but she only took a few bites before putting the cake back on the chipped plate.

"Look at me, kid, I'm finished and that's a fact."

"Don't talk like that, Poll. I've already lost one family and I can't lose you too."

"It had to happen in the end. We all go this way, us tarts. Just you see it don't happen to you."

"How could it?" cried Daisy in alarm. "I can't catch it from you, can I?"

Polly ruffled the soft hair.

"Don't be daft. You know how many beans make five by now my girl. You just keep yourself clean and see that no man takes advantage of you."

"Don't you worry about that, Poll. No man's taking me down."

"Good girl. Thank goodness you can read and do your letters, so we can plan what you'll do when I'm gone."

Daisy sobbed as she stroked her friend's brow. "You're my best friend, Polly. Don't die on me."

As Polly grew frailer, she tried to advise Daisy. "There's money in that black tin box in my bedroom. There's plenty to bury me. I want a carriage with them black 'orses. Gawd knows I worked hard enough for 'em. Should be enough left over to see you through for a couple of weeks but the landlord will want you out. You'd best try for a live-in job."

"Go into service you mean?" said Daisy as she adjusted Polly's pillows.

"It'd give you a roof over your head my girl and some places is good to their staff. You might even make a decent marriage that way. You know," she added, her voice weak. "To some under-footman or something."

"I'm still only twelve."

"Yes, well I haven't gone yet. I'll try to hang on 'till you find somebody to marry you."

Polly started coughing and choking and Daisy supported her until the spasms subsided. Over the next couple of weeks Daisy hardly left Polly's bedside, except to run to the apothecary, and to get some food for herself. Polly had long since given up eating. Sometimes it seemed she didn't recognise her and called her 'Ma' in a thin, wheezy voice. She cried for something to deaden the pain and the doctor prescribed more laudanum, to be given when requested.

One morning, after a particularly bad night, Daisy dragged herself from the couch and put the kettle on the stove, before looking in on Polly. As soon as she opened the bedroom door, she knew her old friend had passed on. She thought people looked like angels when they died, having grown wings ready to fly up to heaven. That's how their passing away was illustrated in scripture books, but in death Polly looked grotesque.

"Oh, Poll," Daisy sobbed as she stroked her friend's blue-veined hand. She ran for the doctor who issued a Death Certificate and told her to go to the local church for advice on funeral arrangements.

Later that week, a carriage led by four magnificent black horses, took Polly to her last resting place. The horses stamped impatiently and tossed their heads as they waited for the small cortege to move off. A few neighbours stood with bowed heads as the carriage, with Daisy sitting beside the driver, made its way to the church on a dull February morning. The service was held in the same place where Daisy had prayed on Christmas Day all those years ago, and Polly was laid to rest in the churchyard later. Daisy beseeched God to save poor Polly's soul, and thanked Him for sending her such a good and loyal friend.

She went back to the flat with a heavy heart and knew what she must do. Together, she and Polly had planned in advance what would be best for Daisy's future. She could hear Polly speaking as she took the paper and pen from the cupboard.

"You'll end up in the gutter if you try to make it on your own. There are too many bad men out there, waiting to pounce on a pretty girl like you."

"But they won't," she'd protested. "I know how to take care of meself and I won't have a baby like Florrie."

"You mark my words, Dais. You should write to that 'ouse you told me about, the one with the lovely kitchen, and see if they'll take yer. God helps them wot helps themselves is what my old mum used to say. A live-in job is what you want. Somewhere that you'll be taken care of, even if it is 'ard work."

Daisy took care in wording the letter, not mentioning her previous experiences. She wrote that her mother had died in childbirth necessitating Daisy to live with her Aunt Polly. The untimely death of her beloved aunt was forcing her to seek a live-in position.

Within the week she received a cream envelope with a crest on the back. Trembling, she withdrew the letter and gasped for joy.

Would she please present herself for interview the following day? as there was a vacancy for an assistant nursery maid.

The next morning, Daisy washed and dressed with care. She tied her curls back with a ribbon and scrubbed her fingernails. In her hand she held the certificates awarded to Daisy Smith by the Sunday school attached to the local church. This time she went straight to the back door of the house in Bloomsbury, where she asked for the housekeeper.

She knew she looked nothing like the waif who'd found the doll more than five years earlier, so held no fear of being recognised. Having established she was at the very least, clean and respectable, Mrs Withers passed Daisy over to Nanny Bruce. The back stairs were covered with worn brown linoleum and the walls had yellowed with age. Daisy followed Nanny who was panting by the time they reached the landing. They entered a large cheerful room that was referred to as the day room and Daisy waited for Nanny to speak. Having been invited to sit down, she sat on the edge of the chair, clasping her knees together in order to stop them shaking.

"I run a very strict nursery, Miss. We usually get staff from the Registry but they had nobody suitable, and since you can write your letters, we decided to take a look at you."

Daisy nodded and pursed her lip as she was inspected. Nanny was Scottish and rather plump but her dress was immaculate and her hair, greying at the temples, was pulled to the nape of her neck in a bun. A crisp white cap was perched on her head and she wore an apron of the same material. She spoke sternly, with traces of a northern accent, but Daisy observed a suppressed twinkle in her eyes.

"Are you listening? What do you have to say for yourself?"

"Nothing, Madam," Daisy replied.

"You'll address me as Nanny, please. The successful applicant will assist the nursery maid who works directly under my control. Should you be lucky enough to be given the job, you'll be up at five o'clock every morning to lay the fires in the nursery suite, and boil the water for breakfast. That's before you rouse me and Phoebe, she's the nursery maid, and make the early morning pot of tea." She went on to tell Daisy that the carrying of the coals for the nursery fires was done by the scullery maid, as was the scrubbing.

"Before she arrives, you'll have to empty the chamber pots. Phoebe will show you how to go about that. After breakfast," she continued, "which the nursery staff take together, the children are woken up and given their porridge, which I make myself." She sniffed, dismissively. "Nobody in the south knows how to make porridge, in my opinion."

"Yes, Nanny."

"The children are out for a walk now but when they come back you'll meet them. There's Lord Harry, who's seven, Lady Adelaide, who is four, and Master George who's almost two."

Daisy nodded but didn't answer.

"Another baby is expected in six weeks time, hence the need for extra help. We usually only take girls by recommendation but as I have said, there was nobody available and we had to resort to the Registry. Why didn't you register for work?"

"I didn't think, Nanny. I knew of this house from somebody years ago, so took a chance."

"Lord Harry," Nanny continued, "Is collected by his tutor at nine o'clock every day and returned at four. He has lunch with his parents when they're at home. At other times he eats in the nursery. You will, should your application be successful, spend your day ironing, mending the children's clothes and making yourself as useful as possible. You'll dust the rooms each day and sweep the crumbs from the floor after meals. Sometimes you'll accompany me on our daily walks in the park, perhaps push Master George in his pushcart. How do you feel you'd cope?"

"I used to help my mother look after the k...children, so I'm used to it."

"I thought your mother died in childbirth. It says so in your letter."

Nanny took the letter from her pocket so Daisy thought quickly. "That's right, Nanny. She already had three of us when she died having our little brother, so Dad took the other kids to Kent — where me grandmother lives."

"I see. Why didn't you go to?"

"My aunt Polly asked for me. She didn't have no kids, children I mean, and she was poorly. I stayed with her until she died a few weeks ago."

Nanny put the letter away. "Well Lassie, you're not to expect an easy life because life in service is not easy, especially with lively children to keep occupied. You'll need two people to give a character reference. Will that be a problem?"

Daisy shook her head but wondered what a reference was. She'd have to find out about that.

"I think that will be all for now, Daisy. By the way, you'll get one half day off each month, probably a Sunday afternoon, but you must be back in the house by 7.30. Do you have any questions?"

Daisy shook her head, unable to absorb all the information the older woman had given her. Nanny rose and rang the bell for somebody to take Daisy downstairs again.

"Don't look so worried, lass," she said, almost kindly. "It's not as frightening as it seems."

Chapter 7

Returning home, Daisy wondered how many girls had applied for the job and whether she'd been over-optimistic to think she might be the lucky one. She wouldn't mind how hard the work was in return for a roof over her head and regular food in her stomach. It was fortunate that Polly had taught her a degree of table manners, having picked up ideas from her gentlemen callers. She'd been particularly fussy about holding the teacup with her pinkie finger sticking out.

Daisy had liked the relaxed atmosphere in the nursery and even though Nanny professed to be strict, she suspected her austere manner masked a mild disposition. And the children seemed happy. She'd glimpsed them briefly when they returned from the park, tumbling on to the top floor while struggling to take off their winter coats.

As she stirred her tea, she wondered about references, and suddenly the solution dawned. She'd ask the vicar at Sunday school about them. She went to see him that afternoon and he explained that taking them up was a normal procedure when employing staff, to ensure they were of good character. He offered to write one himself and suggested she approach the doctor to be her second referee. Since neither were aware of the misfortunes of her past, they would vouch she was clean and honest.

For the next couple of weeks she counted her money carefully each night, and dreaded the landlord knocking for his rent in case he wanted the rooms back. Despite her concern he said little as he noted the payment in his little book, but Daisy guessed he was already looking for new tenants. He'd turn a 'blind eye' while she had enough money to pay the rent, but after that another family would quickly move in. While she was waiting she washed and darned her clothes and kept herself to herself.

Just when she'd given up hope, an envelope came through the letterbox. The embossed envelope and superior quality of the paper was familiar. Tearing it open she read the words and sobbed with relief. She was to be the new nursery assistant to the family of the Earl and Countess of Hartswood. Due to the premature arrival of a new son, would she please report for duty as soon as possible.

Daisy decided it would be best to go to her new job the next day. She left a note for the landlord, which she put on the dresser and taking the bowl from under the bed, boiled a kettle of water. She shook her hair free from its bindings, then washed it with some of Polly's scented soap, leaving it to dry into curls. The following morning she sponged her body all over, taking particular care to scrub her feet and hands.

Before she pulled on her newly polished boots she tied her hair back with a black ribbon and when she was confident she could do no more to improve her appearance, picked up the bag containing her few belongings.

She'd kept Polly's brush and comb as a keepsake but put aside the remainder of her old friend's effects to be taken to the pawnshop. Daisy stored all the money she had in a little bag around her waist, just as Lou had shown her. She was to do this for the rest of her life. Tears sprung to her eyes as she looked around the rooms that had been her home for the past couple of years. Somehow the bright colours that Polly loved so much seemed less glowing without her cheery presence.

Daisy could hear her old friend chattering, ever optimistic and living for the day, seemingly not knowing hers would be so few. Daisy sniffed back the tears and lifted her chin before gently closing the door. Holding her head high, she called into Uncles and her business done, caught the bus. Taking her seat she looked out of the window, remembering when she tramped the streets in all weathers and as the bus rattled along the highway she couldn't help a smug smile. She'd done well for herself had Daisy Smith, and hoped her family were flourishing too.

When she arrived at her destination, an under-footman, took her to the top of the house where she met Nanny Bruce once again.

"I'd hoped to see you yesterday," she frowned. She appeared to be harassed and Daisy apologised for not coming straight away.

"Sorry, Nanny but I didn't like to come too soon."

"Well, put your bag down, since you're here. We've had an eventful few days. The new baby arrived unexpectedly and the maternity nurse can only stay for a week. What with you to train up, we'll be hard pushed with four children to cope with." She opened the door leading to the day nursery.

"By the way, when the children are with us, we don't use titles. His Lordship wants it that way, but you'll address the master and mistress as Your Lordship and Your Ladyship, should they speak to you. Which, they won't. Phoebe!" she called.

"Coming, Nanny!" A dark haired young woman came into the room and Daisy noted she had large brown eyes that crinkled at the corners when she smiled. She wore a pale blue dress with white cap and apron.

"This is Daisy. Take her upstairs with her bag and show her where she'll sleep. She'll wear her own clothes for a few days, until Mrs

Parkins can measure her up. I'll keep my eye on the little ones while you're upstairs."

Nanny bustled into the day nursery and Phoebe led the way to the attic rooms. The wallpaper on the staircase had faded and was peeling at the corners, as was the brown paint on the banisters.

"You'll share with me," Phoebe explained as she opened the door to one of the rooms. It was small, with the walls covered in a dull ochre paper that frowned at the brown paintwork. Single iron bedsteads stood alongside the two longest walls, each with a patchwork cover. A rug made from twisted rags was set on the floor in-between the narrow beds, and under the window there was an old washstand. It had a marble top and on it stood a bowl and ewer, which Daisy noticed was chipped and cracked around the lip.

Although it had seen better days it was still pretty despite the painted forget-me-nots, having long since faded. Phoebe pulled open a narrow cupboard door.

"This is my half and that's yours," she said, pointing to the appropriate sides of what sufficed as a wardrobe.

Although the room was clean it was cheerless, with a discoloured picture of some lambs in a field the only adornment. On the washstand was a Bible.

"Nanny likes to think reading the Bible will keep us on the straight and narrow," Phoebe giggled. "She's all right though, and so long as you do your work properly, she's fair. The food's good too because she always makes sure the nursery staff get a proper diet. We eat the same food as the children and she's strict with what the kiddies are given."

Daisy noted Phoebe spoke with a country burr. Putting down her bag she was overwhelmed by a feeling of homesickness for Polly's cosy little parlour. Tears clouded her eyes and she was ashamed when Phoebe noticed them.

"Here, don't take on," she said soothingly, "the first day's always the worst. You'll get used to it. I'll ask Nanny if I can make a cup of tea." She left Daisy to unpack her belongings.

When she returned downstairs, she was shown the nursery suite, which was shabbily cosy. The paintwork throughout was of the same dark brown, probably to hide dirty little finger marks but the paper on the walls was sprigged cheerily with full-blown roses. The furniture appeared to be cast-offs from more important rooms, some pieces being quite elegant, although well worn. Blue gingham curtains matched the cushion covers, and the table in the centre of the room was covered in a matching pattered oil cloth.

The children spent most of their time in the day-room, it was explained, as Nanny introduced them. Adelaide appeared to be a composed child who nodded politely and flicked back her fair hair when she was presented. Picture books were scattered over the table where Phoebe was helping the children identify objects. A kettle gently hissed over an open fire while flames danced up the chimney. Daisy noticed the fires in all the rooms were heavily guarded against curious little fingers. Nanny's bedroom, which doubled as her parlour, was on the opposite side of the corridor, and was strictly private.

Two more large bedrooms were situated on the same side and one of these was occupied by Lord Harry and Lady Adelaide, with Master George in the other. When the new baby, as yet to be named, joined the nursery suite he'd sleep in Nanny's room for a few months and but when he was old enough, he'd share with George.

Meals were taken in the nursery dining-room where crockery was stacked on the dresser and a row of cook's preserves stood on the highest shelf. Food was brought up from the kitchens by means of a dumb-waiter but there was always fresh bread and jam for hungry little mouths.

"You can start by making us a nice cup of tea before Lord Harry gets back," Nanny said to Daisy. "Show her how we like it made please, Phoebe. Then you can sit with the children while Phoebe helps me make out the menus for the next couple of days."

She took a pen and paper from a drawer in the dresser before adding,

"We have a rule up here. Before any of us uses the kettle, we always make sure one of us is present to watch over the children. Don't want any scaldings."

The morning passed slowly, the only sound being Nanny's pen as it scratched over the surface of the paper. Daisy was later to learn that the pretty silver pen was very precious to Nanny as it had been presented to her by the present Earl when the old Earl had died, as thanks for the service she'd given to the family. When lunch was served Daisy was surprised at the amount of food on offer. Freshly baked bread accompanied every meal along with a mound of delicious butter. Jars of jam were kept on the dresser and there was always a bowl of fruit because, Nanny explained, she encouraged the children to eat fruit after every meal.

"Keeps their blood clear," she expanded. "I'm off for my nap now, so you keep your eye on the children, Phoebe. Wake me up with a cup of tea in an hour and we'll take a walk. Put Master George to bed for a while, but I don't suppose Lady Adelaide will lie down."

Daisy noticed that although the use of titles was not necessary in the nursery it was difficult for Nanny to break the habit of subservience. When the older woman and young George were out of the way, Phoebe became more talkative.

"Nanny used to work for the old Earl, so she was his Lordship's nurse. She came with him when he married her Ladyship. Think the world of her, they do."

"What are they like, the Master and Mistress?"

"Okay. Don't see much of 'em. He's always out at his charities and clubs and she seems to do lots of visiting, and they entertains a lot. Lizzie, the scullery maid, says Albert can hardly keep up with the vegetables. He's the head gardener up in Norfolk. All the veg comes down from there so it's fresh every day."

Phoebe grew more confidential as she captured Daisy's interest. "Got lots of posh friends, they have. Right stuck up most of 'em. And no better than they ought to be from what I 'ear."

"What do you mean?" said Daisy.

"Oh, you know. Assignations with each other's husbands and wives. Goes on all over the place, specially at their country houses."

Daisy changed the subject. "So the master and mistress don't come up to the nursery much?"

"Her Ladyship prefers to have the children taken down to her, so she can show them off to guests. They do try to see them once a day, but you're right, it's not regular. Poor little mites."

"I can't see much point in having babies if you don't see 'em."

"It's different for the likes of them. They needs kids so as they can pass on all their money, and houses. They've got this big place just outside Thetford — that's in Norfolk, like I said, where the family go for the summer. They're different when they're up there. Invite lots of the family, and play with the kids more."

"What happens to us when they're in the country?" Daisy asked.

"Most of the staff usually go with them. It's lovely at Branstead Park. It's near Thetford, where I come from. Everything's much more easy going when we're up there."

"Will I go too?"

"I expect so. There'll be nothing for you to do here."

When Nanny had been roused the children were dressed in their outdoor clothes and they all went into the park. Before they left she told Daisy to pick up the bread left over from lunch. Daisy wrapped it in a brown paper bag and stowed it in her coat pocket, before taking Adelaide's hand and leading her carefully down the stairs. They spent the next two hours in the park, being careful to keep the children off the grass. Nanny sat on a bench with the pushcart while Phoebe and Daisy took the children to the pond.

"Hold their hands tightly now," called Nanny, as the children struggled to escape from the girls in order to feed the birds. George was determined to grab one of the ducks and Daisy had difficulty in restraining him. He was a lively little boy, full of spirit and mischief and made a charming picture in his sailor outfit. Adelaide seemed to be more amenable and was very sweet. Daisy was reminded of the day she and Lou walked in Hyde Park and watched other nannies with their charges. Little had she dreamed then, that one day it would be her privilege to do likewise.

Daisy met Lord Harry when his tutor brought him back to the schoolroom. Percival Peters, the tutor, nodded briefly to Daisy when Nanny explained who she was. He twirled his moustache and looked down on her through narrowed eyes, making her feel uncomfortable so she decided she wouldn't like him very much. Harry shook Daisy's hand solemnly when they were introduced. He looked tired and Daisy felt sorry for him being shut up in the schoolroom with Percy Peters all day.

She soon adapted to the daily routine of the nursery. Her new clothes were delivered by Mrs Parkins within a few days and Daisy felt less conspicuous when she was wearing a uniform like the rest of the staff. Her dress was made of pale blue cotton like Phoebe's, as opposed to Nanny's navy blue.

"Silly colour, if you ask me," commented Nanny Bruce, "But the Mistress insists on that shade. It's the colours they had in her nursery when she was a child."

Daisy soon developed a sense of well-being with her new clothes and regular meals. She began teaching Adelaide to identify animals by their letters and soon the child was able to write the letters for pig, cat and dog.

She caught Phoebe looking at her enviously and when they went to bed that night asked, "Phoebe — can't you write your letters?"

The girl shook her head in shame but Daisy assured her, "I'll teach yer. We'll do half an hour every night before we go to sleep." She added," When we're not too tired."

When roast beef arrived in the nursery on Daisy's first Sunday, she'd sniffed appreciatively. It seemed she'd lived a lifetime since cook gave her soup and bread in the kitchen. She could picture the meat roasting over the fire, even now. Her first full roast meal was a delight and Daisy ate with relish.

As Daisy settled in, Nanny began correcting her grammar so that the children didn't pick up her Cockney dialect and she learned the proper cutlery to use at mealtimes. During the second week of her employment there was a tap on the door while the children were at breakfast. They called a warm greeting to the haughty woman who came into the room carrying a bundle in her arms. Her olive green silk dress whispered as she moved, and she wore an enamelled brooch on her cream lace collar. Pale blond hair was swept to the back of her head into a chignon with loops coiling round her ears. Daisy judged her to be of average height but she held herself erect, giving the impression she was tall. Daisy thought she was quite beautiful.

Nanny immediately stood to attention.

"Good morning, Your Ladyship. I see you've brought the new baby?"

"I have," replied her employer. "We've decided on a name for him. He's to be called William. William Sullivan James."

She handed the child to Nanny who rocked him gently.

"He's beautiful, Your Ladyship," she cooed as she inspected the infant who slept peacefully.

"I brought him up myself so that I could see the children. The wet nurse was in a hurry so I let her go. She'll come in three times a day as she did for the others, and the rest of the time he can have diluted cow's milk. You know the routine." She handed Nanny a list of times and stayed for a few minutes, asking the children what they were doing but taking little real interest.

"How's the new girl coming along?" She nodded in Daisy's direction.

"Fitting in nicely, Your Ladyship."

Daisy blushed with pleasure, but the Countess swept out of the room with only a faint nod in her direction, as Nanny laid the baby in the wooden crib. It had been ready for days, its frills and flounces freshly laundered. The children scampered from the table and looked at the crumpled little face in awe while Nanny bustled about impatiently.

"My word we're going to be busy with four of them to look after." Daisy smiled secretly. How on earth did Nanny think some mothers managed with half a dozen children to care for with no help, and no money?

Chapter 8

During the following weeks Daisy settled into nursery routine. The long hours were no hardship when she was warm for most of the day and well fed. She became adept at starching and ironing the frills on the children's clothes and performing the numerous tasks that were necessary to keep their little world running smoothly. She was allowed to watch the new baby being bathed with Nanny showing how to carefully avoid touching the soft spot on his head, and how to dry him properly. She'd handed Nanny the talcum powder and grease to keep his bottom smooth and although she longed to hold him, knew better than to ask. He was too precious to be touched by a coarse girl from the streets and in any case Nanny was possessive of him.

The children accompanied their parents to church on Sundays, and Phoebe and Daisy went too. The Earl and Countess walked in front, each holding one of the older children's hands, with the nursery staff following behind with little George. Nanny insisted the nursery employees were smartly turned out since any detraction from standards would reflect on their employers. The church was close by and attending the service was both a social occasion as well as a religious one. The congregation was fashionably dressed and when the service was finished and the children had been admired, the girls took the two smallest home. Lord Harry usually stayed behind with the Earl and Countess whilst they chatted with the vicar and their friends. The family usually lunched at home alone on Sundays.

As time progressed Daisy was allowed to carry out tasks involving the older children but Lord Harry was an independent child who spent his spare time reading.

"What are you reading?" she asked him one day. He was curled up in an armchair, deeply immersed in a book but when he heard his name, he looked up and smiled.

"Gulliver's Travels. Jonathon Swift is a wonderful writer. What do you read, Daisy?"

She blushed. "I've never read nothing much. Only prayer books at Sunday school. Don't get much time for reading, really."

"Then I shall find something for you to read during your time off," he replied politely as he shoved his book aside. "Come into my bedroom and we'll choose something."

Daisy glanced at Nanny who nodded her approval so she accompanied him to the bookshelf.

"I like adventure books," he said, "But I suppose you prefer something sissie?"

Daisy giggled. "I think I know a bit about adventure, Harry. You choose something you've enjoyed." She added hastily, "But nothing too hard. I didn't get much schooling."

Harry selected a tattered copy of Grimm's Fairy Tales. "These are wonderful and I know you'll enjoy them. Promise you'll ask if there's a word you don't understand. That's the way to achieve a good vocabulary."

Daisy took the book gratefully. "I don't know what a vocabulary means but it sounds like something good, so I'll try it."

"It means how many words you're able to understand, Daisy."

As the nursery area was isolated from the rest of the household, Daisy didn't come in contact with the other employees very often, except Lizzie who scuttled in and out of the nursery like a frightened mouse. She was scared of Nanny's sharp tongue when something wasn't quite right. Sometimes Daisy might meet a maid on the stairs and they'd nod politely but conversation wasn't encouraged, particularly with the males of the household.

Mr Pike, the butler, ruled his domain with a rod of iron and Daisy felt sorry for any of those working under him who didn't meet his exacting standards. He stood guard at the foot of the stairs, fussing with his shirt cuffs, which he insisted were kept to a certain length beneath the sleeves of his coat. It wasn't unusual to come across a housemaid in tears, as she scurried around with her dusters. What Horace Pike lacked in height, he supplemented with bullying, which he took care to hide when the Earl or Countess were about.

"Do it again, Constance!" he could be heard to bellow along the corridor. The hapless girl would hang her head as she crept in and out of the numerous rooms she was expected to keep clean.

Daisy mentioned it to Phoebe, who replied, "We've got it easy up here, Daisy. Nanny Bruce is an angel compared to old Pike. Mrs Withers is all right but Pike undermines her whenever he gets the chance."

"Don't the Master and Mistress know what he's like?"

"I don't suppose they care, so long as their own lives is made easy."

But there were more pressing problems in the nursery. Baby William wasn't strong. Now three months old, he seemed to have a constant sniffle and despite the patience shown by the wet nurse, often declined his feed. He'd refused nourishment from Sadie Turner's large breasts which seemed to overflow with milk. She'd sit in the rocking chair and sing while cradling the infant wrapped in a shawl of Honiton

59

lace. Nanny explained to Daisy the shawl had been in the family for generations. Milk dripped from Sadie's swollen nipple as it waited for little William to latch on to it. But although he made desultory attempts to suck, more often than not, he turned his head away, whimpering miserably.

Nanny asked the Countess to come up to the nursery to sit in on feed times. Her Ladyship sat by the fire and sniffed distastefully as the wet nurse fumbled at her bodice in order to free her milk supply. They were all silent as they watched, and waited for William to feed.

"I think we'd best call Dr Mortimer, Nanny," frowned the Countess. "The child will never thrive if it doesn't take nourishment."

Nanny nodded. "The others have been such good little feeders and they've all been at Sadie's breast, so there's no problem with the quality of her milk."

The Countess inclined her head in agreement.

"Quite," she said. "I'll accompany Dr Mortimer when he arrives. The baby seems very stuffed up. Does he have a cold?"

"No, I don't think so, Your Ladyship, but his chest often seems tight. He wheezes and it affects his breathing. I rub him with a mild solution of liniment but it doesn't seem to ease the congestion."

That afternoon the doctor arrived. He puffed up the stairs behind the Countess and put his leather bag on the table before warming his hands in front of the fire. He bent over the cradle and put his ear to William's chest.

Nanny looked on anxiously. "I thought it best to keep him in the dayroom, Doctor, where it's nice and warm," she said, as she fussed around William.

"Quite right, Nanny Bruce, we don't want him catching cold." He turned to the Countess who hovered in the background. "I'll take a look at the little lad." He shook his head as he pressed his stethoscope against William's tiny rib cage, listening intently.

He replaced his stethoscope in the bag and gave the Countess a worried glance.

"I think we should get him looked over by Norman Bradbury. He's the finest chest specialist in the country. This poor child's very wheezy."

He repacked his bag and glanced at the Countess.

"Come down to the drawing room, Doctor," she said. "I expect you'd like a glass of sherry before you go?" She turned to Nanny. "I'll let you know when we can expect Mr Bradbury."

They all worried about William, but nursery routine had to go on. The lawns in the park seemed a brighter shade of green and early roses had broken through their buds. The park was warming up and the very air held promise. The children were often too hot as they ran around the pathways in their winter coats.

"Cast ne'er a clout 'till May be out," warned Nanny, when Phoebe suggested scarves could be dispensed with. "But we'll be able to get them out of their thick woollies, if this warm weather continues," she assured her. William was snuggled in the depths of the large bassinette, so that he'd benefit from the fresh air whilst being shielded from the breeze. George, as usual, pulled at the confines of his reins, eager to get to the pond with his crusts of bread.

Mr Bradbury, the consultant from Harley Street called at the end of the week. He accompanied the Countess to the nursery and went straight to the cradle. Small in stature, his movements were deft and efficient as he listened to William's chest. His verdict was immediate.

"I'm afraid the child's asthmatic, Countess."

Her haughty face took on a look of concern as she replied. "Oh dear. What should we do for him?"

"Get him out of town, Your Ladyship. There's nothing worse for an asthmatic than dirty air, and goodness knows London's a filthy place. Are there any others who suffer with their chests in your family? It's often an inherited condition."

The Countess looked perplexed. "I'm not sure." She hesitated. "There was an uncle who lived in one of the Shires: I seem to recall. He wheezed considerably." She gazed out of the window. "The country you say. Are you sure he would benefit from different air?"

Mr. Bradbury fussed with the lapels of his jacket. "Most certainly. He might shake the condition off later. Often these childhood ailments are outgrown by the age of seven." He picked up his bag and began packing his instruments before leaving a list of instructions for Nanny.

"Not much point in my calling again. I'm sure Nanny is quite able to cope," he said, nodding in her direction. "But I'd like you to consider my advice. Talk it over with the Earl. Move the whole family to the country if necessary."

"That would be impossible," murmured the Countess. "We need to be here for the Season."

Daisy waited until she left the nursery before asking Nanny, "Is it serious?"

"I'm afraid it is Daisy, 'though whether the Mistress will take the doctor's advice, I'm not sure."

Nanny was called to Her Ladyship's parlour the following day while Phoebe and Daisy waited anxiously for her return. When she did, Nanny put her fingers to her lips and gestured them not to ask questions within the children's hearing. When they were safely tucked up in bed, she took her sewing basket from the cupboard and told Daisy to make the cocoa.

"Get out the biscuit barrel," she whispered as they gathered round the table. When they were ready she announced with pleasure, "We're all going up to Branstead."

Phoebe's face was joyful. "I'll be able to see me Mum!"

Nanny looked severe. "Of course you will, Phoebe. But only on your afternoon off." She explained what would happen, while they sipped their cocoa. The Earl had decided that as the whole family were due to move up to Norfolk in a couple of months, the children should go up as soon as possible. They kept a skeleton staff at Branstead and in Her Ladyship's opinion; it wouldn't hurt them to work for a change.

"Will Lord Harry stay here?" asked Phoebe.

"No. Mr. Peters will accompany us to Branstead, and tutor him from there. There's no real need for Harry to be in London. Things will be different when he goes to Eton, of course, but he can study just as well in Norfolk."

"What's it like at Branstead?" Daisy ventured.

"Lots of lovely fresh air and gardens," replied Nanny. "It's a world apart from London. I'm sure you'll like it, Daisy. Although you'll still have to work," she added caustically. "Phoebe knows Norfolk better than me. Her aunt works in the kitchens up at Branstead Park. Phoebe came to us by her recommendation."

Phoebe dunked her biscuit in her tea. "Tell Daisy about last year Nanny — with the cholera."

Nanny brushed the crumbs from her bodice before she spoke.

"That was a terrible time. The streets smelled of chloride of lime, and His Lordship sent us to Branstead for four months — because of the danger to the children. But you must have known about the cholera epidemic, Daisy? being a Londoner yourself."

Daisy thought quickly. "But I was in Mile End, Nanny. Me aunt was poorly, so I didn't get up West at all."

Nanny shook her head thoughtfully. "Lots of places were closed and even the public houses didn't open, so I heard. It was dreadful. Not much life in London at all. It didn't make much difference to us, of course."

"I've never been in an ale house, Nanny, so I wouldn't know. I'm beginning to like the sound of Branstead," Daisy added, steering the conversation away from herself.

She was beginning to recognise that she might be safer in Norfolk. She hadn't reckoned with the awkward questions that were sometimes asked, and there was always the chance she might meet somebody from her past in London. Thankfully, she usually spent her free afternoons in her room, reading the book Harry had loaned her.

The next few days flew by as they were all involved in a flurry of packing and although there was a fully equipped nursery at Branstead, Nanny liked her own things about her. "We're to travel on Thursday. His Lordship's ordered the carriage for us and it'll be here at 8.30 sharp!"

There was great excitement on the given day, as the whole party piled into the huge vehicle. The Clarence, commonly known as the Growler, had been manufactured to hold four people but old Earl had ordered his to be adapted to take six. It still gave good service, and meant the family were able to go to and from Norfolk with some ease, although it was still a tight fit to get them all in. Harry was allowed to travel up front with the coach drivers, much to the chagrin of the smaller children. Sachets of pot-pourri were hung strategically from the roof of the carriage in an effort to overcome the odour created by cramped bodies.

The vehicle was drawn by four shire horses which stamped their feet and snorted impatiently while the passengers settled themselves, and boxes and bags were loaded. The coachmen were dressed in the Earl's livery and Daisy felt very important as she anticipated the journey. They were to spend the night at a coaching inn in Ipswich, then travel north-westwards to Thetford the following day. The compartment at the back of the carriage was packed with what Nanny considered necessary for the journey and at last, instructions were given and received, and the travellers were able to sink into the leather upholstery.

Finally, the coach rumbled off and they passed through the outskirts of the capital, then into hamlets, causing little disruption to their inhabitants save the dust thrown up by the horses' hooves. They made a steadier pace when they came to the flat countryside and Daisy looked out of the window in wonder at the patches of woodland and green fields. She nudged Phoebe. "Look, have you ever seen so many trees? It's much bigger than Regents Park. It goes on for ever."

The carriage trundled along the rutted paths, swaying to and fro as it went round corners. The smaller children became fractious but eventually fell asleep as the rocking continued. Nanny tried to talk to Percival Peters but the tutor replied monosyllabically, making it obvious he considered himself superior to the nursery staff so rejected her attempts at conversation. The whole party was relieved when the coachman sounded his horn, announcing their arrival at the inn.

Time passed in a haze for Daisy. She'd experienced much that was new since becoming part of the Bloomsbury household, and was surprised when servants at the inn treated her with respect. When food was brought to the table they nodded solicitously and she copied Phoebe by declining her head politely in thanks.

That night Adelaide and George shared a bed, as did Daisy and Phoebe. Nanny slept on a divan on the other side of the room with baby William in his portable cradle. Harry had to sleep in the same room as Mr. Peters.

There was chaos in their room the following morning with Daisy and Phoebe tripping over the children's boots, while maids arrived with hot water. William howled when Nanny tried to bottle-feed him, and George tugged at Adelaide's ribbons. They were all late for breakfast and the head coachman waited impatiently in the doorway, grumbling and belching. Nanny sniffed her distaste and glowered at him while encouraging the children to hurry with their meal.

They started off for Thetford much later than anticipated and the journey continued monotonously. More fields, and more trees, with the scenery changing only when they went through hamlets. Village children waved as the coach passed by, and although they'd been supplied with food by the innkeeper, the party stopped at a couple of farms for a thirst-quenching cup of fresh milk.

Phoebe nudged Daisy excitedly as Thetford Forest came into view.

"We're nearly there, Daisy. I'll be able to see me Mum." Her face was radiant with excitement.

It was late afternoon when the coach finally lurched through a pair of imposing black wrought-iron gates. They were embellished with the family crest, and underneath was a sign painted in gold lettering which read, "*Branstead Park.*" The horses trotted up a long winding drive flanked with trees, through which could be seen peacocks preening and strutting.

The carriage turned quite suddenly and came to a halt outside the steps leading to a big white house. The clock above the stable block chimed the hour as stable hands ran over to take charge of the horses. The black front door was flanked by rows of windows that twinkled in the sunshine, and flowers bloomed profusely, standing to attention in rows alongside stony pathways that were edged with tiles. Daisy stared in wonder at the fountain on the front lawn which spouted water from a sculptured serpent's mouth, its spray a kaleidoscope of colour in the rays of the sun.

Mrs Girling, the housekeeper stood on the front door step and welcomed them.

"Come along in, all of you. You must be tired out. Your rooms are ready, but first, go into the kitchen and we'll get you some food. My, how the children have grown," she added, as they were herded down a stone staircase and into a spacious kitchen which was similar to that at the Bloomsbury house, but larger. A platter of warm scones, accompanied by jam and cream appeared as if from nowhere, while a muslin cover was whipped off fine china plates to reveal dainty egg and cress sandwiches. Lemonade for the children and tea for the grown-ups soon refreshed the London party, after which their bags were taken up the side stairway to the nursery.

Branstead was typical of an 18th century country house built for the aristocracy. Its rooms were spread over four floors and the nursery suite was in the west wing on the third floor. Portraits of previous Earls of Hartswood adorned the walls along the main staircase and Daisy found them forbidding as she dared stare back at them. Nevertheless the atmosphere at Branstead was more homely than the Bloomsbury townhouse. With fewer staff, there was less restriction on the children and Daisy's heart lightened as they settled into their quarters.

The next few mornings were spent exploring the house. After breakfast, it was Nanny's habit to go down to chat to Mrs Girling, taking William with her. This left Phoebe and Daisy to amuse Adelaide and George, while Harry studied with his tutor.

The girls would put George in his pushcart and wander in and out of the rooms in the east wing, staring in awe at four-poster beds majestically draped in rich brocades. Walking sedately along the corridors they'd inspect locked cabinets where precious porcelain was displayed.

"I wouldn't fancy washing up this lot," said Daisy as she stared in awe at the vast array of china.

"Don't suppose it's ever used," was Phoebe's brief comment.

The children were fascinated by a collection of stuffed birds, brought home from world tours by some distant ancestor. The top floor held the servants' quarters with many of the rooms being used for storage. Daisy, trying to look into the rooms, pushed open some of the doors but was met by cobwebs and dust, so hastily slammed them closed again.

The ground floor was where the family entertained and most of the rooms were very large. Thickly carpeted, they smelled of a mixture of lavender and beeswax and were furnished in grand scale. The walls of the ballroom were lined in deep rose silk and crystal chandeliers sparkled in the bright sunlight.

"I think we should keep the children away from these rooms," said

Phoebe. "They poke their fingers everywhere and might break something. We'd be for it then."

"You're right Phoeb. But exploring is lots of fun. I've never been in a house as big as this before."

Chapter 9

Afternoons were often spent in the grounds, sometimes with Phoebe squinting over her writing block, while Daisy kept her eye on the children. Phoebe's writing was coming along nicely but she found adding and subtraction more difficult.

Daisy thought it wonderful not to have to walk through London's dirty streets to get some air in the park. Here at Branstead the air smelled sweeter with flowers that grew in its *own* park, and wafts of sweet smelling herbs seeped through the hedgerows. Beyond the gardens a herd of deer grazed, dispersing at the sound of a shot gun. Pheasants and rabbits alike scurried from field to field, scavenging in the sun-scorched earth.

"His Lordship'll be here for the shooting soon, Dais, so we'd best make the most of our freedom. It starts on August twelfth and there'll be lots of his friends up here." She tossed her cap in the air and threw herself on to the grass in an expression of ecstasy.

Daisy, who was helping Adelaide make a daisy-chain, looked on wistfully. "Do you know, I don't think I've ever been as happy as I am now. I hope it don't spoil when they all come up."

"We'll be all right Dais, as long as we keep out of the way."

Norfolk basked in a spell of hot weather for the next month and the children were able to run freely through the woods, chasing unsuspecting rabbits as they hopped in and out of hedgerows. Lessons were often held outdoors on the lawn but if the weather was showery Harry and Adelaide, together with Mr Peters, closeted themselves in the summerhouse. They sat on uncomfortable rattan chairs as they pored over their books, while sharing the table with exotic plants. When they were able, the nursery contingent picnicked by the river that ran through the grounds, with William lying on a rug under a tree beside Nanny. He was five months old and growing noticeably bigger as he blew bubbles and kicked his chubby legs. His wheezing had lessened and he greeted them all with a big smile, showing off two new teeth.

The younger children were becoming tanned and Nanny worried about the freckles that had appeared on Adelaide's skin. Her Ladyship wouldn't approve, so the child's face was dabbed night and morning with lemon juice, and as an added precaution she was always shaded by a straw bonnet with a large brim.

One day, Mr Peters, who was going home to Wales for the whole of August, suggested a game of cricket to Harry, and they gathered some of the estate children to join in. Those who weren't playing cheered and clapped as players were bowled out or made runs. Mrs Girling appeared at mid-afternoon with home-made biscuits and lemonade which quickly disappeared down eager throats. It was with sadness that the day came to an end but new friendships had been forged and Harry promised to arrange another match.

The Earl and Countess were expected on August seventh, in order to settle in before the start of the shooting season. As a special treat Nanny arranged for a vehicle to pick up the nursery party a few days before the guests were due to arrive. They all clambered into the wagon and the children were agog with anticipation as the cobs clip-clopped along the lanes. The hedgerows were a tangle of privet and mallow, and poppies clamoured for attention in fields of corn, as they swayed in the summer breeze. The children laughed with glee as they tried to clutch at leaves from overhanging branches with little success. The party eventually arrived at the home farm and waited by the milking sheds as the cows were herded in for morning milking. George squealed with delight as they swished their tails, eager for the milkmaids to take up position on their stools.

The children were given cups of fresh milk in the farm kitchen, before being taken to the orchard where they picked big purple plums that hung from trees heavy with fruit. Wiping them with their aprons, Nanny scolded, warning of tummy ache as juice ran down their chins. Adelaide was entranced with the ducks that had strayed from the adjacent pond. They clucked and waddled around the yard as they searched for tit-bits, aware they were on the territory of three cats and two dogs, as well as a big, fat, pink pig. The farm was a world away from Bloomsbury and the whole party relished the freedom from regulation that was the order in London.

Later, the farmer's wife gave them lunch of freshly roasted ham with salad from the garden, followed by apple pie with cream. The dogs sat close by and looked at them with pleading eyes, so scraps of ham and bread were surreptitiously thrown under the table. Nanny saw every move but said nothing as she nodded conspiratorially to the farmer's wife. They were taken home at four o'clock with promises to return soon, but admitted being weary. Cook was delighted with the baskets of fruit and vegetables they took with them and promised to make a plum duff the following day.

During the next few days the house was in a flurry of activity. Phoebe explained that Mr Danbury, the Earl's steward, would ride over from his house near the farm to take charge. Extra help was hired from the village to give the house a thorough clean in readiness for the Season. Chandeliers were washed and polished until they sparkled. Floors were swept and cleaned, and windows opened so that clouds of dust from the carpets could float outside and come to rest on the plants, much to the annoyance of Pringle, the head gardener.

He'd order his staff to wash the dust off his precious flowers at regular intervals, grumbling about inconsiderate people, but Danbury looked on with amusement. He was used to Pringle's idiosyncrasies. The mammoth task of cleaning all the windows inside and out had been taken a few weeks previously and now they twinkled in the sunshine.

Cook bustled around the kitchen declaring she'd never be ready in time. She wiped her brow as sunlight streamed through the open windows.

"Them jellies'll never set," she wailed as she moved them to the other side of the room. Kitchen maids washed the best china in wooden sinks provided especially for the purpose. Family silver was retrieved from the vaults and cleaned by a temporary butler, under the steward's supervision.

"Mr Pike will inspect it thoroughly, when he gets here," he warned, as the poor man sweated in the heat. Delicious smells wafted through the open windows as the children played hide and seek in the kitchen garden. Laundry maids laid bed-linen out to dry on the lavender bushes, ensuring sweet dreams for guests.

Nanny ceased her visits to the kitchen, a custom, she explained to Daisy, which would be unacceptable when the family was in residence.

It was with great excitement that the approach of the Earl's carriage was eventually heralded as it swept through the gates of Branstead. Harry and Adelaide ran down the stairway to greet their parents on the front steps while the Earl took deep breaths of the fresh country air, as he was assisted from the carriage. He beamed at Harry as he shook his hand.

"Good to be back. How are you, old chap — lessons going well?"

"Yes thank you, Papa. Pleased to see you." Harry turned to the Countess who was smoothing down her crumpled dress. She bent to allow her eldest son to kiss her cheek.

"How's my big boy. Why Harry! You've grown. Your resemblance to my father becomes more evident with every day that passes."

Harry smiled at the compliment as he stood back for his sister to greet her parents. Adelaide offered her cheek to the Earl who kissed it gently. "How's my beautiful girl?" he said, his eyes beaming with affection.

"I'm well, Papa. We're having a lovely summer. We went to the farm last week and saw the cows being milked and. . ."

"That's enough, Adelaide," interrupted the Countess. "Papa and I are tired from our journey. Kiss me quickly and run along back to the nursery. Tell Nanny to bring George and William down to the drawing room after tea."

The children stood back, allowing their parents to pass before joining Phoebe and Daisy who were waiting for them at the foot of the staircase which led to the West Wing of the house. Daisy took Adelaide's hand and led her up the stairs.

You're back soon,' she said "You didn't stay with your parents for long."

Adelaide brushed the comment aside and Harry replied for her.

"Mama and Papa are tired. I doubt they'll send for us after tea. We'll probably see them tomorrow."

When the children were in bed, Nanny took the biscuit tin from the cupboard while Phoebe made cocoa. Anything referring to the children was discussed when they were asleep because, according to Nanny, *little pigs have big ears!*

"Why didn't His Lordship kiss Harry, like he did Adelaide?" asked Daisy.

"It's not done in the upper circles of Society, Daisy. It's just not done to show your sons too much affection. They're expected to grow up far too soon in my opinion. It's different with girls though," added Nanny thoughtfully, as she sipped her drink.

"If you ask me, Her Ladyship's jealous of Adelaide," suggested Phoebe as she dipped a biscuit into her cocoa. "She always gets her away from the Earl as quick as she can."

Nanny frowned, conscious she may have been disloyal.

"Don't dunk your biscuits Phoebe," she scolded, "I've told you about it before. You'll have the children copying you. And don't talk about Her Ladyship like that. It's none of your business. It's how the likes of them carry on. It does the children no harm. It toughens them up."

"I never see them sit on their laps when they come up to the nursery. Or have a cuddle," persisted Daisy.

"Hush, Girl. It's nothing to do with us. Our job is to look after the children and make their lives as pleasant as possible."

"I cuddle George, and I kiss him."

"That's all right, Daisy. I've seen you. Just don't let the Master or Mistress catch you, that's all."

70

The Earl and Countess were pleased with the change in William when Nanny took him down to the drawing room next day. "My! How he's filled out. And two teeth!" said the Earl as he handed the baby to his wife.

"The country air certainly agrees with him," she replied. "How is his chest, Nanny?"

"It seems to be getting better, Your Ladyship. Difficult to tell when a baby's teething because they all get snuffled up. But I do believe the little lad's breathing's improved."

"And the other children?"

"They're doing very well, Your Ladyship. Harry's been working hard, as usual. Adelaide is still doing her letters and little George; well, he's into everything at the moment. He's a lively little chap, but good natured."

"I hope they're getting plenty of fresh air Nanny?"

"Oh, yes, Your Ladyship. They go walking in the woods and play in the fields. One of the gardeners made them little nets on a rod so they can catch tiddlers in the stream."

"Oh dear. I hope you're careful they don't fall in?"

"Of course, Your Ladyship. I've got Phoebe and Daisy watching them all the time. They wouldn't let them come to any harm."

Satisfied, the Countess handed the baby back to Nanny.

"Good. Now you know the rules when we have guests. You and the children must always use the West Wing stairs, and the side entrance. Make sure the new girl knows. We can't have her wandering around the estate when the shooting begins. The children can take their exercise in the back meadow and we'll send for them when we need them."

Nanny nodded. "Very good, My Lady."

"That's all, Nanny. By the way the Dowager Countess will be coming home for a few weeks. She'll want to see the children, so make sure they're always tidy. Sometimes I think they look like street urchins when we're in Norfolk." She turned her back. "You may go."

Nanny grumbled as she returned to the nursery.

"Daisy! You're good with ribbons. For goodness sake keep Adelaide's hair tied back nicely. Her Ladyship has just mentioned the children's dress to me. And you," she added, nodding at Phoebe. "Try to keep George under control. I've got enough to do with looking after William."

"I thought I might try putting Adelaide's hair in curling rags, Nanny. She'd look ever so pretty," said Daisy.

"No. No. Just brush her hair thoroughly every night. A hundred strokes, that's what it should be." As Nanny began to sort the baby's clothes she relayed the Countess' instructions for the nursery. "We're always told to keep to the back of the house while they've got visitors. They play croquet on the front lawn and cricket in the large field. The shooting takes place in that direction." She waved an arm towards the east of the estate.

"Do you think they'll get the boats out this year, Nanny?" asked Phoebe.

"If the weather holds, I should think so."

The next few days saw the arrival of liveried carriages, from which beautifully dressed ladies and fashionable gentlemen stepped down. Daisy and Phoebe peeped through the windows from the West Wing, fascinated by their appearance. They overheard them being called names like Veronica and Tabitha, Guy and Miles. There was an elegant man they referred to as Bunny and it seemed to Daisy they all had one purpose, and that was to enjoy themselves. They sipped tea and lemonade on the terrace as they watched the others guests play croquet, or the ladies talked quietly amongst themselves. Their dresses swished gently as they walked through the grounds, with satin rubbing against silk and taffeta.

The men played cricket or bowls and organised rabbit shooting parties. The reception rooms echoed with chatter, and hummed with muted laughter and music. As Nanny had said, the house came alive for August.

"They're getting ready for August Twelfth!" she declared to the nursery in general. "There'll be plenty going on then. You mark my words."

"What's so important about the Twelfth, Nanny?" asked Daisy, as she folded the children's clothes.

"It's the start of the grouse-shooting season — one of the highlights of the social calendar. You hear what I say, there'll be such goings on! Shooting, fishing, games on the lawn, picnics." Nanny was obviously looking forward to it.

On Sunday, Phoebe was going home for the afternoon. She'd already been home once but wanted to look her best today as she was getting a lift. Daisy helped to button up the back of Phoebe's dress, which she'd made from green, sprigged cotton. The girls usually spent their evenings darning stockings and mending the children's clothes, but if they had time would work on an item of clothing for themselves. Phoebe was helping Daisy to make a dress for Sundays. They planned to buy cheap straw bonnets from the village shop to decorate at home but meanwhile, they'd bound the crown of Phoebe's old cloth hat with ribbons that matched her dress.

"You look lovely, Phoebe," said Daisy as she admired the result. "Your Mum will be surprised at how you look. What time is Jimmy Fawcett coming?"

"He said as soon as he could get away."

Jimmy Fawcett worked on the farm and the girls had met him when he brought fruit and vegetables over for Cook. He came from the same village as Phoebe and offered to save her the five-mile walk.

"I hope he got permission from Mr Jennings to use the cart?" queried Nanny caustically as they waited for it to come down the track.

"I'm sure he did. He usually has to make deliveries from the farm on the way. That's how he manages to get home most Sunday afternoons."

"I see," she replied. "Well, don't get any ideas about joining him every time because you're only due one afternoon a month."

Phoebe grimaced and shrugged, knowing there was no point in arguing.

They were interrupted by Harry who was waiting at the window, "He's coming. Hurry, Phoebe."

She gathered her things together and ran down the stairs. They closed the door behind her and watched from the window while she climbed into the cart. With a smart crack of the whip the horse began to trot down the drive and the children settled down to play while Nanny dozed in her rocking chair. Daisy thought how peaceful the room was and how lucky for her that she was with a good family. The kettle hissed on the stove that, despite the heat of the summer, was still lit, and Daisy closed her eyes. She still dreamed of her family and hoped they were in a nice room somewhere, but in her heart she knew it was unlikely. Not many workhouse families were able to elevate themselves from such a humble position. She almost nodded off but came back to reality when there was a soft tap on the door.

They all looked up as a short figure stepped into the room. The children's faces lit up with delight as they ran to an elderly lady. Putting their arms round her waist, they squealed excitedly crying, "Grandmamma, it's Grandmamma."

"Goodness. Those stairs," the visitor panted, as she took a seat.

Nanny snorted as she shook herself awake and beamed when she recognised their visitor. She rose immediately, patted her hair and bobbed.

"Why! Your Ladyship, how nice to see you."

Daisy watched as the children plied their grandmother with questions. Her chins wobbled as she spoke and her plump body, clothed in black silk, seemed to ripple too. Even though her dress and coat were trimmed with black ribbons the effect was still severe, relieved only by a white lace collar. She wore a black feather in her tiny hat and a marquisette and jet brooch on her bosom. The children obviously adored her and treated her with far less deference than they did their parents.

"Would you like refreshments, Lady Charlotte?" enquired Nanny, as the children crowded round their grandmother.

"Please. A glass of that delicious lemonade Cook makes, would be very welcome," she replied. "And, some of her cakes, as well. Perhaps the children could join me?" she added, her eyes sparkling. Nanny put a note under a brass weight and pulled at the ropes on the dumb waiter before it rumbled its noisy way down to the kitchen.

Chapter 10

"Have you been home for long, Your Ladyship," Nanny asked as they cleared the children's books from the table.

The Dowager watched her stack the books neatly on a side table.

"I arrived back from Europe a couple of days ago — can't stand the dower house when the estate is quiet. But I wanted to come back for August to see my little darlings." She patted Harry's head as she glanced in Daisy's direction.

"I see we have somebody new in the nursery."

Daisy stood and bobbed, not knowing what to say, but Nanny explained. "This is Daisy, Your Ladyship. She came to us at the beginning of the year and is doing nicely."

The older woman beckoned to Daisy. "Come over here."

Daisy trembled as she stood before her but the Dowager wasn't unkind and did her best to put the newcomer at her ease.

"Don't be frightened, girl. I don't bite! Now, tell me all about yourself."

Daisy repeated what she now believed to be true, that her mother was dead and her brother and sisters were living in Kent. The Dowager nodded sympathetically.

"Do the children like her, Nanny?" she asked, as if Daisy wasn't in the room.

"They do, Lady Charlotte. She's very good with them."

Daisy blushed and was relieved when the refreshments arrived.

"Come along. All of you."

The Dowager made it clear that Daisy was to be included as they jostled for places around the table. Nanny poured the lemonade and helped them all to cake. When they'd finished their grandmother said:

"Children, if you bring me that bag over there you'll see what I've brought you from Europe."

The children heaved the big tapestry bag along the floor, their eyes beaming with anticipation as they stood at her side. She handed a parcel to Harry.

"I bought you Æsop's Fables, Harry, dear. I know your head's always in a book. And for you?" She addressed Adelaide and withdrew another parcel from the bag, "A doll. A doll from Germany. She's very special."

Adelaide unwrapped a china doll with an exquisitely painted face.

"Oh thank you, Grandmamma," the child cried and rushed into the

75

Dowager's arms, smothering her with kisses and nearly knocking her hat off in the process.

George, who thought he was being left out, yelled, "Me!"

His grandmother beamed and handed him a puppet. "I wouldn't forget you, my little sunshine boy." She showed him how to make it dance on its strings while he looked on, his face alight with wonder.

Nanny rolled her eyes. "He'll have us doing that all day long," she grumbled gently. Daisy watched the family scene with interest. The children, although restrained with their parents, were uninhibited with their grandmother. It was a delight to see.

"And I have a special treat in store for you," the Dowager continued, addressing the two eldest children. "I'll send my carriage for you at eleven o'clock tomorrow morning and we'll have lunch together at the dower house. Then perhaps we'll take a drive in the afternoon."

She turned her attention to Nanny. "Supposing I have them back by five o'clock Nanny? Will that be all right? I've spoken to my daughter-in-law and she's agreeable."

"Of course, Your Ladyship. I'll have the children ready."

"Good. That just about gives me time to cuddle William, then I must go home and get dressed for dinner."

The Dowager left a trail of excitement in her wake as Harry escorted her down to the waiting carriage. Daisy was aware the atmosphere in the nursery had been lightened by her presence and mentioned it when the Dowager had left.

"She's not from the aristocracy," Nanny explained. "The Old Earl wasn't expected to inherit the title you see, so he was allowed to marry beneath him. The Dowager Countess, that's what they're known as when the titles pass on to their son, was the daughter of his tutor."

"She was still respectable though?"

"Yes. But it was hard for her at first. It wasn't the family, it was their friends who made life difficult for her."

"I thought she was lovely."

Nanny continued sorting the children's washing and for once was prepared to indulge in a little gossip. "She is. Bright as a button too, doesn't miss much that goes on around her. She prefers to be called Lady Charlotte but I forget sometimes. Hates being a Dowager, she does. Well educated, with her father being a scholar, but not quite top drawer, if you get my meaning."

Daisy was confused about the titles and laws of inheritance. She'd never had to bother about it before and all she knew was that Lady Charlotte was kind and smelled of lavender.

"The eldest son, he being the Earl's older brother, should have inherited the title," clarified Nanny. "But he was killed out in Africa. Went out there shooting lions, so serves him right, if you ask me."

Daisy missed having Phoebe to chatter to, but just before tea they heard the clatter of Jimmy Fawcett's cart as it drew up outside the back door.

The following day there was much excitement as the Dowager's carriage bore Harry and Adelaide to the other side of the park to lunch with their grandmother.

There was nothing much to do after they'd eaten their own lunch, so Nanny suggested Phoebe and Daisy go for a walk while the two younger children had their afternoon nap.

"Be back by three, so we can take George and William out for some fresh air. Don't be late!" she warned as they digested their good fortune. She adjusted the footstool, and closed her eyes as she settled in the rocking chair to doze.

"Thank you Nanny," the girls called out, pleased at the prospect of an hour or so away from the house. They tied on their bonnets and strolled in the deserted back meadow, listening to blackbirds and thrushes as they clucked in the bushes. They laughed when a bird ventured into the open ground, only to dash back quickly when it heard footsteps.

They ambled towards the woods that flanked the field and Phoebe suggested they shelter from the heat of the sun, looking longingly at density of the trees. "It'll be lovely and cool in there."

"We aren't allowed in the wood though, are we?" asked Daisy.

Phoebe was undeterred and ignored Daisy's hesitation as she replied, "I'm not really sure. The children aren't, but nobody comes here so we're not likely to meet anybody. Come along."

They slipped through a gap in the bushes and Phoebe was right, it was cool under the trees and the girls were soon enveloped in a welcome silence as their feet padded over the rich smelling soil. Now and again a bird twittered and fallen branches crackled as wildlife scurried about its business in the undergrowth.

It was very peaceful and they walked silently enjoying the feel of the damp earth, until they took a little-used path that led deeper into the wood. They were about twenty feet along when Phoebe pulled Daisy up short. She indicated ahead with her finger before putting a hand to her mouth, her eyes open wide in astonishment.

Daisy was equally bewildered when she looked to where Phoebe had pointed. The Earl was embracing a woman in a clearing and the girls were rooted to the spot, not knowing what to do. If they turned back, they might be heard and they couldn't go forward without being seen, so in silent agreement, they carefully moved sideways and hid behind the trunk of a tree while they decided what to do. They peeped from behind the tree, knowing they shouldn't, but were fascinated by the unfolding scene before them.

Mesmerised, they saw the Earl remove the lady's hat and kiss her on the lips, a long, lingering kiss, to which the woman responded by putting her arms around his neck. He began to unbutton her bodice before bending to expose and kiss one of her breasts. Then he grabbed at her skirts and they heard a gasp, as the woman cried,

"No. No. Not here, Gerald. We might be seen!"

The Earl responded impatiently. "Don't be silly, Hermione. Nobody comes here. This area of the estate belongs to the children but the woods are out of bounds. Anyway, they're visiting my mother today so this is the least likely place we'll be seen. Come along, be a good sport, eh?"

Surrendering, Hermione leaned forward and shrugged both breasts free, allowing the Earl to fondle and kiss them. Wide eyed, Phoebe looked at Daisy who wasn't sure what was happening but knew they were witnessing what they shouldn't. She whispered, "We should go."

"We can't. They'll hear us."

They looked again to see the Earl's dropping his trousers. Eyes agog, they watched him turn to lay them on a nearby bush, exposing the engorged flesh which sprang from his groin. Hermione was hurriedly divesting herself of her underskirts and neatly stepped out of a hooped petticoat, which she dropped to the ground. Her body was almost shielded by the Earl but when she was ready she smiled at him wantonly with her dress hitched up, revealing long white legs with a dark shadow between them. The Earl moved towards her and took her in his arms, kissing the exposed breasts again before he moved into her, as she supported herself against the trunk of the tree.

With their hands over their mouths Phoebe and Daisy watched as his body moved in and out of the woman's with increasing rhythm.

"Just like horses," exclaimed Phoebe in a loud whisper, her eyes open wide with astonishment. They turned their faces away and, overwhelmed by what they'd witnessed, didn't utter another word to each other. Crawling noiselessly under some nearby bushes, they waited for the couple to be done with their business and get dressed. They passed within feet of the girls as they returned along the path. Hermione was tucking her hair back with tortoiseshell combs as the Earl whispered endearments in her ear. As they got further away the girls could hear them laughing softly, unaware they'd been observed.

When it was safe, Phoebe and Daisy crept out of their hiding place and continued walking into the wood in silence. They took the long way back to the meadow before circling the house to go in by the west entrance stairs. Still in shock, neither mentioned what they'd witnessed.

Nanny was furious with them.

"It's nearly four o'clock. Where have you two been?"

"We got held up, Nanny. Sorry," whimpered Phoebe.

"Held up, Miss. What could possibly have made you an hour late."

Phoebe gulped. "We saw His Lordship, Nanny. He was in the back woods, by the meadow."

Daisy tensed, but was relieved to see Nanny shrug.

"You went into the woods? You know you should stay in the meadow."

Phoebe explained, "We didn't have the children with us, so we thought it would be all right. It was very hot."

Nanny dismissed the subject with a wave of her hand.

"Oh well, if you were talking to His Lordship, I suppose there was nothing you could do. Come along now and help me with the boys!" Thankful not to be questioned further, Daisy put on George's bonnet while Phoebe rummaged for a change of clothes for the baby.

It was a relief to get into the open air again where there was plenty to distract Nanny and the boys. She appeared not to notice the uneasy silence that enveloped her assistants and when they went up to bed that night, the girls discussed what they'd seen.

"I couldn't believe what the Earl was doing with that woman," said Phoebe.

"I know. He's married. I thought it wasn't allowed."

"My auntie says the rich are worse than the poor, for goings-on — that is. I didn't realise people did it like animals, did you?"

Daisy shook her head, denying the stirring in her stomach when she pictured the Earl's naked body.

"No. I didn't, Phoeb. I knew they did something but I didn't realise they put their 'things' together. Horrible, wasn't it?"

"Oh, yes," said Phoebe, as she struggled into her nightdress. "I'm not getting married, if that's what I've got to look forward to. Imagine!" Her eyes widened. "I wonder if me Mam and Dad did it?"

"Must have done. I expect that's how you got here. I remember now. My dad used to grunt when he went to bed, but I didn't know why. That's what they must call it, Phoeb. Grunting!"

Phoebe leaped into bed and replied with certainty.

"Well, I'm not going grunting with anybody, I can tell you that."

"What about when Nanny bawled us out? I thought you were going to split on the Earl!"

"I very nearly did. I was all of a dither. I hate lying to Nanny but she'd have been upset to hear the truth."

The sun was beginning to set, casting a rosy glow over the room.

"Night, Dais," Phoebe yawned.

"Night, Phoebe." The last thing Daisy remembered was the look of happiness on Hermione's face and the tenderness on the Earl's. Perhaps grunting wasn't so bad after all?

A message arrived for Nanny the next morning. The Countess wanted to talk to her about William's progress.

"Was her Ladyship happy with the baby, Nanny?" asked Phoebe when she returned.

"Very satisfied. Said he's come on a treat. Haven't you my little darling," she tickled the child under the chin before continuing, "His Lordship was in the morning room with Mr Danbury. I thanked him for being so nice to you when he met you in the woods yesterday." She waggled a finger. "I assured him you won't go there again without permission, so don't you let me down."

Daisy busied herself with the children's clothes, willing herself not to make eye contact with Phoebe, but when she stole a glance at her a few minutes later she noticed how flushed she was. There was no opportunity for them to speak to each other before they took the eldest children out for a walk, when to their horror; they saw the Earl walking towards them. He held a balloon each for Harry and Adelaide and bade them run in the breeze, before turning to Phoebe and Daisy.

"You were in the back woods yesterday afternoon, I understand from Nanny." The girls were rooted to the spot and failed to reply.

"Come along, come along. Answer me!"

Since Phoebe seemed unable to speak, it was Daisy who blurted out, "We were, Sir, but we didn't see you with no clothes on, honestly."

The Earl sneered and played with his moustache as he contemplated his reply, whilst Daisy realised her mistake. Phoebe found her tongue.

"We won't tell anybody, Sir. We didn't tell Nanny, did we Daisy?"

The Earl narrowed his eyes. "Too right you won't tell anybody. If a word of this ever reaches the Countess, or Nanny for that matter, I'll see you're dismissed immediately — and without a character. Meantime. . ." He put his face nearer to theirs as he sneered, "Should I ever feel the need for quick gratification, I'll know where to get it. You've seen all there is to see, so you won't mind, will you?"

Having issued the threat, he called to the children and began to run around the field with them. The girls cast their eyes down as they digested his words of warning.

August passed in a golden haze and having frightened the girls, the Earl kept out of their way, so they made sure they didn't go near the woods again. They hadn't understood what he meant by gratification but assumed it was something nasty. The whole household spent as much time out of doors as possible. Lying on the grass helping to amuse the children, the continual pop-pop of guns became a familiar sound as dogs barked and grouse fell from the sky. Distant cries of farm workers could be heard as they gathered in the harvest, and Daisy had never known such contentment. One day melted into another, each giving exquisite pleasure.

Tension mounted as the Season came to an end. New friendships had been forged and enemies made. Bunny paid too much attention to the Countess, who in turn, watched the Earl flirting openly with Hermione. Daisy noted these indiscretions and learned the ways of British aristocracy.

"They all carry on like that." Phoebe assured her. "My aunt Floss, who works in the kitchens, says some of the women are as bad as the men. Once they've had their children and provided their husbands with an heir, they do what they like."

The end of the Season brought news for Harry. He stopped Daisy as they passed on the stairs, having been to see his parents. "I'm to go back to London with Mama and Papa."

She commiserated. "Oh, that's a shame."

"No, really. I'm looking forward to it." He nudged her conspiratorially. "They're dismissing Mr Peters. Oh, he won't suffer," he added. "He'll get three months severance pay and a good reference. I overheard Papa telling Grandmamma."

"But, why on earth?" interrupted Daisy.

"Mamma doesn't want me growing up like a country yokel, so she says. I'm to share a tutor with my Harrington cousins who live in Woburn Place. I shall go there by carriage every day."

"But, who'll look after you. Make your cocoa at night?"

"I shall be eight years old on September fourth, Daisy. I don't need babying any longer. Mrs Withers will make my cocoa and Mama's maid will look after my clothes."

"But, what about washing behind your ears?"

Harry grinned. "I shan't need to any more."

Daisy was thoughtful. With Harry back in London, it would hardly take three of them to look after the rest of the children.

"What are you thinking about?" asked Nanny when the children were in bed.

"What'll happen to me, when Harry's gone?"

"To be sure I don't know." She frowned. "Her Ladyship hasn't spoken to me about it yet, but I must warn you, Daisy. I can't see her keeping you on, under the circumstances."

Daisy cried silently into her pillow that night. She'd been so happy here in Thetford, with the children and everything. Why did it all have to change? But the hoops used for croquet were put in store for the next summer along with the mallets and balls, temporary hire dismissed and covers put on the furniture in the unused rooms. Branstead was quieter, and wild life returned to the grounds as gardeners prepared for autumn.

Chapter 11

Something disturbed Daisy in the night and she woke with a start. She lay still, trying to identify the faint crackling that seemed to come from the centre of the house. Sitting up in bed, she heard the rustling and scraping again. Was it a mouse? Although they were used to hearing mice scampering about in the attics, this was different. She glanced out of the window, expecting to see the usual silvery shafts of light cast by the moon. Instead the far side of the room was bathed in pale orange and Daisy was puzzled by the change. Then, she sniffed and panicked!

"Oh my Gawd," she screamed, "Phoebe, Phoebe. I think the house is on fire. Get up." She shook Phoebe as hard as she could and shouted into the girl's dazed face.

"Get up, Phoebe — get the kids. The house is on fire!"

Thrusting her feet into her shoes, she ran into the nursery and picked up George, who roared with anger at being woken so abruptly. Ignoring his protests, she held him close while she ran to Nanny's room. "Get up, Nanny. Get up."

The older woman growled at being disturbed then put her hands to her face and stared.

"Daisy, have you gone mad. What do you think you're doing?"

"I think the house is on fire, Nanny. Quickly — you'd best get up!"

Nanny pulled off her nightcap and slid out of bed, fumbling for her slippers before hurrying over to William. She took him from his cradle before asking,

"Where's Phoebe?"

"I'm not sure. I told her to get up. I'll go and shake her again."

A dazed Phoebe appeared, with a sleepy Adelaide in tow. She pulled a coat over the child's nightgown as they all made their way down the West Wing stairway. Unbolting the door, the little party crept into the moonlit garden where the reek of smoke was overpowering. Other members of staff had been roused by the smell of burning and were slowly gathering at the front of the house to watch the flames as they crept through the far side of the house.

One of the grooms was quickly despatched to alert Mr Danbury who would take charge of the situation.

"Where on earth shall we go?" asked Phoebe. Nanny had been deep in conversation with the housekeeper who reckoned the kitchens were unaffected by the fire.

"I could do with a nice cup of tea," declared Nanny, looking at Cook. Before long they saw Mr Danbury's tall frame outlined against the trees as he approached them.

"Are you ladies all right?" he asked.

"We are," replied Nanny. "But the baby needs his milk and a change of napkin. What am I to do?"

"I can't let you back into the house, I'm afraid. But I think your wing is pretty sound. Tell me what you need and I'll go up there myself and get it. I've asked one of my men to bring the wagon round so he can take you over to my place. You and the children will be safe there for the rest of the night. And you, Mrs Taylor." he nodded in the cook's direction.

"My woman, Mrs Jones, knows you're on your way. She's a kindly person and will help you with what you need."

He returned holding a bag containing of William's napkins, some muslin squares and a couple of feeding bottles. So, rubbing their eyes, the little party wearily hauled themselves into the trap. It was a couple of hours later when, after a soothing drink, they sank gratefully into the soft beds Danbury's housekeeper had prepared for them.

The estate had its own fire engine but it took an hour for it to trundle up the drive. All night long, workmen passed buckets of water to and fro in an effort to quench the fire, which seemed to have started in one of the guest rooms. By morning, the exhausted estate workers, their faces, blackened with smoke, declared the fire out.

The beautiful house was a mess. Carpets and expensive drapes were saturated where water had been thrown carelessly, and priceless works of art had been ruined. Until the house was examined for structural damage, it was declared unsafe.

Daisy and Phoebe were up early the next morning. The children were fractious due to their disturbed night and the girls didn't feel much better. Nanny was short-tempered and tut-tutted noisily when she was unable to find all the wanted. The good natured housekeeper prepared breakfast for them, gossiping as she ladled porridge into earthenware bowls.

"I thought the world was coming to an end when I saw them flames. Such a terrible time for the Earl and his Lady."

Nanny's reply was caustic.

"They're in London," she said. "Have you seen Mr Danbury this morning?"

"Oh, 'e was out early, Nanny Bruce. 'ad hardly a wink of sleep last night, he did. Said I was to take care of you as best I can." She bustled around happily. "I think I'll do a nice steak and kidney pudding today.

The little ones can have veg mashed into the liquor."

Nanny was appeased. "Thank you, Mrs Jones. That sounds very nice."

Daisy spooned porridge into her mouth thoughtfully. Things were going from bad to worse. No job and now the house was in ruins. Phoebe commiserated with her when they took the children for a walk after lunch.

"Something'll turn up, Dais. We'll put our thinking caps on — there are lots of big estates in Norfolk,"

They were eating lunch when they heard the approach of a horse. It whinnied as it was pulled up outside the house and dragging the curtain aside, Mrs Jones saw Mr Danbury jumping down. He came through the front door, refusing his housekeeper's offer of food.

"I've had something to eat, thank you, Mrs Jones. I've far too much to do — can't stop now."

"Perhaps I can put some aside, Sir, and warm it up for your supper," she insisted.

"Very good. But, I've come with news."

He looked at Nanny and the children. "You're all to go to the Dower House with the old Countess. Some of the staff from the big house are preparing rooms for you and Cook, as I speak."

"That's welcome news, Mr Danbury and very kind of Lady Charlotte," replied Nanny. "What about the equipment from the nursery?"

"That's being sorted out. I said I'd get the trap out and take you over there at about four o'clock. Will that suit?"

"I suppose it'll have to," Nanny mumbled in reply, and not wanting to appear ungracious she added, "Thank you. You've been very kind." She turned to the housekeeper. "And you, Mrs Jones, you've looked after us magnificently."

Lime Lodge, referred to on the estate as the Dower house, was much smaller than Branstead, but still a substantial house. Built in the seventeenth century for the mother of the Earl when he married, the outside was gothic in appearance. It took its name from the lime trees that lined the drive and gave off a pungent perfume in the summer. The present Dowager had laid large Persian rugs over the stone floors and hung tapestries on the walls. The new furnishings bestowed the effect of warmth and almost, cosiness.

"Thank goodness I don't have to live with those grim ancestors staring down at me any longer," Lady Charlotte had been heard to say, when obliged to leave Branstead.

Rooms had been prepared for the nursery party on the second floor but Daisy was to join the other servants in the attic. However, she did at least have a room to herself since the house was run with a much smaller staff. She received the message that Lady Charlotte would like to see her at four p.m. The Dowager was in her sitting room when Daisy knocked on the door.

"Sit down. I want to talk to you."

Daisy nodded anxiously and sat on the edge of her chair, feet dangling and with her hands clasped in her lap.

"I'm aware of the situation with the children, and the fact that you might no longer have a job now that Harry has gone," the Dowager Countess said. "In the past, since I'm often away, I haven't been in need of a large retinue to attend me. Lime Lodge, the same as Branstead, is run with a skeleton staff and we hire extra help when I'm in residence." She paused as she looked at the cuff of her dress.

"You see this? A button has fallen off, and Mildred's eyes aren't as good as they were. She's missed it."

Wondering what the buttons had to do with her, Daisy waited for the Dowager to resume.

"Mildred is my personal maid, and has been for many years. My dressmaker is in London and Mildred does any small repairs for me. There used to be a good little dressmaker in Thetford, but she married and moved away. Unfortunately," she added irritably.

"Yes, Your Ladyship," replied Daisy.

"What I've decided is this. Mildred isn't getting any younger and perhaps you can help her. Can you sew?"

Daisy hesitated. "Well, yes I can sew a bit, Your Ladyship. I can turn a neat stitch and sew on buttons. I made me Sunday dress, with help from Phoebe."

"Good. Nanny says you iron well, so you can press all my clothes and keep them in good condition. Also, you can keep my personal rooms clean and tidy. That will help Mrs Sargent, she's my housekeeper."

Daisy blushed with pleasure. "You mean I can stay?"

"Yes, I think you'll do very well. Nanny says you're polite and considerate. I really need a little extra help."

"But, Nanny says you don't spend much time in the Dower House. Is it only until you go away again?"

"Of course not." Lady Charlotte looked pensive. "I'm not as young as I was. We're all getting older, I'm afraid and I get fed up with travelling. Anyway my son will be returning to Branstead in a couple of days. He's bringing an architect with him, to assess the damage." She stared out of the window, before continuing. "I expect he'll want me to keep an eye on the rebuilding of Branstead, so I'll need more staff anyway. Especially while the children are here."

Daisy looked down at her hands and asked, "Will I be able to see the children?"

Lady Charlotte looked sympathetic. "I'm sure you'll see them during the day, Daisy. They'll be around the house. You may go now."

Daisy fled to Nanny to tell her the good news. She was allowed to have tea with the children, as she wasn't to commence her duties until the next day. Mildred was a bit dour and although the thought of getting help pleased her, she was resentful of another person being involved with Lady Charlotte.

"She won't keep you if you don't pull your weight," she advised coldly. "I hope you can sew a decent stitch. She's always losing buttons and ripping her clothes."

Daisy was diplomatic. "I'm not too bad Mildred, if I can call you that, but I'll need help. Lady Charlotte told me how much she relies on you and said you can teach me a lot."

Mildred was mollified and set Daisy to repairing a seam on a chemise. "Nice neat stitches, mind you!" she warned.

Daisy slipped into a routine and for the next eighteen months life passed pleasantly. Mildred mellowed a little, and Lady Charlotte was kept busy overseeing the rebuilding of Branstead. As Daisy's fourteenth birthday neared, the house was declared safe.

She enjoyed looking after the Dowager's clothes and tidying her rooms, but found Mildred dull company so was often lonely because she had little contact with the younger members of staff. The year of the fire, the children had gone down to Bloomsbury for Christmas and sadly, in Daisy's opinion, didn't return. The doctors considered William better able to deal with his asthma and their confidence seemed to be justified. He was now a normal, happy toddler.

Daisy was overjoyed to see the children when they came for the summer in 1860. Harry had been at Eton for two years and Adelaide had a governess whom she shared with the irrepressible George. Daisy always accompanied Lady Charlotte when she took the children for picnics. She saw little of Phoebe but it became obvious that summer that Phoebe was being courted by Jimmy Fawcett.

"Don't say anything, Daisy," she'd pleaded when they met in the village. "The Countess don't approve of followers."

"I won't say a word. When are you getting married?"

"Next year. Jimmy wants me to give up working in London and come back to Thetford. He's going to apply for a job on one of the bigger farms — one that comes with a cottage."

Daisy beamed. "You, a married woman, Phoebe. I hope you don't live too far away, then I can visit on my day off!"

"Oh Daisy. That'd be nice. I miss having someone young to talk to in London."

"I get lonely too, Phoeb. But Lady Charlotte is easy to work for and I'm happy enough."

The year of the wedding seemed to arrive quickly and on the eve of Phoebe's big day Daisy was given permission by The Dowager to attend the wedding in the village church.

"Mildred tells me you're quite a little seamstress now, Daisy," remarked Lady Charlotte as she examined the hem of a velvet dress. "I like the way you inserted a panel into the sleeves, as well. Pagoda sleeves are very fashionable just now."

Daisy blushed with pleasure. "I like altering garments, Your Ladyship. I thought the royal blue brocade could be brought up-to-date with a bertha collar and if we trimmed the black toque with matching feathers, it would look quite charming. I can do much more with your clothes now that you don't wear mourning any more."

There had been quite a change to the Dowager's mode of dress since she'd stayed in the country. Having worn mourning for years, it had been ruthlessly abandoned when a certain Sir Algernon Fox began making regular visits.

Sir Algernon owned an estate on the outskirts of King's Lynn and when Lady Charlotte told him about Phoebe's marriage, he'd set about finding Jimmy employment on his farm. Although elderly, he was charming and courteous, and it was obvious Lady Charlotte enjoyed his company.

Algi, as the Dowager called him, was about medium height and portly. His breeches buttons always looked as if they were about to pop as his stomach strained at its confines. Totally bald, his head shone as though polished, and his chins shook when he laughed — which was often. He entertained the Dowager immensely and the atmosphere at Lime Lodge lightened when he visited.

The day of the wedding dawned fair and Daisy was driven into the village on one of the carts belonging to the estate. She'd made a new dress for the occasion with material bought from the village shop.

Making her way into the church she sat at the rear and waited for the wedding party. Phoebe was prettily dressed in pale blue checked muslin, with a bonnet to match, whilst Jimmy wore a new suit of clothes that would stay in his wardrobe until the next family occasion.

Daisy was touched when Phoebe made her vows and earnestly wished in her heart for the bride's happiness.

The guests went back to Phoebe's parents' cottage for the wedding feast which consisted of ale or lemonade, chunks of honey roasted ham with potatoes baked on the old range. This was followed by a deep apple and blackberry pie topped with clotted cream. It was delicious, and Daisy sang and danced outside until it was time to return to Lime Lodge. She said her goodbyes and waited on a bench by the chicken shed for the cart to take her home. The ale had made her sleepy and she sat contentedly recalling the day's events and how Phoebe's serious little face had lit up when she promised herself to the man she loved. It was then she heard a soft footfall.

"Well, if it ain't little Daisy. Snivelling little Daisy from the cellar. I thought it was you when I saw the red 'air."

Startled, Daisy turned to look at her accuser. Her world fell apart when she recognised Rose. An older Rose, a dirtier Rose, but she still had the meanness in her eyes that Daisy remembered so well. She stared with her mouth open as Rose pranced in front of her.

"Well now. Quite the little lady, ain't we? Doing well for yerself I 'ear. Oh yes," she crowed as she strutted up and down. "I asked questions when I see you. Work for the aristocracy, don't you? Nice pickings there for a sensible girl, I reckon."

"What do you mean, pickings?"

"Well, I bet they don't know you've been locked up for thieving, do they?"

Daisy declined to answer and Rose thrust her face nearer as she continued, "I won't tell 'em, if you do as I say, gel. I'm 'ungry. I need food. Bring me some tonight."

"Food from where? I can't take food from the pantry! Cook'll know. Anyway I should tell on you. You got me into trouble. You got me sent to prison."

Daisy looked around furtively, anxious that nobody was listening. She thought quickly. She had to get Rose away from the village.

"What are you doing here, anyway?"

The girl sniffed as she wiped her nose on the back of her hand.

"I heard what happened to you from one of me contacts. We all 'ad to leave the cellar before the Peelers found us. One of my men decided London was too 'ot and we got the mail coach to Ipswich. Planned to go into business once we got there, but he let me down." She kicked at some stones with worn boots while she thought about her plight. "I've been getting work where I can. I was living with me grandparents but they said they couldn't keep me any longer. So I've just bin walking for the past week."

Had Daisy not known better, she'd have felt sorry for the girl who looked thin and worn. "I'll try to pop out later, after my mistress has retired. I'm not sure how I'll do it, but I'll get you some food."

She thought quickly. "There's a quarry by the road that runs round the east side of the estate. Meet me there." She pointed in the direction of the house. "Take the track that leads off the left side of the road — just before you get to the gates. You can't miss the entrance. It says *Branstead Park* in gold letters. Sorry." She apologised, remembering that Rose couldn't read very well. "Go down the track opposite the gates and you'll come to the quarry."

Rose narrowed her eyes. "What time?"

"Between eight and nine — I can't get away before then. I'll try to sneak you out some food. Okay?"

Rose's eyes narrowed but she nodded. "No tricks now."

"Of course not." Daisy looked up. "Here's the cart coming to take me back. I'll have to go."

Chapter 12

Daisy's heart was leaden but she forced a smile when she returned to Lime Lodge. She saw to Her Ladyship's needs and at about seven o'clock went into the kitchen where Cook was labelling up jars of preserves.

"Hello, Daisy!" she greeted her favourite. "How did the wedding go off?"

"It was lovely," Daisy replied. "Phoebe looked really happy. I danced all afternoon."

They settled down for a gossip and when she'd given Cook the details of the afternoon's events, she asked for some food.

"Oh, I'm sorry. . ." Cook went to the pantry and brought back some ham and bread. "I didn't think you'd be hungry after the wedding feast."

"It's all the dancing, I expect," replied Daisy, feeling guilty at deceiving Cook whom she both liked and respected. "I've got a headache coming on. You wouldn't mind if I took this to my room, would you? Just this once?"

Cook hesitated, then frowned. "You know it's against the rules. Oh, all right then, but don't let anybody else see you. They'll all want to do it."

Daisy hid the plate under her apron and said goodnight. She turned round to call out *thank you,* but Cook had her back to her and was already preparing Lady Charlotte's supper, so Daisy snatched a pie from the dresser and put it in her pocket.

Later she called in on Mildred who was darning some stockings. "I'm just going out for a walk," she explained. "I've got a bit of a headache. Probably the excitement of the wedding, and a stroll through the grounds might help me get rid of it."

The sky was still bright at half-past eight and as Daisy strolled through the garden, perfume from the flowers mingled with the scent from the herb garden. To an onlooker her demeanour might have appeared casual but her heart hammered in her chest as she passed through the grounds and walked towards the gatehouse. She scrambled through a gap in the hedge, not daring to go through the half open gates in case the gatekeeper saw her. Running over the road, she slid down the embankment and looked for her tormentor.

"Psst....psssst." Rose thrust out a claw from behind a bush. "I'm here. Got the food?" Daisy sauntered towards her with deliberate steps before whipping the food from under her apron. She'd made the bread and ham into a sandwich and placed the pie on top. Rose grabbed the food and stuffed it eagerly into her mouth. It was obvious she hadn't eaten for some time. Daisy turned to go but the girl detained her.

"Be here the same time tomorrer. And bring me something to drink next time."

"Really, I can't," protested Daisy.

"Got a fancy way of talking now, 'aven't we — must be mixing with all them fine people. You'll find a way," snarled Rose. "I've bin thinking. A trinket or two from the old girl's rooms wouldn't go amiss. Get me some bits and pieces I can sell. And the food and drink, mind you."

Daisy slowly returned to the house in a quandary. The Dowager Countess had been very kind and trusted her. She didn't want to steal, but what could she do? Rose would tell on her if she didn't give her some things she could sell and surely the Dowager wouldn't miss some very small items? If only she could keep Rose quiet for a day or two, maybe she'd think of a way of dealing with her.

Daisy dusted Lady Charlotte's private rooms while she was at church the next morning. Trying to hide her uneasiness; she hummed as she flicked the feather duster to and fro, before slipping a little Viennese beaker decorated with tarot cards into her pocket. This was followed by a cut glass scent bottle, hastily taken from the back of a cabinet.

At lunch, she secreted some bread and cheese into the capacious pocket of her white frilled apron, smiling at the thought of the food being contaminated by her polishing rags. She grinned and said to herself — should make the bread quite tasty, that.

When she met Rose again later, she said "Here you are, and this is the last time I'm thieving for you. If you don't go away, I'll take my chances." Daisy shoved the food into Rose's outstretched hand, and then carefully retrieved the trinkets she'd hidden in the waistband of her dress. Rose inspected them.

"They look all right. Should get something for 'em."

"I'm not coming again tomorrow," Daisy began, but Rose interrupted her by shaking her head.

"It'll take me best part of a week to get to Norwich, sell this china and get back again. Say six days from now. Next Saturday. And you be 'ere."

"I'll do my best Rose but I can't promise. I never know what Mildred'll ask me to do."

"Who's Mildred, for Gawd's sake?"

"She's the mistress's personal maid. I help her."

"Oh dear, it's all so lah-di-dah now, isn't it? You make sure you get here, young'n, or 'eaven help you."

Daisy fled back to the house and spent the next day wondering how on earth to get rid of Rose, and even contemplated taking Mildred into her confidence about her past. But, she wasn't close to Mildred, as she had been with Phoebe and didn't think she'd understand.

How Daisy wished Phoebe was back in the village, but she was serving out a terms' notice in Bloomsbury. She'd begin her married life with Jimmy in the service of Sir Algernon when she left London for the last time. Meanwhile events left Daisy little time to think because Mildred, climbing a ladder in the library to get a book for Lady Charlotte, missed her footing and fell. She was taken to the infirmary where her leg was found to be broken, so the bone was set, necessitating convalescence with her mother.

The Dowager sent a message to Daisy who was ironing in the wardrobe room. Daisy put the iron back on the range and hurried downstairs.

"I'm in trouble, Daisy," puffed Lady Charlotte. She paced up and down the room, her crinolined dress swaying as it brushed over the carpet.

"I've received an invitation to a wedding in Paris, France, which necessitates my leaving here as early as next Sunday. It's a very sudden affair." She frowned as she adjusted the cuffs on her gown. "How inconsiderate of my niece to marry in such haste — you'll have to come with me. Do you think you could manage?"

Daisy demurred. "Well, Your Ladyship. I've never dressed you completely on my own but I've watched Mildred do your hair. I'm sure I can look after your clothes all right but I'm not sure about the rest. And, the travelling and all that. I've never been out of England. Would I have to talk in French?"

Lady Charlotte laughed. "Oh, Daisy. I can see we're going to have to help each other. Meantime, you can practice on my hair and we'll see about getting you a passport. As for my jewellery, well, there's no reason why I shouldn't look after it myself, I suppose." She stood at the window, deep in thought. "Most unfortunate that Mildred broke her leg. I hope you won't be seasick. And, moreover, I hope my niece won't live to regret taking on that philandering young man. I can't understand her parents allowing it. Oh... I see...." Her voice trailed and she snapped her fingers. "Of course — she's with child, I'll wager. Stupid young woman!"

The following week saw Daisy dressing the Dowager's hair, and doing it quite successfully. Having had her hair well brushed, Lady Charlotte wore it turned under and drawn into a low chignon, with a plait across the top of her head. Daisy didn't have time to think about Rose as she pressed and refreshed the garments Lady Charlotte had chosen for the visit. Unsurprisingly she'd appealed to Sir Algi for help and he offered to partner her. Together with his valet and private secretary, the party were to be taken by carriage to the port of Harwich. Thence they'd go by sea to Ostend before travelling by road to Paris. Daisy was in a high state of excitement coupled with anxiety. Not only was this to be her first trip to another country, but she was worried about the situation with Rose.

On the day she was to meet her at the quarry, Daisy stole a diamond and ruby necklace. She hated deceiving Lady Charlotte but stealthily unlocked the wooden cabinet, and put the necklace in her pocket along with some food. When she reached the quarry that night Rose was in a foul mood.

"Is this all the food you've got? Not enough to keep body and soul together."

"It's all I could get," Daisy muttered. "And this." She held out her hand with the necklace, which Rose quickly snatched.

"I didn't get much of a price for the other things, but this looks better."

Daisy drew herself up to her full height.

"This is the last time Rose. I'm going away with my mistress tomorrow, for about a week, and when I come back, I want you gone. You'll get no food while I'm away so there's no point in staying. If you insist on threatening me, I'll go to Her Ladyship and confess."

"You silly little cow." Rose's face was contorted as she screamed abuse. "You can't treat me like this. I'll turn you in. Don't forget the things you stole for me."

Daisy replied calmly, although her heart was thumping in her chest. "You don't have proof of that, Rose. Nobody has seen us together." She took a deep breath before continuing. "I shall say you broke into the house while the Dowager and I were away. Nobody will believe you. Look at yourself — who'd take notice of a scarecrow like you?"

Rose roared with anger and went to strike Daisy on the shoulder but Daisy jumped aside and to her dismay, Rose fell headlong into the quarry. Horrified Daisy watched from the embankment as Rose went tumbling down, coming to rest on a hawthorn bush. There was a sickening crack as Rose's neck snapped. She lay in an awkward position like a limp rag doll and Daisy guessed rightly there was nothing to be done.

She was stunned — and rooted to the spot as her heart thumped fit to burst. Should she see if her tormenter was still alive? Common sense told Daisy to leave the girl alone, so she scuttled through the hedge and back to Lime Lodge.

She felt uneasy as she looked in on Lady Charlotte to see if there was anything she needed before she retired.

"Why Daisy! You look flushed. Are you feeling all right?"

"Yes, Your Ladyship. I'm fine. I've been finishing off the ironing. Do you need help undressing this evening?"

"I don't think so but I'll ring if I do. Just hang up my gown for tomorrow and put the jewellery back in its case, then you may retire. We have to be up early tomorrow. I take it you're packed?"

Daisy assured Lady Charlotte that all was well. "The largest trunks are in the hall already, Your Ladyship." The last thing she remembered that evening was to pray that Rose's body wasn't found until the travellers were crossing the channel.

The young man was dressed elegantly. "I think we shall have good weather for the rest of the crossing, Miss Smith."

Daisy looked up into Vernon Fenn's grey-blue eyes. "Do you think so? That's good news for me. I've never been on the water before and I'm not sure I'll like it."

They stood at the railings encasing the deck of the ferry and watched the waves ripple across the deep green waters of the English Channel. Daisy sniffed the air. "It certainly smells differently from London, or the Norfolk countryside, come to that."

She realised Vernon was studying her and was pleased she'd chosen her lemon silk dress, with the front bodice fastening. He probably guessed she didn't have the benefit of his education, but her manner of speech had certainly improved. With a well-developed bosom and narrow waist, she made an attractive figure. And this, with a milky complexion topped by flaming red hair, rendered her very desirable indeed.

Daisy was very direct and asked, "Why are you staring at me?"

Vernon was taken aback and replied, "I'm sorry if I was being rude but I think you're awfully pretty." He bowed his apology and Daisy grinned.

"I'm sorry too. I'm not used to people looking at me, especially young men. I don't meet many." She blushed and looked towards the water then the two young people continued their stroll around the deck, Vernon having been told to escort Daisy, by Sir Algi. She found herself telling him how she came to be in Lady Charlotte's employ and why

95

she, instead of Mildred, was accompanying her mistress to France. Vernon came from a middle class working family, he told her. His father had a string of butcher shops around the country, some of which supplied Foxlands, being Sir Algi's estate. The latter offered the young man a post as his private secretary when he left college, and Vernon had been employed by him for a couple of years.

"What do you do, as his secretary?" asked Daisy.

"All sorts of things. Answer letters, see to the accounts on the farms and the house. Look after invitations. Run personal errands."

"And do you enjoy your employment?"

"Oh yes. Sir Algernon is very good to work for. Shall we sit down for a while?"

They found an unoccupied space next to a French family with young children, and sat in companionable silence as the ship rocked gently on the calm sea. Daisy noticed the strong calves under his tight trousers and felt a quickening in her stomach. His nearness made her stiffen with anxiety and she rose suddenly.

"I think I'll go and see if Lady Charlotte needs anything," she explained. Vernon nodded and said he'd stay on deck for a while.

"Ah, there you are, Daisy," beamed the Dowager, when Daisy tapped on the half-opened cabin door. "It can't be very long before we dock. I say, that's a pretty dress you're wearing. Did you make it yourself?"

Daisy blushed with pleasure as she answered in the affirmative. She was even more pleased at the Dowager's reply.

"I think you might try making a simple day dress for me when we return to Lime Lodge. Do you think you could?"

"I'd love to. We've got several pattern books your Ladyship. Those short stand-up collars are fashionable this season. Mildred and I like to keep up with the latest."

"Really, Daisy. I had no idea you knew about high fashion."

"I suggested we try making up something for you once, just for day-wear, but Mildred didn't think you'd like it. She said you buy all your clothes in London and wouldn't want to wear things we made. I do love sewing."

Lady Charlotte peered at Daisy. She thought the girl was getting far too pretty for her own good, and took too much interest her clothes. She sighed, and wondered how much longer it would be before some young pup turned up to deflower her.

"You're not allowed followers, Daisy. You do realise that? It's my duty to take care of you."

"Of course! I don't have followers, Your Ladyship," cried the horrified Daisy. "I know they're not allowed and in any case, I never meet any boys."

Lady Charlotte touched her lightly on the arm.

"I know you're a good girl." Daisy felt mean when she remembered taking the woman's trinkets. She'd grown quite fond of her mistress and was determined not to let her down again.

They left Ostend and travelled by carriage to a villa on the outskirts of Paris. The estate was owned by the Compte de Este, who'd been a friend of Lady Charlotte's first husband. Daisy was allotted a room in the servants' quarters and smiled tentatively at the other maids, trying to convey a feeling of friendliness, whilst not being able to converse in their language. She was rewarded by some merry smiles in return and one young girl brought her a glass of lemonade.

On the day of the wedding, Daisy dressed Lady Charlotte in a black and gold striped satin dress with bishop sleeves and a small black lace collar. On her head she wore a black toque with a marigold ostrich feather. Rows of jet beads were strung round her neck and she carried buttoned satin gloves and a parasol made from material matching her gown. Her crinoline was now fashionably flatter at the front.

Daisy admired her handiwork. "You look lovely, Your Ladyship," she ventured.

"Thank you. I do look rather fine, don't I?" She pirouetted in front of the mirror, admiring herself. Before she turned to go, she looked at Daisy anxiously.

"What will you do with yourself while I'm away?"

"I haven't thought about it, Your Ladyship."

Lady Charlotte snapped her fingers, "I know! You can take a walk around the estate, perhaps read in the grounds. I shall be away until very late, so make sure you get something to eat. I'll get Sir Algi's valet to take care of you, and Vernon speaks French, so none of you will starve."

Daisy watched the carriage roll down the drive and decided to walk in the grounds. The rose gardens were exquisite, with huge blooms and fallen petals scattered throughout the flower beds, their perfume saturating the air. She sat on a bench and closed her eyes, trying to capture the moment for future years. This, she thought, must be the most beautiful place on earth, more lovely even than Norfolk.

Some time later a bell tinkled from somewhere within the house and Daisy decided that since her stomach felt rather empty, it must be nearing lunch time. She met Henry Carter, the valet, in the main hall.

"Ah, Daisy, I was looking for you. Mr Fenn says we're to meet him in the upper-servant's dining room for lunch. Follow me."

Daisy walked behind him and they entered a large, noisy room where the staff were waiting to be served. They looked up when the pair entered and the butler called over to them,

"Je m'appelle Louis. Comment vous appelez-vous, et le madamoiselle?"

As if from nowhere, Vernon appeared and introduced them in French. After conversing with Louis, he took them to one side.

"You gathered his name is Louis. Nice chap. He says to sit on the side-table over there." He indicated with his hand. "And the servants will bring us food." They took their seats, while the rest of the staff gave them curious glances. The meal was very tasty consisting of beef braised in garlic and onion sauce, accompanied by baby potatoes and crusty bread. A peach flan followed, washed down with red wine. Daisy wasn't used to drinking wine and felt her cheeks flush. Vernon laughed and suggested some fresh air was needed, so a walk through the vineyard might be in order. The valet interrupted.

"Do you think you should, sir? Take the young lady out alone, I mean?"

"Nonsense," came the scathing reply. "She'll come to no harm with me."

Chapter 13

Vernon waited while Daisy fetched her bonnet so they could walk around the estate. They found themselves in a small vineyard and Vernon told Daisy about his conversation with a valet.

"Apparently the owner attempts to grow grapes in unsuitable soil, with the result the fruit is quite puny," he explained, as they walked through the vines, sheltered from the strong sun.

"France is so beautiful," replied Daisy as she a cupped a bunch of small grapes in her palm. They lay there as she stroked them tenderly and a strange look came over Vernon's eyes.

"Let's walk further," he suggested hastily, and they ambled onwards, through a meadow until they came across a gate in a hedge.

"Do you think we might be trespassing onto somebody else's property?" asked Daisy as they contemplated the other side.

"I'm sure no one will mind us taking a walk," Vernon replied. "Oh look, there's a hut over there. Let's see what's within."

He helped Daisy through the gate and they cautiously opened the door. Vernon peered inside. "Thank goodness, a seat. There's somewhere to rest. It must be somebody's summerhouse, or some such thing."

He sat down and patted the bench. "Come — rest."

Daisy sat down and he moved to be near her. She could feel him looking at her and became confused when Vernon began tracing her eyes with the tip of his finger.

"You're so lovely, Daisy," he whispered. He began stroking her face softly, running a finger along one of her cheeks, then covering her ears with both his hands. "Kiss me, sweet Daisy," he murmured, as he bent his face towards hers. He gently untied the strings to her bonnet and lifted it from her head as his lips found hers. Her bonnet fell to the floor and his kiss was light as a feather. Daisy found herself responding, gently at first, then fiercely, as his kiss became more urgent. She felt the same stirring in her inside as when she'd seen the Earl naked in the woods but when Vernon's fingers toyed with the bodice of her dress, she made to push him away.

"No. No. You're not taking me down, Vernon."

The young man look startled. "But I wouldn't do anything to hurt you, Daisy. I love you. Don't you know?"

Daisy demurred. "You love me, Vernon? But why didn't you say?"

He smiled at her confusion. "I'm saying it now, you little silly. Let me just touch you, Daisy? Let me feel your sweet body, just once. I'll not ask again." He buried his head in her bosom and she could feel the warmth of his lips through her cotton dress.

"You'll mark my frock," she cried.

"Then let me unbutton it, so that nobody will know, you little enchantress," he sighed then began to unfasten her bodice. Daisy's head was in turmoil as he uncovered her breasts.

"You're so beautiful, my little love," Vernon breathed into her ear, as he tried to control his mounting passion. "Just let me feel your skin. I promise not to do anything you don't want me to."

She wanted to be touched, but was also frightened of the outcome. Vernon took her silence as approval and began lifting her skirts to stroke her leg. She could feel the warmth of his flesh through her cotton bloomers as his fingers crept towards her thigh. So she wavered, her body longing to be close to his. Suddenly common sense prevailed, and she pushed his tormenting hands away.

"I can't Vernon. I can't."

Vernon jumped up and went to the other side of the hut, turning his back as he adjusted his trousers to accommodate his swollen groin.

"You're a tease, Daisy Smith," he growled, his face flushed with excitement. "You've been leading me on ever since we started on this trip."

"Please, Vernon. No," replied Daisy as she covered her breasts and buttoned up her dress. "I didn't lead you on. I like you, you know that. And I'd love to lie with you, but not like this."

Vernon hooted with derision. "You don't think I'd actually marry you, do you?"

Daisy was aghast. "You said you love me. If you do, then you'd want to marry me. If you don't love me, you shouldn't try to take me down."

Vernon was curt. "Marry you! I can't marry a servant girl. My father would be furious." He sneered as he looked her over and found her wanting. "But I know how you feel now, Daisy." He took her hand and placed it over his groin. "And now you know how I feel, and you'll want to again."

Retrieving her hand, Daisy picked up her bonnet and fled. She crossed the field and ran between the vines, hoping she wouldn't meet Henry Carter, who might well wonder at her distress. She cried with shame when she reached her room. How could she allow herself to be treated so? She was as silly as any scullery maid who thought it was an honour to be abused by her master. But however much she protested, she still had the longing inside her and was relieved when she felt the start of her monthly flow. At least she'd have some protection against the attentions of the persuasive Vernon Fenn.

Daisy was relieved when Lady Charlotte returned and rushed to her side immediately she was sent for, walking swiftly along the corridors hoping she wouldn't meet Vernon on the way. She excused herself from any effort made by Vernon to be alone with her at the chateau for the next couple of days, keeping to the servants' rooms, pressing and re-pressing her mistress's clothes, causing considerable amusement to the Compte's valet and wardrobe mistress.

The Dowager enthused about the wonderful attire worn at the wedding, as Daisy brushed her hair.

"Those Parisienne ladies are very chic. They dress in a way that is so subtle; you'd think they'd taken no trouble with their appearance at all. Everything they wear is of the finest quality and I've become aware of how dowdy my wardrobe has become"

She fussed with her collar. "I must get myself some new clothes. I don't know where the last sixty years have gone," she said as she preened herself before the mirror. "I feel like a girl of seventeen."

Daisy wondered at her Ladyship's high spirits. Most of the mourning wear had been relegated to some disused closets and although never flamboyant, there was now a certain éclat when she walked and talked. Although it was her nature to be garrulous and warm-hearted, she'd begun to bloom in a way that gladdened Daisy's heart.

She appeared to be younger than when Daisy had first set eyes upon her in the nursery at Branstead. It was a pleasure to help her dress and to brush the long, sleek hair that still retained much of its original colour, making Daisy wonder just how old she was?

Vernon nodded politely when the carriage called for them on the morning of their departure but he cast sidelong glances at Daisy when he thought nobody was looking. She felt uncomfortable under his gaze and lowered her eyes in case he should see the desire that burned in them. She kept the Dowager company in her cabin on the sea journey, declaring she was too tired to walk on deck.

They played cards to pass the time and it wasn't until the port of Harwich came in sight that Daisy allowed herself to think of Rose. She wondered whether her body had been recovered, or indeed if she'd only imagined Rose was dead at all.

Storm clouds were gathering as the party waited for the ship to dock and where the weather had been warm and sultry for a few weeks, there was now a distinctive crackle in the air. Daisy looked up at the purple clouds scudding across the sky, reminding her of witches with their skirts billowing as they rode their broomsticks. Large drops of rain sent the party scurrying for the carriage that was waiting at the dockside, laughing, as threw themselves inside.

Lady Charlotte and Daisy were exhausted when Sir Algi left them at Lime Lodge, and the former gave instructions for both of them to be served with hot chocolate, before she dealt with any household problems that may have arisen. Daisy drank hers in the servants' dining hall, aware Rose's body might have been found. She trembled at the thought, with the chocolate drink spilling into the saucer as she set it on the table. All had seemed so different in France but now she must be prepared for any gossip that might arise. Mildred was still with her mother and would be for some time to come so Daisy decided to take her empty cup along to the kitchen to chat to the cook.

"How was Paris?" Cook asked, as Daisy entered the room.

"Lady Charlotte said it was wonderful. I didn't go into the City, of course but she was full of all the latest fashions and says the Parisiennes are very smart."

Cook wanted to hear about the wedding so Daisy repeated what Lady Charlotte had told her, and continued, "I stayed out at the villa, don't ask me the name of the place, it was something French. The gardens were lovely and there was a little vineyard where the owner was trying to grow grapes. It was very interesting." She felt herself flush as she thought of Vernon and his attempt to seduce her but came back to the present as Cook continued:

"I'd love to go to Paris, but I don't suppose I ever will. Not unless I finds meself a rich husband." She rocked with laughter, her jowls juddering at the impossibility of such a thing ever happening, and Daisy joined in.

"Has there been any word from Mildred?" asked Daisy. "Perhaps Lady Charlotte will allow me to visit her."

"I haven't heard anything," she replied. "It's been very dull round here, with everybody being away. Mind you, there was talk of a vagrant being found in the quarry. Dead she was, poor soul, but I don't know any more about it. I dare say she won't be missed by anybody."

"Mmmmmm," agreed Daisy, by way of reply.

The following day two policemen came to Lime Lodge, wanting to talk to Lady Charlotte. A quarter of an hour must have passed before Daisy was summoned by her mistress, and with beating heart she went to meet her.

"Come in, Daisy. Something terrible has happened."

The policemen were standing in front of the Dowager who looked perplexed.

"Sit down. Sit down," she commanded them, before turning to speak to Daisy.

"These two gentlemen want to talk to you. A body's been found nearby and they seem to think you may know the person, although for the life of me I can't think why?"

Daisy felt her throat constrict, and she replied in a squeaky voice,

"I heard about the body in the quarry, Your Ladyship. Cook told me yesterday. Is it about that?"

"Yes." Lady Charlotte indicated a seat before resting her ample form on the chaise-longue by the fireplace.

The senior policeman cleared his throat.

"It's like this here, Miss. We've been making enquiries in the village about the body of a woman found in the quarry, as you already seem to know. It appears that there was a wedding a few weeks ago and you was seen talking to the said person. What do you have to say to that?"

Daisy thought quickly. In a flash she remembered that Rose was responsible for her spending a year in prison, and how she made her steal from her mistress. She owed her nothing and wasn't really sorry she was dead, so she answered firmly.

"That's quite true. A woman did speak to me at Phoebe's wedding."

"What about?"

"She seemed to know I worked for Her Ladyship and was asking me questions."

The policeman coughed loudly. "And did she speak of her intention to rob your mistress?"

"No — of course not. She asked me why I was waiting for the cart and how long it would take to walk back to Lime Lodge. I thought she might ask for a lift but she didn't." Daisy was aware of the man studying her.

"And she said nothing else?"

"No, Sir. I formed the opinion that she'd been begging for food. She was very grubby and I remember being relieved when she didn't ask for a ride in the cart. There was an awful smell about her and she was most unpleasant to be near."

"So," the policeman persisted, "you wouldn't know how she came to have the Countess's necklace in her hand?"

"Her necklace?" Daisy had forgotten Rose snatching it. In fact, in her desire to be done with the whole tawdry episode, she'd put the

103

subject right out of her head, so she was able to reply convincingly.

"I know nothing about any necklace, Sir."

The policeman seemed satisfied and turned to Lady Charlotte.

"I think that about clears matters up, Your Ladyship. The girl must have sneaked into the house by the back way when nobody was looking. They're crafty, is these thieves. Brought up to it by their parents."

"I only hope she took nothing else," commented the Dowager, as she rose to ring her bell. "Thank you for restoring my jewellery to me."

Daisy breathed a sigh of relief as she watched the men walk to the waiting police wagon.

"Thank goodness that's over," said Lady Charlotte. "It's of great concern she had one of my necklaces in her hand. You remember the diamond and ruby circlet that was locked in the cabinet?" She held it up for Daisy to see.

"I'm not really sure, Your Ladyship," Daisy lied, as she inspected the necklace. "You have so much jewellery."

"The police brought it for me to identify. They gave it back since they can't possibly prosecute the girl. They think she must have broken in while we were away, though goodness knows how. I must have left the cabinet unlocked. Very careless of me." She shrugged as she replaced the necklace in its hiding place. "I suppose we'll never know exactly what happened. Now I'm wondering what else she might have taken?"

"But wouldn't the police have found it? If she took anything else," said Daisy, trying to appear as natural as was possible under the circumstances.

The Dowager sighed. "I suppose you're right. But it's very disconcerting."

Within a couple of months Mildred returned to work and she and Daisy began making a day dress for Lady Charlotte. Between them, they decided on deep-blue heavy cotton with a low neckline to be worn over a chemisette. The sleeves would be very wide and fitted into a tight bodice, while the skirts would be full enough to accommodate a crinoline.

Mildred, a typical spinster in her forties, was no companion for Daisy who longed for Phoebe's return to Thetford. She'd heard from Lady Charlotte that Phoebe was with child and would be six months gone before she came home to live with her husband permanently.

"Isn't it exciting," exclaimed Daisy as she and Mildred worked at their sewing. Mildred looked sad. "I shall never have children now. She's very lucky."

Daisy frowned as she inspected her stitches. "I'd like children, but I'm nearly sixteen and I'll never meet a husband round here. It's far too quiet." She was surprised at Mildred's response.

"If you want a husband and children, you should get away, Daisy. Or you'll end up like me, a dried up old woman with nobody but aged parents to care for."

"I don't even have those," replied Daisy, sadly.

Things were soon to change for the household at Lime Lodge. Sir Algi had asked Lady Charlotte to become his wife and she'd accepted his proposal without hesitation. Mildred relayed the news to Daisy.

"Her Ladyship says they're not going to have a formal engagement and will marry almost immediately. No time to lose, she reckons. Both she and Sir Algi are in their late sixties so delay is pointless."

"What'll happen to us?" asked Daisy, ever conscious of her dependence on a job.

"We'll go with her. Sir Algi is very rich and says she's to take who she wants."

Daisy was ecstatic. Jimmy Fawcett worked for Sir Algi, so Phoebe would be close by and they'd be able to spend time together on her day off. She realised Mildred was still talking.

"She's chattering like a girl of about eighteen. Wants to go to London for a new gown to get married in and says, I'm to go with her. They've made all their plans."

"When is the wedding?"

"In a couple of weeks, I think. Just as long as it takes to call the banns. Lady Charlotte and I are going to London the day after tomorrow. She says you're to go over her entire wardrobe while we're away and discard anything you think unsuitable for her new life."

She saw Daisy's mouth droop. "Don't worry — I'll check on what you think should be thrown away. And by the way, she's making up a list of furniture she wants to take with her. Just personal things like her davenport and cabinets she's fond of. Oh, and some rugs. While we're away Vernon Fenn will come over and do a proper inventory of what's left."

Daisy's heart skipped a beat. She thought about Vernon and the heat from his groin and hoped he wouldn't approach her but she'd be very formal if he did, she decided.

But when she met him on the stairs a few days later, she was conscious of how handsome he was, and responded to the admiration in his eyes with a flirtatious smile.

"How have you been keeping, Daisy," Vernon asked, as he noted how the autumn sunshine gave an added glow to her burnished hair.

"I'm very well. I heard you were coming over. How long are you staying?"

Vernon continued to gaze at her as he replied softly, "Another two days should do it, but Daisy, I must see you."

She felt elated and knew he felt the same as she did. Her laugh echoed down the staircase.

"But you're seeing me now, Vernon." She snatched her hand away as he tried to take it into his own. "Please — the servants will see us."

"Then see me alone?"

"I can't," she replied, but he persisted.

"Yes you can. Just to chat."

She thought quickly and suddenly relented. "The summerhouse at three o'clock. We'll talk there."

Chapter 14

Time passed slowly with Daisy checking and re-checking the grandfather clock in the lower hall. What if Vernon tried to seduce her again? He couldn't possibly. Not after last time. But, she remembered his kiss and thought of him with longing, although she blushed with shame when recalling how he'd stroked her thigh. Perhaps he loved her after all. She ran her hands down her body and wished she was in his arms, knowing that if he tried to take what he wanted, she'd be powerless to resist.

At half past two she sauntered into the garden and inspected the roses, blowsy now, as they basked in the late sunshine. She walked slowly but purposefully, so that should anybody see her they'd think she was taking her usual afternoon stroll. When she reached the edge of the kitchen garden, she opened the gate and passed through the high wall and on to the path that led towards the summerhouse. It stood by the stream and clematis still trailed its blooms over the roof. Pushing the door open slowly, she heard Vernon say. "Come in my sweetest, I'm waiting."

"You said you wanted to talk, Vernon." Daisy spoke with a confidence she didn't feel.

He sat on the window seat and beckoned her towards him. She took a few steps forward but kept out of his reach.

"It's all right," he said. "I've being doing a lot of thinking, Daisy. I can't get you out of my mind. I'm sure I could persuade my father to let us marry, but I have to be sure of you first."

"Sure of me?" Daisy questioned, as she fell into Vernon's trap.

"Sure you love me enough to do anything for me."

Daisy felt her determination falter as she looked into his eyes. Her heart melted as she was drawn towards him and her feet slid softly over the floorboards. He held out his arms and her head swirled as she was encompassed by his warmth, her limbs turning to liquid as his tongue searched her mouth. Pausing, he took off his jacket and shirt before unbuttoning her bodice. They stood before each other shedding the rest of their clothes and when they were quite naked, he groaned.

Guiding her gently to the floor he buried his head between her breasts, whispering endearments until he could contain himself no longer. Then he moved over her and she put her arms around him, wanting to be close, closer than she'd ever been to anybody. She felt him pierce her body and gasped as he broke her fragile defence.

He spent himself quickly upon Daisy's innocent form, dismounting carelessly when he was satisfied.

"There," he said with a smile, "that wasn't so bad was it?"

Disappointed, she agreed reluctantly, but the experience hadn't been as wonderful as she'd hoped. For all its promise, it left her wanting and she felt vaguely irritated as Vernon helped her stand up. She dressed herself and bade him goodbye, wanting him to stop her, to take her in his arms and say she was his only true love. But he didn't look at her as he buttoned his jacket.

"We'll have to be careful," he said. "You go first. We don't want to cause any gossip."

We won't, she thought to herself as she crossed the lawn aware of the stickiness between her legs. You've allowed yourself to be grunted on, she acknowledged, you're no better than any other silly girl. Instinct told her that what she'd experienced wasn't love, she'd allowed herself to be used.

Holding her head high and with bitterness in her heart she vowed never to be taken again unless it was by a man who loved her.

Daisy avoided Vernon the following day. She deliberately kept away from the areas he'd be working in, and heard from Mrs Sargent later that he'd left Lime Lodge in the afternoon. He hadn't asked for her and left no message, so she spent the rest of the day in the sewing room, wiping her eyes before the falling tears stained the garment she was working on.

Lady Charlotte and Mildred returned home and there was much flurry in the household. The wedding was to be held in the village, in the same church where Phoebe had married Jimmy Fawcett. This time however the pretty little church was to be decorated with garlands of flowers, and the service attended by London's aristocracy.

The Earl and Countess were bringing the older children up from London and guests accommodated at Branstead. Whilst the couple honeymooned in Scotland, the dower house would be vacated and some of the household moved to Sir Algi's estate at King's Lynn.

Daisy dreaded seeing Vernon when she moved to her new address and considered whether she should find other employment. But, she'd have to ask for a recommendation and this would be difficult since she had no obvious reason to leave. In any case she liked working for the Dowager, or Lady Charlotte Fox as her mistress would be known after the wedding. Why should she be driven away by Vernon? What really worried her, she acknowledged, was that her body would let her down, and should she look into Vernon's eyes, she'd be overcome with longing.

Meanwhile there was much to do. Daisy was allotted the task of packing clothing and any personal items Lady Charlotte needed to be taken to Foxlands, her new home. Mr Danbury would provide the trunks and accompany Daisy to King's Lynn in a carriage made available from Branstead. He'd help unpack and hang the gowns. This would entail an overnight stay and Daisy was glad of Danbury's company in the carriage, and as protection against Vernon when they were at Foxlands. She didn't know Danbury very well, but remembered his kindness on the night of the fire. She found him to be an amiable man and whilst they were journeying to Foxlands, he talked about his family.

"Are you a Norfolk man?" Daisy asked.

"Born and bred in these parts," he replied with a slight burr. "My father was gamekeeper to the old Earl. There was more game around then and the job entailed a lot more than it does now, so I act as gamekeeper as well as steward and estate manager, but it's a good life."

The carriage rocked and Daisy worried about the trunks strapped on the outside, as they made a steady pace northwards.

"So you were brought up on the estate, Mr Danbury?"

"Call me Simon," he replied in his unhurried way. "Yes. I went to the village school at first but after a while the old Earl offered to have me tutored with the present Earl until he went on to Eton. He'd have been about nine then."

"That was good of him. Are you and the Earl friends?"

"Not really. We live in different worlds. Although I'm better educated than my father was, my interest is still with the countryside. I was always out with Pa learning about the trees and gardens, and all the creatures that live in the grounds. He taught me about trapping vermin, shooting rabbits and game, and sewing seeds, planting — everything I need to know about running the estate, really. I used to help him with the bookwork and that, but I hated being indoors when he was out there, in the fresh air." He paused and grinned at Daisy. "Give me a chance to talk about my job, and I'll go on forever."

She laughed at his enthusiasm. "Do you share your house with your parents?

"No, they passed on a couple of years ago but I've lived there all my life." A look of sadness came over his weathered face and he scratched his head. "I even brought my bride to the same house some fifteen years ago"

Daisy was surprised. "I didn't realise there was a Mrs Danbury. We didn't see her the night of the fire."

"No. You wouldn't have. She died before we'd been married a year — in childbirth," he explained. "Ma and Pa went within the next two years and I've been on my own ever since. But that's enough about me. What about you? You speak like a Londoner."

Daisy told him how she'd lost touch with her family.

"I was too young to write down an address, so I don't know where they are. I vowed one day I'd find them but I don't want to go back there any more. I'm used to the country now, it's so clean."

"And are you looking forward to working at Foxlands?"

"I'll let you know when I've seen it," she replied cheekily.

Sir Algi's estate was impressive and Daisy looked with interest at the cattle grazing in the fields. "Does this all belong to him?" she asked Danbury.

"Don't ask me, young lady," he smiled, "I've never been here before and don't suppose I'll ever have reason to come again."

Vernon was waiting to greet them as the carriage came to a halt at the side entrance. The trunks were taken upstairs while Daisy and Simon Danbury were given lunch in the servants' hall before meeting in the afternoon again to unpack. Dinner was also taken in the servants' hall so Daisy didn't see Vernon alone. She was shown to her new room by the housekeeper, and was pleased to find she'd not be sharing. The room was pleasant and adequately furnished, and the housekeeper said Daisy was to ask if there were anything else she needed, adding that a small armchair was available, if required.

When she went to bed Daisy fell asleep straight away despite being in strange surroundings. She and Danbury has worked hard all day, lifting heavy garments from trunks to wardrobes, and planned to return to Thetford early the next day.

The village church was packed to capacity on the day of the wedding and Daisy helped Mildred put the finishing touches to their mistress's toilette, dabbing a little cologne on some cotton wool before tucking it into her chemise. Lady Charlotte was waved off in style by the staff, who stood on the front steps calling out their good wishes. The Earl was holding a reception for the happy couple at Branstead, and staff from both houses were invited to feast in the grounds of the larger house. Long tables were carried to one of the big barns and jugs of ale were provided, together with hams and pies of all sorts. During the feast, Simon Danbury, as head of the estate, proposed a toast to the newlyweds after which the dancing began.

Daisy stood at the side of the barn with Mildred, feeling shy as the ale began to have its effect on the revellers. Before long most of the younger staff were tipsy and Mildred excused herself, saying she had things to do before her Ladyship returned. Daisy was about to follow her when she felt a tap on her shoulder.

"Like to dance?" She turned to see Danbury who was dressed in his Sunday suit.

"I'm not sure I can," she laughed, "but I'm willing to try."

He showed her how to dance a make-shift jig as the musicians ran their bows over well-worn fiddles. The couple flew around the floor as the crowd stood aside, shouting and clapping, and stamping their feet to the beat of the music. When the tune came to an end the exhausted pair collapsed onto a bench, gasping for breath and laughing at the same time.

"Stay there. I'll get you some lemonade," instructed Danbury. He returned with a mug brimming with cooled lemonade for her and ale for himself and they sat together watching the antics of the merrymakers. Long before the revelry finished Daisy decided to go back to Lime Lodge. She turned to her companion and smiled.

"Thank you for your company, Mr Danbury," she said, surprised that this man she'd thought rather remote seemed to be enjoying himself.

"Call me Simon," he replied, lowering his eyes "Think nothing of it. You're easy to be nice to, Daisy Smith."

"And you're very kind, Simon," she responded, curtsying prettily before leaving the barn.

Sir Algi and Lady Charlotte stayed in Scotland for the rest of October and all November, leaving Daisy and Mildred plenty of time to settle into Foxlands. The main residence was larger than the Dower house at Thetford but not quite as big as Branstead. The estate encompassed some arable land, plus fields left fallow and a cattle farm. Daisy loved the outbuildings where chickens were housed and she was encouraged to harvest the warm eggs left by squawking hens. She was fascinated by the way they tossed their heads as they strutted up and down the yard, much to the annoyance of the cats who appeared to hate them.

The front of the house was much more formal with Italian gardens and graceful statues. But the days were becoming shorter and the trees began shedding their foliage, with showers of red and gold leaves falling slowly to the ground, aided by a light autumnal breeze. Berries appeared on bushes that were sometimes shrouded in fog and the house began to smell of log fires. But the deteriorating weather wasn't Daisy's only worry. Her monthly occurrence failed to materialise and she waited for mid-December anxiously.

Fortunately she was kept busy by the return of Lady Charlotte as she fussed about her ornaments and music boxes. Nevertheless, the fear she may be with child was uppermost in Daisy's mind. Surely, she reasoned, not when it happened only once? However, she learned later that fate wasn't selective when it struck its cruel blow. December wore on, with her mind in turmoil, and as she helped prepare the house for Christmas celebrations, she knew she was in trouble.

Her sixteenth birthday passed unnoticed and on a quiet day, when the Foxes were visiting Branstead, she sought out Vernon in his office.

"Yes, Daisy," he smiled, as he looked up from his ledgers. "What can I do for you?"

"I'm going to have a baby," she blurted out, forgetting the speech she'd rehearsed the previous day.

"I hope you aren't suggesting the culprit is me?"

Shamed, she bowed her head. "You are the only one I've ever been with, Vernon."

He tapped on the desk with his pencil. "A likely story. What do you want me to do? Marry you!" he added derisively.

She met his eyes. "You said you loved me but I don't think you do."

"Quite right, Daisy. I don't love you and never have. I warned you I couldn't marry a servant girl, and that's what you are."

Wringing her hands in distress Daisy pleaded. "But what's to become of me? I can't possibly have a baby."

"Then get rid of it, if you don't want a little bastard hanging round your skirts."

Daisy couldn't believe he could be so nasty.

"But it will be your child. Do you want me to kill it?"

Vernon stood up and walked round the desk to confront Daisy.

"It's not mine and I'll deny I ever touched you. If you spread rumours about me I'll have you dismissed. Do you understand?"

"Sir Algi's valet knows you were after me in France," threatened Daisy. "I could tell on you."

"Who do you think would believe a little trollop like you. You servant girls will lift your skirts for anybody. Get rid of it. I'll give you the money."

Daisy's face crumpled as she began to weep with humiliation.

"But how?"

"You'll find a way. And now leave me to my work please, Miss, before I really lose my temper." He took her by the arm and thrust her outside the door.

She went straight to her room and sat on the bed. How could he do this to her? She'd been stupid to think he loved her but even so, he could have been nicer. And how was she to get rid of the thing that was growing in inside her? He seemed to think there was a way. She remembered the birth of Florrie's baby in the cellar and knew there was no place in the world for a child born out of wedlock. There was only one person she could think of who might be able to help and that was Phoebe.

The next Sunday was Daisy's day off and she announced her intention to spend it with Phoebe and Jimmy who were now settled in one of the farm cottages. She sent a note and received the reply that she was expected at midday. She spent the rest of the week cutting and stitching the softest flannel into a little gown and bonnet for Phoebe's baby. When it was finished she wrapped it carefully in tissue paper.

Her friend was overjoyed to see her. "Come in, come in." She took her hand and led her into the cosy sitting room where a fire was blazing in the hearth.

"You look peaky, Dais. Are you all right?"

Daisy nodded as she put her mantle on the armchair.

"I'm fine, Phoebe and look at you? You're blooming with health."

Phoebe patted her stomach. "I think I've got three of them in here, with all the kicking they do." She chatted excitedly saying how wonderful it was to be living in her own house with Jimmy, who was proving a very considerate husband.

"He won't let me get the water from the well or do anything that might harm the little one. I'm very lucky."

Later, Jimmy came back to the cottage for his lunch and Daisy noticed how tender he was towards his wife, helping her to sit comfortably and insisting she rest. His plain, honest face lit up when she smiled at him and before he left he made certain there was enough wood for the stove.

"There'll be a frost tonight," he warned in his country dialect as he gazed up at the sky. "I'll be off to check the cattle in the far field, then I'll bring them cows in for milking."

The girls sat by the fire getting drowsy as they caught up with each other's news. The clock ticked hypnotically over the mantle shelf and Daisy felt herself nodding off. Phoebe suddenly sat up.

"I'll make some more tea," she said, rising awkwardly. "Then you can tell me what's wrong." She held up a hand. "I know you, Daisy Smith, and something's wrong."

Chapter 15

Phoebe filled the kettle and put in on the hearth before placing the cups and saucers on a tray. "Right — now talk to me."

To Phoebe's horror Daisy burst into tears.

"I'm with child," she blurted out, searching for her handkerchief.

"No." Phoebe gasped, with horror. "Are you sure? Who's is it!"

"I've been such a fool. Such a fool." Bit by bit she related her story while her friend made tea. "I've got to find a way of getting rid of it. Please help me. And don't hate me. I know I've been a fool but I only did it the once."

"I don't know what I can do, but I'll help in any way I can. But getting rid of it, that's very dangerous and you could die. How far gone are you?"

"I've missed three times now. I might as well be dead as have a child when I'm not married. Who'd employ me? I'd have to go to the work'ouse." She almost added like her mother and father but stopped herself.

Phoebe spoke with a wisdom Daisy hadn't known she possessed.

"Things happen. Things we can't control." There was bitterness in her voice. "Since you've told me your story I'll tell you mine. You remember the day we saw the Earl in the woods? Yes? Well when I was in London he used to make me do things — you know."

"No. I don't know. What are you talking about?"

Phoebe's eyes filled with tears as she explained what happened. "It was only a few times, when the Countess was out. The first time was when I got back to London, after the wedding. The Countess took the children to a birthday party at her sister's in Woburn Place." Her face was pained as she continued, "He got me alone downstairs. I'm sure Nanny knew. She was afraid to say anything when he sent for me, but I saw her looking at me funny sometimes. What would he want me for in the drawing room, I ask you?"

"Was it awful?"

"Terrible. I wanted it to be my Jimmy but he made me lie there with my skirts round my waist, going at me with that 'orrible thing of his. I hate him. I really 'ate him. The worst thing is. . ." She paused and bit her lip before bursting into tears. "I'm worried that my baby might be his." Phoebe looked round the room miserably. "Not my Jimmy's at all but his, and I've just got to live with it." She added bitterly, "That's what happens to the likes of us."

Daisy rushed to her side and put her arms around her.

"You poor thing. Your secret's safe with me, just as I hope you won't tell about mine."

Phoebe blew her nose and sat up straight, declaring, "That's enough snivelling from the two of us. At least I've got a husband, but what are we going to do about you? I'll go over to see me Auntie Nellie next week and see if I can get the name of somebody from her."

"Supposing she asks you who it's for? You won't tell will you?"

"No. Course not. I'll have to tell Jimmy of course, but he'll understand. I'll think of something to tell Aunty Nellie but it's ever so dangerous getting rid of a baby, you know?"

Daisy shrugged. "It's my only option."

"Do you feel well?" asked Phoebe, a look of concern on her face.

"I'm a bit sick in the mornings but nothing much. Nothing I can't hide but I've got to be free of it soon. I can't walk round with a big belly."

At four o'clock Daisy rose and began the short walk back to Foxlands. They'd agreed that Phoebe would get Jimmy to borrow the trap and take her down to Thetford where she'd visit her mother. Whilst there, she'd go to see her aunt and bring the conversation round to getting rid of unwanted babies. Her writing was just about good enough to send Daisy a note via Jimmy when she had some news. The staff knew the girls were friends and would think nothing if they saw Daisy talking to Phoebe's husband.

It was the middle of February before Daisy saw Jimmy walking along the boxed hedge that ran alongside the Italian garden. He greeted her casually and she glanced round furtively to ensure they couldn't be overheard.

"How's Phoebe?" she enquired.

"She's well but getting quite 'eavy now. She's found someone to do the job for you."

"That's wonderful, Jimmy. I'm so sorry to put you to all this trouble."

"It's not that I approve, like, but I understands your problem. I can't pretend to 'old with what you're doing, but needs must and all that. There's an old woman over at Marsden about five mile away. She's got a place about a mile from the village. When's your next day off?"

"I'm due a whole day on Thursday in two weeks time."

"Good. If you can meet me by the main track then, I'll be ready with the wagon."

Daisy was relieved that at last something was happening and her

115

heart leapt for joy. "Thank you. Thank you. I don't know what to say."

Jimmy looked worried. "Phoebe says to get all your savings together and any clothes you can sneak out because you're likely to be ill after you've had it done. I can't take you right up to the cottage in case I'm seen. You'll have to walk the last mile by yourself."

Daisy nodded her understanding and Jimmy continued, "I'll be able to pick you up at the gate when it's been done as it'll be getting dark. You do realise you might not be able to come back here, don't you?"

"I'll be all right, Jimmy. I'm strong and healthy. But I'll do what Phoebe thinks best."

They parted, with Daisy waving to him cheerily before continuing her walk. It was imperative she act as naturally as possible. Should she tell Vernon Fenn? He'd offered money which she'd be wise to take. No, she decided, she wanted nothing from him and while she was waiting for her day off, she counted out her precious savings, collected most of her belongings together and hid them in the copse.

It was snowing on the day in early March when Daisy went to the old woman. They saw no sign of life when Jimmy dropped her off, as he'd proposed, just outside the village. The wind howled as it whipped around her, swirling and churning into drifts as she walked the last mile. As she pulled her shawl further over her head it snatched at her skirts, lifting them as it coiled around her legs. She stopped frequently to regain her balance and pull down her petticoats, while snow seeped through her knitted mittens making her fingers red and numb. She blew on them, hoping to bring them back to life with her warm breath.

Daisy struggled onwards over the white meadow, which was becoming slippery where the pale morning sun melted the surface as it shone intermittently through the clouds. Snow-flakes danced into her eyelashes and she wiped them off with the back of her hand, the hem of her petticoats growing wetter as the snow settled into a crisp white blanket.

The cottage came into view, its roof melting into the hills that rose above it like great white clouds, relieved only by smoke curling from the chimney. She opened the dilapidated gate that creaked as it swung drunkenly off its hinges, and walked up the path that led to the old clapboard cottage. It stood forlorn amid the cold beauty of the countryside, its rotting wood and peeling paint contributing to an air of neglect. Daisy tapped on the door and it was opened by an elderly woman wearing grubby clothes.

"On yer own, I 'ope," she snapped, looking out across the fields suspiciously. "I bin expecting yer. Come on in. Weather's bad though, ain't it gel?"

The stench in the interior of the cottage was a shock to Daisy, now used to Lime Lodge which was always well supplied with fresh pot-pourri and lavender water. She could smell animals and suspected that like many country dwellers, the woman sometimes kept chickens in the scullery. Stale cabbage and dirty boots contributed to the dank odour that pervaded throughout the main room, as well as washing that hung on hooks from the blackened beams.

The woman pointed towards the fire on which a kettle had been set to boil. "Warm yerself up, gel," she muttered, humming to herself as she placed a cover on the table. Daisy nodded and crept towards the warmth where a one-eyed cat got to its haunches and stretched, its tail twitching with annoyance.

"Get away, you moth-eaten, mangy animal," growled its owner, as she kicked it viciously in the rump before addressing Daisy again.

"Have you got the money?"

Daisy fumbled in her cloth bag and found her purse. The woman counted carefully, wiping her nose with the back of her hand, before putting the coins in a tankard that stood amongst the clutter on the dresser.

"Right," she sniffed, "We may as well get started. And you know, don't you?" She stopped speaking as she wagged a dirty finger at the frightened girl. "If anything goes wrong, I've 'ad nothing to do with it. You don't know me and I don't know you. Is that clear?"

Daisy nodded and whimpered, "Is anything likely to go wrong?"

"Not if you lies still, and does what I tells yer." She nodded towards the middle of the room. "I want you on the table, naked from the waist down. There's only one way to get that bastard thing out of you and that's with this."

She went to the dresser and picked up a long, slim piece of metal with a hook at the end. Daisy cowered at the thought of was to happen next and watched with dismay as the woman busied herself about the room, assembling bowls and tinctures. "And it 'as to come out the same way as it got in, if you gets my meaning?" she warned, catching her breath as she coughed so severely that dribble ran down her chin.

"Don't s'pose you know who the father might be. None of 'em does what comes 'ere. Promised yer riches, did he?" She cackled to herself as she spoke. "They all does that. None of 'em's no good, not a single bastard one of 'em." She sniffed again.

Wide eyed with horror, Daisy nodded again, as her tormentor wiped her face on a tattered apron. "Up you get then, let's be getting on with it." She went to a cupboard and took out another medicine bottle. "This 'ere's laudanum. It'll make you drowsy. When it's over you can rest here for a bit. Your friend said 'e'd pick you up at four o'clock."

Daisy removed her boots and stockings and then her petticoats and drawers. Knowing she had to pursue the course she had chosen, she climbed onto the table and the crone folded a piece of cloth and placed it under Daisy's head.

"Now I want you open wide at both ends. Here, take this mixture." She spooned some of the liquid into Daisy's throat, saying, "Hold on to the sides of the table — hard." The terrified girl screwed up her eyelids and felt leathery hands on her thighs, then cold metal between her legs.

"Are we ready?" she heard and then she felt something searching and digging into her flesh. She screamed in agony, shock reverberating through her body. Then the old woman was at her head again. "Here, 'ave some more of this." More laudanum was poured into her mouth and the woman's voice receded into the distance, as she complained, "Try not to make so much bleeding noise, gel, will you?"

Daisy cried with tears of terror as she felt the cold steel again. This time it found its target, clawing at the very core of her being, pulling and tugging, inflicting such anguish, she felt as though her heart would stop. Excruciating pain ripped through her body, but mercifully she passed out as she heard an ear-splitting scream from a distance.

When she came round, the woman was standing by her side. Daisy felt her stomach being rubbed to release the bloody mass of congealed matter that followed the tiny corpse of her child. Blood poured profusely from her body as it rebelled against the violation inflicted upon it.

"A girl, it was," said the woman matter-of-factly.

"Looks like we got it all out okay. It seems to be in one piece." She inspected the contents of the bowl before putting it to one side. "Want to see it?"

"No. No," wailed Daisy, as she felt rags being stuffed between her legs, before being helped from the table. She was led to the truckle-bed under the window and could hear the wind still howling round the hovel, sneaking through the loose window panes to cause a sharp draught. Covering her with an old blanket, the crone started humming to herself again as she began to clear away the mess.

Daisy couldn't get warm. A dull ache clamped around her heart when she thought of what she'd done. She hadn't been prepared for the feeling of loss in the aftermath of destruction brought about by her own stupidity. A girl? She wondered what her child had looked like, but didn't really regret not seeing her. She couldn't have borne seeing the tiny half-formed body, floating naked in a sea of blood. Although still convinced she had no alternative, the untimely birth and death of her daughter would remain forever on her conscience.

When Jimmy came to collect her, he was able to bring the wagon up to the gate as it was already getting dark and there was little fear of being seen. Daisy crept along the path bent over in an effort to alleviate the pains in her stomach, supported by Jimmy and the old woman. The latter wrapped shawls around Daisy and with Jimmy's help she managed to climb on to the vehicle.

"Let her rest for a couple of days and she'll be all right," the crone assured Jimmy carelessly, giving him the benefit of an almost toothless grin.

The snow had abated a little by now but the horse could only plod slowly through the lanes that were carpeted in white, as were the trees and distant rooftops. At last Jimmy's house came in sight, smoke curling from the chimney and welcoming lights in the windows. Phoebe was waiting for them. She undressed Daisy and put her into a makeshift bed behind a curtain in the kitchen, where it was warm. Daisy wanted nothing to eat and half-heartedly sipped the blackberry cordial that Phoebe held to her lips. Its syrupy smell made her retch, and as evening drew on her temperature rose, causing Phoebe and Jimmy to sit with her all night. They wiped her brow and spoke to her in soothing tones but by morning she was sweating profusely and talking nonsense.

"What shall we do?" a terrified Phoebe beseeched her husband. "We can't get the doctor from the village."

Jimmy held his wife's hand. "I know we can't, sweetheart. This is a bad business. I've bin thinking about it. Daisy's ill, very ill." He pulled off his cap and scratched his head. "She can't stay here and there only one person I know who'll help her and keep his mouth shut. That's Mr Danbury."

"But supposing he's away?"

"He won't be. He never goes off the estate and I don't know who else to turn to."

Phoebe wrung her hands. "I suppose you're right, Jimmy. It's for the best."

"You get her ready and I'll take her down to Thetford." He put his arm around his wife's shoulder, and gave her a hug. "Come along, Gel. We'll make her comfortable and I'll put some logs round her on the inside of the wagon so no one'll notice her, then I'll scout around for Danbury when I gets there. I hopes to goodness I finds him because if I don't, she'll surely die."

"What do you think it is? What's the matter with her?"

"It's poison. That's what happens. I've heard about it. She'll most likely perish of the poison."

Phoebe started to weep again and her husband looked worried.

"You stay 'ere and take care of yerself. Okay? I'll be back as soon as I can and if anybody asks after me, say me mother's bin taken poorly and I've gone down to Thetford to see 'er."

Wrapping Daisy in a large patchwork quilt, Jimmy carried her out to the wagon, making her as comfortable as he could within the confines of the logs.

"The last part's true enough," he muttered. "And you look after yerself, Phoebe. Keep inside out of the wind and don't go out in case you slip on the snow. There's plenty of wood stacked by the fireplace."

Phoebe threw him a grateful glance. "You're a good man, Jimmy Fawcett. You take care of yourself and I'll see you when you get back."

"I hope to make it tonight, but if not, first thing tomorrer. Depends on the weather." He tugged at the reins and the horse moved slowly forward. Phoebe waved her husband off and wearily closed the cottage door, her brow creased with concern.

Snow threatened again as Jimmy drove the wagon over the tracks. He stopped once or twice to make sure Daisy was comfortable, and was relieved when she moaned softly in reply to his words. It was late afternoon when he reined the horse outside Simon Danbury's house, his nose as red as a cherry and his fingers frozen with the cold.

Mrs Jones opened the door in answer to his knock and told him Danbury was out somewhere on the estate.

"But I've got to see him right now," pleaded Jimmy. "Don't you have no idea where he is?" He knew that if Danbury wasn't found, Daisy would surely die.

Chapter 16

"He said something about going down by the river. Let me give you some hot soup, Jimmy. Then you can go and look for him."

"No, Mrs Jones. I've got to fetch him now. I've got something for him. It's urgent."

Puzzled, Danbury's housekeeper watched him plod through the snow towards the river, wondering what was so urgent that he'd come without warning. Surely not just some logs for the fire? They had plenty of timber hereabouts. She wondered if something was wrong with Phoebe and hurried to the vehicle in case the girl needed help. Just logs, she said to herself, peering over the firewood. Why such a fuss about such a silly thing. Then she heard something stir, and moved a few logs aside. She saw the bundle of coverings and gasped with surprise as she pulled them aside.

"Oh, my God, it's young Daisy," she exclaimed. "You can't stay out here girl. You'll catch your death. Come along, let me lend a hand."

She helped Daisy into a sitting position, which enabled her to drag herself feebly along the wooden floor.

"Put your arms round me," she said as she helped Daisy to her feet. "I don't know what the great big secret is but I'm taking you inside."

They progressed slowly into the house where Daisy sunk onto a sofa. Mrs Jones made some tea and tried to get the girl to sip it, to no avail.

"Just rest there then, until Mr Danbury comes back."

She put warming pans in the bed in one of the spare rooms before lighting a fire in the hearth. She was a kindly soul but no fool, and knew there was a serious problem if Jimmy Fawcett was seeking Mr Danbury's help. She fussed around Daisy trying to make her comfortable, wringing her hands, as the girl slipped in and out of consciousness.

Meanwhile Jimmy trudged through the crisp fields towards the river. Snow-laden clouds hung mournfully from the sky as he glanced upwards at the cry of a bird. Trees, stripped of their summer glory and coated with snow, formed a dejected tableau against the misty heavens. He heard movement as he approached the bank and felt relieved when Danbury emerged from behind some bushes. He was holding a duck under his arm and stopped in his tracks when he saw Jimmy.

"Why, hello young Jimmy, what brings you here? Nothing wrong, I hope. Mother Okay?"

Jimmy nodded. "What's wrong with the duck?"

"Broken wing, I think. I'll take him up to the barn and try to tie it up. You can give me a hand if you will?"

Jimmy nodded and blurted out, "Course — but I've got something to tell you first."

Danbury looked at him curiously. "Oh yes. What might that be?"

Jimmy struggled to find the correct words. "I've got a sick woman in my cart, Mr Danbury and I couldn't think of anywhere else to bring her to. Anybody we could trust, like — me and Phoebe."

Danbury was curious. "Sick? What's the matter with her? Who is she?"

Jimmy hesitated but the older man persisted, "Come along. Who is it?"

"It's young Daisy!" Jimmy started to sob. "She's awful sick, Mr Danbury. We; that's me and Phoebe, think she might be dying."

"Dying. Why bring her to me? Didn't you call a doctor, boy?"

Jimmy shook his head and tufts of snow fell from his woollen cap.

"No. Not with what ails her. I got to tell you, Sir. She's 'ad one of those abortions, like."

He stood still, waiting for Danbury's reaction. The older man's face took on a look of consternation. "Where is she?"

"In the cart. In front of the 'ouse."

Ignoring Jimmy's last words, Danbury strode back through the meadow and upon reaching the wagon, pulled aside some of the logs. He cast them aside when he realised nobody was there and let himself into the house, followed seconds later by Jimmy. Daisy lay on the sofa in a stupor, her skin like marble, her breathing shallow. Forgetting all about Jimmy, Danbury called for Mrs Jones, as he picked Daisy up like a baby and took the stairs two at a time. Between them they settled Daisy into the warm bed and stoked the fire.

"We should call the doctor," advised his housekeeper.

"We can't," he replied curtly. "I'd like to find the devil who did this to her. She's got rid of a child."

Mrs Jones shook her head. "I knew it was bad. Little Daisy? Never. The poor, foolish girl. What on earth are we going to do?"

Simon Danbury looked at the still head on the pillow before turning to Mrs Jones. "This stays between these four walls, you understand?"

"Of course, Sir."

"I'll sit up with her all night and if she survives, you can nurse her by day. Not a word to any of the tradesmen or the Branstead staff. Just treat her condition as a fever and see if we can get her temperature down. We'll have to wait for the poison to pass through her system.

Perhaps you will look after her. . . her wounds. . . and things. I'll go down and have a word with Jimmy Fawcett."

He went downstairs to where Jimmy was waiting, rocking anxiously on his heels, cap in hand.

"You did right to bring her here, lad. We'll take care of her as best we can. Now I insist you have some hot soup before you journey back. What shall I say brought you here, should anybody mention it?"

Jimmy looked at him gratefully.

"I told Phoebe to say me mother was sick. I'll pop over to see her then make me way back to King's Lynn. That should cover me tracks. Daisy won't die, will she, sir?"

"In all truth, I don't know," Danbury replied, patting Jimmy on the shoulder. "But she won't if I have anything to do with it. Though goodness knows how we'll explain her presence if the worst happens. Come into the kitchen and I'll get that soup. Don't want you being ill too, what with your wife expecting. How is she, by the way?"

"Getting 'eavy. I'm needing to get back to her. She's really cut up over Daisy. Very fond of each other, they are."

"Daisy's a silly girl," growled Danbury. "Does anybody else know about this? I wonder who the father is?"

"Phoebe says she don't know. Daisy wouldn't tell her, so I doubt anyone else knows. And the only ones who know about the abortion are me and Phoebe, Daisy and the woman what did it."

"She wants shooting," growled Danbury as he led Jimmy to the kitchen where the soup was simmering on the stove.

The next three weeks saw Daisy drifting in and out of consciousness, with Danbury and Mrs Jones mopping her brow and applying poultices.

"Blood letting might help her," said Mrs Jones. "But we can't do that without no doctor."

As the weeks passed Danbury grew more tired. Lines were etched down his cheeks and his skin had taken on a grey appearance. He'd heave his weary body from the chair each morning before going out to supervise the grounds-men, his eyes red-rimmed from lack of sleep.

He appeared to have aged about ten years and Mrs Jones hovered over him anxiously. Despite his protests, she insisted sharing the night duty and they moved a daybed into the sick room, taking naps when Daisy was quiet. They were careful not to invite any callers into the house.

The door to Daisy's room was kept locked in the mornings, lest some curious housemaid should discover their secret. They explained there was wine-making equipment the room and it was imperative the temperature wasn't disturbed.

At last, after a terrifying night when a delirious Daisy tossed and turned, the fever broke, and she fell into a peaceful sleep. Danbury and Mrs Jones were left with the memory of the girl crying out for her lost baby, her tortured mind unable to rest.

The following morning the housekeeper was about very early, enabling her to wash the patient and change the sheets before going downstairs to see the maids.

Jimmy came by one evening to enquire after Daisy's health and was told she was a little improved.

"Sit down. Sit down," Danbury insisted after offering him a drink. "What are the gossips saying?" he continued as he filled his pipe.

"I understand Lady Charlotte is very disappointed in Daisy's behaviour, Sir, and says she must have run off to London with a lover."

"Humph," replied Danbury, throwing his taper into the fire. "Well I suppose things could be worse. At least they don't think she's been murdered and feel obliged to call out the police."

Jimmy didn't stay for long. Phoebe was very heavy with child now and the birth was imminent.

Two days later he returned, hammering on the door.

"It's a boy! Phoebe had a boy last night." He waved his hat into the air to Danbury who bounded down the stairs at the sound of his voice.

"Congratulations, Jimmy. You're a lucky man," he beamed. "I've been talking to Daisy while she eats a little of the trout I caught this morning. Come up and see her?"

"Just for a minute then. I can't stop. I'm off to tell me mum she's a grandmother again."

As they mounted the stairs Daisy called from the bedroom. "Congratulations. It's good of you to call, Jimmy."

As he entered her room, Jimmy was taken back by how thin and pale Daisy was. She looked almost as white as the mountain of pillows that supported her and when she spoke her voice was feeble.

"I haven't had the chance to thank you for all you did for me. Please give Phoebe and the little one my love. And Jimmy?" She stumbled over the words as she continued, "I can't tell you how grateful I am for all the trouble you've been to, and the risks you took. You and Phoebe are true friends. Mrs Jones told me all about it."

"No trouble, Daisy. I'm sure we'll be bringing the baby to see you soon enough."

Jimmy almost danced down the path, eager to spread his good news. Daisy wept when she was alone. Phoebe's little boy should have had a playmate under different circumstances. She cried once again for her aborted child.

By the end of April, Daisy was able to sit in the armchair for short periods and a little colour began appearing in her cheeks. She was allowed downstairs when the staff had gone home and in the evening Simon Danbury read to her, hesitating over sentences when the candles flickered as the skies darkened.

Another week passed and one morning, Daisy took a few faltering steps towards the bedroom window to look at the fields where daffodils swayed in the breeze and newly born lambs were bleating in the distance.

"You've been so kind to me," she said to Mrs Jones when the older woman gave her a bowl of porridge. "I can never hope to repay you."

"We don't need no thanks. It's pleasing that you're getting better. What d'you think you'll do. When you're better, like?"

"I've been considering it. Obviously I can't stay in Norfolk. I'll probably go to London and try to get work as a dressmaker."

"What's all this about a dressmaker?" Mr Danbury came into the room carrying a bunch of flowers. "You're not ready to leave yet. Not by a long chalk."

Daisy smiled gratefully as she looked directly into his eyes. "I'll have to leave soon, Simon. I can't impose on you any longer than necessary."

"You're not strong enough yet, my girl. You might be feeling better but you need fattening up, doesn't she, Mrs Jones?" he asked, turning to his housekeeper, who was plumping up the cushions on the faded chaise-longue. She smoothed the antimacassars that rested along its back before replying.

"We were just having a word about it, Mr Danbury, and I was going to say she can't think of going yet." She put a fresh jug of water on the table and continued, "Goodness me, you can only just manage to creep down the staircase."

Danbury concurred. "I should think not. We'll talk more when I come back for dinner tonight. You can start having a glass of port, it might put some colour into your cheeks."

Weakness made Daisy cry again as he left to go about his duties. They'd both been very good to her and she couldn't take advantage of their hospitality for much longer. She'd chat to Danbury about it over dinner. Mrs Jones broke into her thoughts. "I've got a nice bit o' beef on the stove and I can do it with some dumplings, so I'll be off to the kitchen."

Daisy wondered what she'd done to deserve two such good people and that evening she described her plans to Simon Danbury.

"I've always been careful with my money," she explained. "I don't want to talk about what happened to me, with the illness and everything, but it's obvious I have to get away from Norfolk and the only other place I know is London. I can find work there."

"What work do you plan to do?"

"I thought I'd try for dressmaking. I've been making clothes for Lady Charlotte." She caught her breath. "Poor Lady Charlotte, she must be very disappointed in me but what's done is done and I must earn some money. Anyway, as I said—" she paused to sip her wine, "I was working under Mildred and feel quite confident I can sew well enough to get work."

Danbury cut in. "But where will you live?"

"I've enough saved to get some cheap lodgings for about a month. That should do it. It's quite exciting really. I'll be sorry to leave the friends I've made but I'll keep in touch."

"You're tired," replied Simon. "You must let me help you up to bed now and I'll do some thinking myself."

He gave her his arm and they made their way slowly towards the bedroom door. Daisy turned and said softly, "Where do the clothes come from that I've been wearing?"

He tossed the question aside nonchalantly. "They were only in a trunk, doing nothing."

"They belonged to your wife, didn't they?"

"They did," he agreed, "but they weren't doing her or anybody else any good up there. Time to put the past behind me, I reckon."

"You're such a good man, Simon. I'll never be able to repay you for what you've done for me."

"Stop going on about it," he growled. "And get yourself into bed." He practically shoved her into the room and closed the door after her.

Over the following weeks Daisy began helping Mrs Jones prepare the vegetables and began doing some sewing. Simon Danbury had given instructions that the housekeeper was to open the trunks of clothing that had belonged to his wife, so that Daisy might take anything she felt could be useful. There were gloves and hats and undergarments as well as pretty dresses. She worked on these garments in her room in the morning and part of the afternoon when he was out in the fields. She altered some of them to fit her, sometimes adding trimmings she found in Mrs Jones' sewing box.

When it grew dusk and there was little chance of them being seen, she took Danbury's arm and they went for walks. Sometimes they'd stroll to the river and at others to the orchard where the smell of fruit trees perfumed the air.

"I shall miss all this," she said sadly, one evening as she stood on tip-toe to sniff the apple blossom. "London will seem so dirty and I've grown used to country life."

"There's no need to go back," replied Simon as he studied her profile, silhouetted against the darkening sky. If only you knew, he whispered to himself, how I've grown to love you, sweet Daisy

"There's every need," laughed Daisy, unaware of his thoughts. "I'm stronger now and must look out for myself."

"I've an aunt who lives in London," Danbury said reluctantly. "She has a shop near London Bridge somewhere. A sweet-shop. I'll write to her and ask if she has a room to let, if you'd like. I'd feel a whole lot happier if I knew you were with somebody I know."

Daisy's reply was caustic. "Don't worry, Simon, I shan't be getting myself into trouble again. I've had enough of men."

He was apologetic. "I didn't mean any such thing. I know just how unsafe London is but you'll meet a decent chap one day, somebody will soon snap you up." Lucky devil, he added under his breath. "Would you like me to write to my aunt?"

"Oh, yes please," Daisy replied, reaching up to kiss him on the cheek. "And I'm sorry if I sounded irritable. I always seem to be thanking you for one thing or another."

Three weeks later a letter arrived from Danbury's aunt. Yes, she had a spare room and would be glad of the rent, if he was sure the proposed lodger was of good character. She'd expect Miss Smith during the first week of July and assumed her favourite nephew would accompany her, since too many years had passed since she'd seen him.

Daisy was feeling much stronger now and having gained some weight, looked almost her old self. She was eager to start her new life in London and a note was sent to Phoebe telling of her plans, asking if it would be possible to bring the new baby to Thetford before she left.

Daisy was sewing in the parlour when she heard the rumble of wheels. She ran to the window to see who had come to call, just in case she'd have to run upstairs and hide. To her delight she saw Jimmy helping Phoebe alight from the cart, and in her friend's arms was a bundle of white covers. The happy couple had called in, they later explained, on their way to the village where Phoebe planned to stay with her mother for a few weeks before the child was christened. The girls' joy at seeing each other was mingled with sadness since they had no idea when they'd meet again. Daisy took Phoebe's son in her arms while his mother looked on anxiously.

"He's beautiful," Daisy cried as she stroked the chubby cheek before turning to Jimmy, "He has your mouth Jimmy, but Phoebe's eyes, I think." Her friend threw her a grateful glance, knowing that Daisy must have recognised the likeness to the Earl, in that the child was so fair, whereas Jimmy and Phoebe had dark hair and eyes.

Chapter 17

"But Phoebe's eyes is brown," interrupted Mrs Jones innocently. "Still, their eyes don't go their real colour 'til they're about a year old. Oh, do let me have a cuddle of the little darling." She beamed as she took the child from Daisy, leaving her free to discuss her plans for the future.

"I've no option but to get away from Norfolk," she explained once again. "But I'll write often and who knows, perhaps you'll be able to come to see me one day?"

"You never know," replied Phoebe doubtfully, thinking she wanted to be as far from the Earl as possible. "We're sorry you won't be able to come to the christening," she said to Daisy looking at the baby as it began to cry. She unbuttoned her blouse and Mrs Jones handed him back.

"We're calling him Ned," she said as the child sought nourishment, "After Jimmy's grandfather. It's short for Edward."

"Edward James," explained Jimmy, "after me, too."

Daisy felt sad when the little family left and Danbury commented on it over dinner.

"You'll settle in London, it won't be long before you've forgotten all about us."

She replied, "I very much doubt that. Seeing Phoebe has made me realise how much I *shall* miss everybody. It's funny," she reflected, "They say you never know what you've had until you've lost it."

"Don't worry, Daisy," said Mrs Jones as she ladled thick custard onto the syrup pudding, "You'll most likely meet a nice young man in London and be married yourself within a couple of years."

"I don't think so," replied Daisy as she took the plate from the housekeeper, "I don't intend to marry."

They decided to go to London by train. The railway companies had been operating in East Anglia for some years but were very unreliable and journeys took ages. It was all very well for the Earl to go between Thetford and London in his private carriage, but since the advent of the railway several of the public coach lines had ceased to operate. So having pored over maps and timetables, they decided to hire a carriage to take them to Bury St Edmunds and arrived at the station just a few minutes before the train was due to arrive. It wasn't long before they heard it rumble round the bend and into the station.

Danbury stowed their cases on the luggage rack and Daisy bobbed up and down in her seat excitedly, as the engine was fired up again and the train began to shunt out of the station. Simon snapped the windows shut as smoke blew into the carriage and smuts drifted on to their faces. Laughing, Simon wiped Daisy's face with his handkerchief and she brushed his with her fingers. She caught his gaze and, slightly embarrassed, turned her attention to the ticket collector who suddenly appeared.

To hide her face from curious eyes, Daisy wore a bonnet with a deep brim. Her red hair was tucked up into her hat and she was careful to keep her gaze downwards. Simon assured her there was little chance of anybody from King's Lynn being on the train and local folk were too busy going about their business to take any notice of the couple. Nevertheless, Daisy was grateful there were very few passengers.

After a tedious journey they arrived at Shoreditch railway station and were glad to alight in order to stretch their limbs. There were plenty of cabs outside the station, so Simon hailed one and the last lap of the journey began.

Everything is the same, thought Daisy, as she leaned forward to look about her. Having so recently left the countryside, she couldn't help but compare the mood of London and its inhabitants. There were still too many people scurrying along the littered streets and the atmosphere almost crackled with activity. As the cab rolled over London Bridge the Thames was alive with traffic, bringing back memories of her days with Tom when they'd watched mudlarks scavenging for treasure and wood along the banks of the Thames.

The sooty smell of the water was evocative and Daisy inhaled deeply in order to capture its overpowering tang. She smiled to herself as barges warned of their impending approach, throaty horns being a familiar noise on the river. Somehow, despite her misgivings, she felt she was coming home to a place that, although it held many bad memories, was exactly that, home. Again, she thought of her family. Tears of nostalgia welled in her eyes at the sounds and smells of her childhood but she brushed them aside, determined to look to the future.

Daisy almost broke her resolve when they stepped into the little shop and the bell above the door tinkled, just as it had in Mr. Tibbet's establishment. She almost expected a cat to come sidling round the counter.

"And this is Daisy, my new lodger?" A small, stout woman beamed as she looked Daisy over critically. Her face reminded Daisy of a currant bun with two small raisins for eyes. Simon Danbury replied on her behalf.

"Hello there, Aunt Millie, this is my young friend, Daisy Smith."

"Come along in, the both of you. I'm sure you'll be wanting a nice drink after that 'orrible journey. I remember coming to see your mother when she was ill the last time," she went on, as she led the way into the back kitchen. "The journey on the mail coach was terrible. All sorts were getting on, all the ruffians you can imagine — I was jolly glad to get to Thetford. Don't suppose the trains are much better." She took hold of a cloth and picked up the steaming kettle from the hob, pouring water into the teapot.

"Just take your 'at off, Daisy. It's 'ot in here. Perhaps you'd have preferred lemonade."

Aunt Millie grumbled amiably while she took a slab of cake from the larder, doing her best to make Daisy feel at home. She was disappointed when Simon said he couldn't stay overnight as he had to catch the first train the next day, so would sleep at an inn near the station.

"The Earl and his family will be up for the shooting next month," he explained, "So there's a lot to be done. The house has to be got ready for them and if I don't keep an eye on things. . ." He made a gesture as if to slit his throat. Daisy laughed but would be sad to see him go. He was such a kind man, who had been good to her. She said as much when she kissed him on the cheek under the watchful eye of Aunt Millie. She didn't know what Simon had told his aunt about her but realised he'd only speak in confidence to somebody he could trust.

During her entire stay with Aunt Millie, her past was never spoken of except when Daisy volunteered any explanation of her knowledge of London. But on her first evening, when the shop was shut, they sat in the back parlour and mulled over Daisy's plans to find a job as a seamstress.

It was cosy in the small room. The furniture was pleasantly shabby with rag rugs spread over the linoleum. An aspidistra stood on a mahogany plant stand in one corner and the mantelpiece was crowded with cheerful ornaments, alongside a wooden clock that chimed the hour. The older woman advised Daisy to sign on at one of the new employment agencies.

"There's one near Regent Street that a friend of mine went to. Said it was a nice class of establishment. Why don't you try it?"

On her advice, Daisy went to the agency on the very next day and was taken to a booth where she was dealt with by a friendly young woman. She watched as details of her experience were transferred to a card, the pen scratching loudly over the paper.

"That seems to be all right, Miss Smith," the girl confirmed as she rummaged through some cards. "You've had some useful experience, and I'm sure Lady Charlotte would give you a good reference?"

Daisy put her hand to her mouth in panic. "I didn't realise I'd need references. How silly of me."

"All the good fashion houses need a character. I was hoping to place you with one of the big establishments and they insist on character references."

"I'm afraid I can't provide one," Daisy said, embarrassed that she hadn't thought things through properly.

"Well," the girl answered as she put her sheaf of papers to one side, "In that case, there's not a lot I can do for you. If I were you, I'd go away and think about it. Call in from time to time. We do get the odd dressmaker who wants help on the quick and isn't too fussy."

"Thank you," replied Daisy, upset at the last remark. She was disconsolate as she rose to go. "I may see you again."

Dejected, she walked home and discussed the situation with Aunt Millie. "I didn't think about references when I made my plans. I can't ask Lady Charlotte to give me one, nor the Countess, seeing as Lady Charlotte is the Earl's mother."

Aunty Millie patted her hand. "I don't know why you've come back to London, dearie, and don't intend to ask but I can guess by the shadows under your eyes that something nasty 'appened to you. That's the trouble with working in service. You fall out with the master or mistress and you've got no reference for your next job."

She stopped to serve a small boy with an ounce of brandy balls before speaking to Daisy again. "Tell you what, why don't you go down Cheapside and look at the cards in the shop windows. They sometimes advertise jobs that way when they don't want to pay the agency fees. Then there's all the Jews down Whitechapel, they take on sewing people but you don't really want to work for them. Word has it their places are sweat shops and their premises are dark and dirty. You're a cut above them sort of people."

She finished serving the boy who ran out of the shop gleefully poking his chubby fingers into the paper cone of sweets. The cash drawer closed with a thud and she turned her attention back to Daisy.

"Make us a nice cup of tea and then put your feet up. You look exhausted after being out all morning."

Daisy appreciated Millie's kindness and thought about her predicament.

"Perhaps you could teach me how to serve in the shop?" she suggested as she put Millie's tea on the counter. "Not for pay, but I'd like to help out while I'm with you."

"I must say I'd like some time off now for a nice cup of tea now and again. Open seven days a week I am. Finish your tea and come outside when you're ready. I'll show you the ropes — but I'll still need my rent, mind."

Daisy spent a pleasant afternoon weighing tobacco and snuff, and learning how to chop slabs of toffee into little pieces with a tiny hammer. Since the confectionary shop was the only one in the parade, there was a steady stream of customers during the day.

"Have you been here long?" asked Daisy, as she twisted the lid on a jar of boiled sweets.

"Lordy, yes. Me and Jack bought the shop when we left the service of Lord Ogden up West, nigh on thirty years ago. We'd saved up for years we 'ad and as soon as we was able, we bought this place. Used to be a little gold mine but not so much now, although I can't say as I'm doing badly."

"Did your husband die?"

"No. No. We was never married you see. Lived over the brush, as they say — then along comes this little trollop and he's all of a dither. I think it was because we never 'ad no children and she went and got pregnant. Already had two of her own. I couldn't fall, see."

"That's very sad. What about the shop?"

"Ah well, we'd had the deeds drawn up proper like and I owned 'alf. Like I said it 'ad been a gold mine so I'd saved and said I'd give 'im a quarter of what it was worth to have it all put in my name. He was desperate because of the child, see, so 'e took the money and made the shop over to me."

She wiped the counter down with a flourish. "I 'eard as 'ow they run a flower stall outside Euston station. Bit cold in the winter, I reckon."

Daisy stared out of the window. "It's funny isn't it, Millie. I thought I was the only one in the world who has problems, but everybody's the same."

"That's right, dearie. I was cut up when Jack left but I'm used to being on me own now. And, at least I'm an independent woman and that's a good feeling, I can tell you."

"I want to be like you, Aunt Millie. I want to stand on my own two feet and not have to answer to a man."

"That's my girl," replied Millie. "But you'll be lonely, and that's the truth of it. Nothing's perfect. I'd like to meet a decent bloke, I don't mind saying, but they don't grow on trees — not round 'ere, anyways."

The next morning, Daisy walked over London Bridge and on to Cheapside. The road was bustling with activity and she peered in shop windows at cards offering all manner of second hand goods for sale, and jobs. Some were for maids or cleaners and Daisy realised she may have to take one of these jobs until she could find something suitable; however, there was no necessity for that now, so she sauntered East, carefully keeping to the main thoroughfare, until she came to the entrance to Petticoat Lane.

It looked just the same as it had when she went there with Tom and Blanche, dusty and just as busy. She'd forgotten the cries of the street vendors and wondered what had happened to Tom and Jake, and whether she'd meet them in one of the markets. Perhaps she'd see dear Lou again, or maybe her own parents had returned to Mile End. They might even work in this area. Would she recognise them after all these years? More to the point would they recognise this nicely dressed girl as their own dear Daisy? Choking back the tears she pretended to examine the fruit that was on sale and eventually bought some apples to take home to Millie, but she felt conspicuous in her nice clothes, aware people were staring at her. Perhaps she'd make a mistake in coming and vowed should she ever visit again, she'd not come alone. With bowed head, she slunk to the where the bus stopped.

Daisy was soon able to look after the shop on her own and took to seeking work as a seamstress in the morning, and serving in the shop in the afternoon while Millie put her feet up. She became acquainted with the local children and enjoyed weighing their sweets or selling them bars of chocolate wrapped in silver paper.

Sherbet dabs were another favourite with the little ones, as were sugared almonds and tiny marzipan mice with waxed, string whiskers. One or two ladies she recognised as prostitutes came in for snuff, and left the shop heavily perfumed with cheap scent. All manner of artisans and labourers came in for their 'baccy' and most had a cheerful grin for the new girl behind the counter.

In the middle of August, Daisy was taking her usual walk along Cheapside, when she heard a commotion outside an ironmongers. The shopkeeper was standing at the door shaking his fist at a woman who was walking away unhurriedly with her head held high. In fact she didn't see Daisy until she collided with her, spilling packets and parcels on the floor.

"Oh dear," she cried. "Now look what I've done."

Daisy helped her retrieve the things she'd dropped and waited while the woman stuffed braids and ribbons into her reticule.

"Damned man," she complained, "All I did was return a pair of scissors that didn't cut properly and the stupid man objected to giving my money back."

Daisy found herself being appraised by a pair of large brown eyes that were set in a somewhat equine face. The woman was tall with large bones, albeit they were not well covered with flesh. She wore a brown bombazine dress, cut in the latest fashion and bore herself with grace.

"Thank you very much for your help," she said as she rummaged in her bag. "Hell and damnation, I knew there was something I forgot."

Daisy looked at her questioningly.

"I meant to put a notice in his shop window," the woman explained. "I need to replace one of my workers and forgot all about it in the rumpus."

"Some of the other shops will do it for you," suggested Daisy. "I should know. I've been looking for work for about two weeks." She pointed to a green doorway opposite. "I've seen them in the window over there."

"Thank you," said the woman, "One of my seamstresses has left me suddenly to take care of her sick mother and I've a lots of orders to fulfil for the winter season. I must find somebody quickly."

Daisy's heart beat faster. "I'm looking for sewing work. Perhaps I could help you out until you find a permanent person?"

The woman thrust out her hand. "I'm Vi Goodbody. Short for Violette." She looked around dubiously at the beer shop where women and children loitered on the road outside. The unruly bunch were shouting and swearing at their children, obviously the worse for drink. "I wish there was somewhere we could talk."

"Why don't we walk," suggested Daisy, "Which are you going?"

"Towards Ludgate Hill."

"It's not much out of my way, I'll walk with you if I may. I'm free to help you out, but I warn you I don't have a reference."

"Where did you work?" asked Vi as they made their way along the thoroughfare.

"In Norfolk — for a Countess. I worked under her dresser and when Mildred had an accident, I took her job over. As well as doing her Ladyship's hair and looking after her generally, I kept her clothes in good repair and after a while began making some for her, too. Just simple day dresses and underwear at first then I started trimming bonnets. I turn a good stitch."

"Why are you looking for work in shop windows? Aren't you registered with an agency?"

Daisy spread her hands in explanation. "Unfortunately, as I already mentioned, I don't have a reference."

135

Vi gave her a knowing look. "I see. Trouble with the master, eh. Not surprising, a pretty girl like you. I'll tell you what, I'm stuck, so why don't we give it a try. I don't care about references so long as you can do your job and are honest. My place is near St. Paul's."

She felt in her bag for a piece of paper and hastily scribbled an address. "Come along at eight tomorrow morning and we'll set you to work. See what you can do. What's your name, by the way?"

"I'm Daisy. Daisy Smith."

"Very well, Daisy Smith, until tomorrow." She swept off with a flourish of her hand and Daisy couldn't wait to tell Millie what had happened, so hurried back over London Bridge with the good news.

Chapter 18

"My word, what a stroke of luck," cried Millie as Daisy explained about meeting Vi Goodbody. "Do you know what you'll have to do?"

"Not really, just straightforward sewing I presume. I'm to present myself at this address at eight o'clock tomorrow morning."

Daisy thrust the scribbled note towards Millie who peered at it and said, "It's a good address by the looks of it. It could be the new start you're looking for."

It was an excited Daisy who pushed open the glass-panelled door of the premises in a side street near St. Paul's Cathedral. Violette was behind the counter, measuring a length of blue ribbon for a nanny who had a fractious infant in tow.

"Good morning," said Vi as she snipped the ribbon and put it into a bag. The customer paid before scooping the child up with a few encouraging words as she hurried into the street.

"You turned up then? I thought you would," said Vi, using what Daisy was to learn was her usual abrupt manner of speech. She pointed to a prettily upholstered seat usually reserved for clients. "Sit down. Sit down."

Daisy lowered herself onto the fragile frame, afraid it would buckle under her weight.

"I serve in the shop until nine when Pam comes in," explained Vi, "she's my shop assistant. We rarely get early morning callers so I take the opportunity to keep my eye on things out here. I find it useful to stock haberdashery; it helps to get the shop known."

She put the reel of ribbon back on the shelf and turned her attention to Daisy once more. "After nine o'clock I go into the rooms at the back. It's where I do all the designing and cutting. I've got three regular women who sew and another two girls who come in as and when they're needed. They do the beadwork and most of the trimming."

"Really! So you've a small manufactory going on here? I imagined you worked on your own with just one assistant."

"I used to. In fact I started by doing all the work by myself but fortunately, by keeping my prices down and turning out good work, the business grew. I've got some very rich clients now."

Vi stopped talking as another customer came into the shop, returning her attention to Daisy when she was free again. "A lot of my clients come to me for evening wear, so you'll often be working on rich, heavy materials where mistakes are costly. Do you think you'd be up to that?"

Daisy nodded. "I'm accustomed to matching and repairing beautiful silks and satins, and I promise to be careful, if you'll only give me a trial."

"Right," agreed Vi, as the girl Daisy assumed to be Pamela, arrived to begin work. "Let's take you into the back and get you started."

She led the way through pristine muslin curtains into the rear of the shop where two other women were bent over their sewing. She introduced them as Betsy and Maud and told them to answer any questions Daisy may have. "I want her to start on the black and green striped for Mrs. Smythe."

When Vi had left the room Betsy smiled at Daisy tentatively.

"You sit over there." She pointed to a chair on the far side of the table. The workers sat round a large wooden table, sharing the various silk and cotton threads. Dummy forms draped with half finished clothes stood around the room looking, Daisy thought, like headless bodies after an execution.

"Miss Goodbody's very fussy about clean hands, especially in summer when our hands sweat There's a bowl over there," Betsy pointed towards it as she continued, "You'll be doing the seams on the bodice of Mrs Smythe's dress. They need to be done in a very small running stitch and later on they'll be feathered."

Daisy washed her hands and selected a needle, then nervously set about threading it with a matching silk twist. This was her chance to prove what she could do. She bent over the material and sewed tiny stitches until her eyes and back ached. She heard Betsy and Maud speaking to each other in low tones but didn't join in the conversation, preferring to concentrate on her work.

Later, they stopped for something to eat. "The pie man's on 'is way," called out Pam as she popped her head through the curtain.

"Good," chorused the other two women, "We're starving. Coming to buy a pie, Daisy?"

She followed them to the front of the shop where the vendor took his tray from the top of his head.

"Come on, gels," he jested, "Five is it today? Let's be 'aving yer money." He gave them their pies before continuing on his way, calling, "All best beef. Penny each!"

"Blimey, they're half cold, as usual," grumbled Betsy. "I reckon we should change to the eel pie man, 'is stuff might be 'otter."

"Still, it's something to eat," Maud explained, "This is the end of his round. We only get a fifteen-minute break. Me and Betsy bring in some lemonade from home — you can share ours for today."

They stood outside the shop gobbling down the pies and swigging lemonade from the bottle.

Pam explained, "We mustn't eat in the shop, in case we get marks on the material."

"What happens when it rains?" asked Daisy as she swallowed the last of the warm pie.

"Vi let's us use her sitting room. She's good like that. She lives above the shop, so that's where she usually eats herself."

"She seems very nice," remarked Daisy.

"She's a good sort if you do yer work properly." With that short comment Maud wiped her hands down her apron before returning to the shop to wash them properly. Daisy finished stitching the bodice of the brown and yellow striped dress and had almost completed the seams of skirt when Vi came into the sewing room at seven in the evening. She inspected what Daisy had done and nodded approvingly.

"That's fine," she said. "You're a bit slow but you'll learn to work more quickly. Get that finished in the morning and you can make a start on the little bridesmaid's dresses for Lady Olive Garner's wedding."

She put Daisy's finished work down on the table, before adding, "It's to be a big affair, they'll all be dressed in white with orange blossom sewn round the waist. The trimmers will do that." She clapped her hands. "Right girls. I'm closing up."

Daisy's eyes were tired as she hurried over the bridge, anxious to tell Millie how her day had gone.

"You sit down, Millie. You've been on your feet all day while I've been sitting. I'll make the tea and look after the shop." While she brewed the tea she described all the rich materials and the joy of working with them, breaking off intermittently to serve customers.

"Do you think this Vi Goodbody was satisfied with your work?" asked Millie as she sipped her tea.

"I think so. She said I was a bit slow but it's better to be slow and do the job properly. I'll get quicker, and in any case she wouldn't have asked me to go back tomorrow if I was no use." She pursed her lips before asking doubtfully, "*Would* she?"

In the event Vi Goodbody offered Daisy a permanent job at the end of the week and she settled into the routine quite happily. As the months wore on she grew more confident, although she never became really friendly with the other girls who lived at home with their parents and seemed to have large families. Daisy felt apart from them as they discussed the ailments and antics of their siblings, and she deliberately gave the impression that although she had no immediate family herself,

Millie was her real aunt.

They heard from Simon in November. He'd said he'd like to visit before the Earl took his family up to Thetford for their winter holiday, and Aunty Millie hastily responded to his request with delight.

"We'll have an early Christmas, Dais," she said. "Tell you what, we'll get a turkey from Leadenhall Market and I'll make a plum pudding. He was always my favourite, was Simon. He was in a terrible state when his wife died, along with the little one, then his parents went so soon after. Mind you, I thought he looked more like 'is old self last time I seen him."

"What was she like? his wife," said Daisy.

"Pretty little thing. Hung on his every word. I always hoped he'd meet somebody else, but he hasn't. Not yet, any way."

She cast Daisy a sideways glance to see what effect her words had, but Daisy didn't take the bait.

Simon was already drinking tea in the back parlour when Daisy returned from work on Friday. He jumped out of his seat in front of the fire to help take off with her shawl.

"You look really well now, Daisy. Come and warm yourself while I make a hot drink."

They settled themselves for an hour's gossip about Thetford while Aunty Millie served in the shop. Friday night was pay night so there was a steady stream of customers all evening. Daisy slipped off her boots and wriggled her toes.

"Have you seen Phoebe and the baby?" she asked.

"Yes. Jimmy usually stops off for an hour or so when he's taking Phoebe to see her mother. The little chap's doing fine and I wasn't exactly told but I shouldn't be surprised if there isn't another little Fawcett on the way."

"What makes you think that?"

"By the size of Phoebe's stomach. Mind you, she's put on some weight since having young Ned."

He brought Daisy up to date with news from the estate and she told him about her job.

He nodded thoughtfully. "So you're settled there, d'you think?"

"Oh yes. I like the girls and Violette of course, but mostly I enjoy working with quality materials. Then there's Aunty Millie — she and I really get along well."

"Yes," said Simon as he raked the coals on the fire. "She told me. Serve in the shop as well, don't you?"

"Yes. Which reminds me, we'd better put the pudding on to heat. Aunty Millie made it last night especially. I'll peel some potatoes and carrots while we're talking. I want it ready for when she closes up. She'll be tired by then."

Daisy pottered around the back scullery, with Simon calling out to her as she bustled to and fro.

"I think Aunty Millie looks a bit peaky since I saw her last?"

Daisy put the pan of potatoes on the big black range. "She wasn't well last month but I thought she's looking better. I suppose I don't notice it since I live with her. She does get tired but I think it's probably her age."

"I'd like you to keep an eye on her for me, Daisy."

"I will, don't worry."

Millie closed the shop while Daisy put the vegetables on the plates and they gathered round the table to eat. Steam rose from the steak and kidney pudding and they all sniffed with anticipation as Millie cut into it.

"Now tomorrow," she said, pausing between mouthfuls. "I want you to call in at the market, Dais, and get the turkey. Get one about sixteen pound. That'll last us into next week. And some sausages too."

"That's a bit heavy for Daisy to carry," interjected Simon. "Tell you what. I'll come and meet you from work and we'll go to the market together so I can carry the bird."

"Now there's a good idea," trilled Millie. "Shame Daisy has to work of a Saturday but she does, and that's that. What will you do during the day, Simon?"

"I thought I'd take a walk round London. Look at St Paul's first, then go down into Fleet Street and see where my fancy takes me. Don't you worry Daisy, I'll be outside the shop at seven, if you'll give me the address."

True to his word he was prompt the following evening and Daisy said goodbye to the girls, amid curious stares. She'd explained he was Millie's nephew.

"He'll be your cousin, then?" asked Betsy.

Daisy disseminated quickly and replied, "By marriage, yes."

Since working for Vi, she'd become much more aware of clothes and was delighted to note Simon was dressed for the city. She thought how smart he looked in his clothes tailored from a discreet worsted cloth, the waistcoat being complete with pocket chain. His feet were well shod in the latest square-toed shoes and on his head he wore a high hat. She proudly tucked her hand into his arm and they walked to Leadenhall market.

The area was crackling with activity as customers inspected and dithered before making their purchases. Amid the bustle they managed to find a turkey that was just the correct size for Aunty Millie's roasting dish. Trade was coming to an end and they bought the bird for a good price, along with two pounds of beef sausages. Simon hoisted the turkey onto his back and they made for London Bridge which was already swathed in fog. Gas lamps hissed and cast an eerie glow on the faces of the pedestrians as they crossed the river.

They were glad to reach home where Millie banked up the fire, as the bird would be left to cook slowly during the night, but first it was stuffed with herbs and sausages and its breast smothered in butter.

As Daisy lay in bed that night she appreciated her good fortune, she enjoyed her work, had a comfortable bed and Aunty Millie for company. The little shop had become home to her in a way that the country houses had never been. The smell of herbs wafted up the stairs and Daisy felt safe in the knowledge that Simon was sleeping on the couch in the parlour.

The shop had to be kept open during the morning, so Daisy served customers in order to leave Millie free to supervise the cooking. Simon helped peel vegetables and kept them both supplied with cups of tea, although he produced a bottle of brandy as a treat for Millie, after their meal. There was great excitement as the turkey was taken from the oven, its breast singed to a golden brown. It was placed on a large blue and white china plate in the centre of the table ready for Simon to carve. Daisy watched as his strong hands deftly guided the carving knife over the succulent flesh. He has nice hands, she thought, I like the way he keeps his nails short and clean. The wrists were thick and covered in fine fair and she found herself thinking of Vernon Fenn's hands. She pulled herself together as she heard her name called.

"Daisy, wake up, girl! Can you stir the custard for me? Don't want it going into lumps." Aunty Millie was putting the Christmas pudding to warm while they ate the traditional Christmas lunch.

It was a merry occasion with Simon keeping the ladies amused with tales from the Branstead estate and Daisy telling them about the customers who came into the dress shop.

"We're not allowed to call them customers, of course," she said, as she popped a Brussels' sprout into her mouth. "They're clients, not mere mortals like us."

"You're really happy with your new life, aren't you?" Simon observed rather sadly.

"I am," agreed Daisy. "What more could I want? I enjoy my job and get on very well with Aunty Millie." She smiled indulgently at the older woman. "My cup runneth over, as they say."

"And my life's much better with Daisy here too," said Millie, patting the girl's hand. "I must be getting old because sometimes I don't feel so good. She helps in the shop and can cook a decent meal. I don't know how I ever managed without her."

"And how often don't you feel so good?" queried Simon.

"Oh it's just a bit of indigestion now and again, nothing to worry about."

They raised their glasses, agreeing that life was treating them well.

Simon started his journey back to Thetford the next morning, with Daisy and Aunty Millie accompanying him to Shoreditch where he was to make his connection to Bury St Edmunds. They said their sad goodbyes and waved their handkerchiefs until the train was out of sight, then Daisy went to St Paul's and Millie walked back over London Bridge.

Christmas came and went with Aunty Millie buying Daisy some expensive dressmaking scissors for her seventeenth birthday.

Both work and home settled into a routine and apart from Simon Danbury making trips to London a couple of times, 1862 passed uneventfully. Daisy wrote to Phoebe who had had another son in May and according to Simon, was pregnant for yet a third time, when he came to London the following October.

Simon remarked again on Millie's deterioration and once again asked Daisy to keep an eye on her. By now they had slipped into an easy friendship and she'd even brought up the subject of her miscarriage when he walked her home from work one evening.

"I shall be eighteen this Christmas Day, Simon," she'd remarked as they walked through the fog. "It's funny how when you're little you can't imagine being grown up. I wouldn't be alive if it wasn't for you."

"Stuff and nonsense. Mrs Jones did most of the hard work. She asked after you, by the way. Always does, and threatens to come down to London to see you, even."

"From the way she speaks, she's obviously a Londoner so I expect she'd enjoy being home again. I wonder what made her go to Norfolk in the first place?"

"I'm not sure — I must ask her some time but I dare say, like my mother, she married a Norfolk man."

"Anyway, it would be wonderful, if she could come and stay for a few weeks, why don't you arrange it? I'll have a word with Millie. Mrs Jones could sleep in my room and I could use the sofa in the parlour, like you do, when you visit."

"Hold on. Hold on," he chided, pleased with her enthusiasm. "What would I do, all on my own in that big house on the estate?"

"Oh, don't be so difficult, Simon. You could manage. You've got a small army of maids to take care of you. You wouldn't miss Mrs Jones for a week or so, surely?"

Simon laughed in response, holding up his arm as if to protect himself.

"All right. All right. I know when I'm beaten. I'm just not sure it's such a good idea with Aunty Millie looking so peaky."

Chapter 19

Daisy watched over Millie carefully, insisting she take some herbal products the apothecary had recommended, but the indigestion persisted so Daisy asked the doctor to call. He left a bottle of white medicine with instructions it had to be taken after meals, and for a while Millie seemed to get better.

Daisy wrote to Simon, asking if he'd thought any more about Mrs Jones visiting them as perhaps it would cheer Millie up. She'd agreed she'd like to meet Simon's housekeeper and would welcome some company with Daisy being out at work every day. She'd even proposed Mrs Jones might like to help in the shop.

Daisy was a little concerned that Millie would like assistance, knowing how independent she'd always been.

Simon replied: "I've explained the situation to Mrs Jones, and kind soul that she is, she's prepared to come to London for an extended stay until Aunty Millie recovers fully."

Arrangements were hastily made and it was just a week later that Daisy met Mrs Jones off the train. They hugged and cried with pleasure at seeing each other again and chatted non-stop while walking home.

"I've had the doctor in to see Aunty Millie," explained Daisy, "and he prescribed some medicine — anti-acid I think he said it is — sometimes I see her wincing with pain but she won't admit she's not getting any better. Perhaps she'll talk to you when you get to know each other. You don't know how glad I am that you're here."

"I bin pestering Mr. Danbury to let me come for ages, like, but he likes 'is comforts, like any man."

"I'm so pleased to see you," Daisy repeated. "By the way, Aunty Millie doesn't know about my... my "illness." I wouldn't mind her knowing now that so much time has passed and I've grown fond of her. But somehow, the right time to tell her hasn't presented itself. Sometimes I think she guesses, anyway."

The two women walked in silence for a while, each deep in thought until Mrs Jones said, "I'd forgotten how breezy it is down in London."

Daisy laughed. "It's because we're nearing the river. The bridge is just round the corner. It means we're nearly home."

The shop was still open and Mrs Jones was delighted when the bell tinkled as they crossed the threshold.

"Oh, the smell of it. All them wonderful smells!" She sniffed appreciatively as Daisy introduced Aunty Millie.

The two women appeared to get along well and Daisy went to bed that night, happy to hear them deep in conversation. On returning from work the next day, she heard from Kate Jones, who now insisted on the use of her Christian name, that she'd learned to serve in the shop so Millie could rest.

"This idea of yours was a good one," observed Millie who by now had insisted Daisy dropped the 'aunty' too. "Kate picked up serving the customers in no time so we've struck a deal. She's going to see the sights of London in the morning and serve in the shop in afternoon, just until I'm better, that is."

"That's wonderful," cried Daisy with relief.

"There's just one thing, mind. I've insisted she take my bedroom. You pay me rent for your room and you're a working girl so it's too inconvenient for you to sleep downstairs on a permanent basis. No." She held up a hand. "Me mind's made up — I insist. Kate shall 'ave my room and I'll sleep downstairs. Any rate," she added, "It'll save me walking up those stairs." It was settled.

Christmas came and went with Simon putting in his usual appearance beforehand. Since Millie was now sleeping on the couch he put up at the nearby inn. They all spent a cheery few days together and exchanged small gifts. Millie gave Daisy a bottle of perfume for her eighteenth birthday and Kate produced some pinking shears that Daisy had coveted for some time.

Aside from being allowed to cut into expensive materials, she'd now progressed to making patterns, although they were readily available from the suppliers of haberdashery. Vi liked to make some of her own patterns from heavy brown paper as they lasted longer and Daisy had become adept at reducing and enlarging pattern pieces of popular designs.

The next couple of months passed uneventfully with the three women taking turns to serve in the shop and sharing the household chores. Daisy began to think Millie was better until she went downstairs early one morning to find her retching over the stone sink, her face twisted with pain.

"Millie, Millie, what on earth's the matter," Daisy cried as she witnessed her old friend's distress.

"I'm in awful pain, Daisy. Right here." She tapped the area of her breastbone and Daisy made her sit in an armchair. She ran upstairs and roused Kate Jones before scuttling off for the doctor. His face was grave and he called Daisy to one side.

"She's very ill, Miss. Come back to my surgery with me and I'll give you some laudanum to ease the pain."

Daisy was perturbed. "How ill is she, Doctor?" she asked sharply. He turned to his portmanteau and began scribbling on a pad. Daisy stood by nervously remembering how lost she'd felt when Polly had died. Surely Millie wasn't that ill? She bit her lip as she waited for the doctor to reply, aware of the smell of sweat that was embedded in the armpits of his jacket.

He turned to face her. "Very ill, my dear," he said gently, "You must be prepared for the worst."

There was nothing much they could do for Millie, except to see she was made comfortable and supplied with medicine to help with the pain. Daisy continued going to the shop, although Vi Goodbody was sympathetic.

"We're not too busy. I'll understand if you can't make it to work." But Daisy continued to work on Millie's good days and Kate looked after the sweet shop. Between them they muddled through the next few weeks until they deemed it time to summon Simon. He took leave of absence, which again wasn't a problem due to the time of year. In the early hours of the morning towards the end of the second week of Simon's stay, Daisy heard a cry.

She rushed downstairs to find Millie had fallen back on the pillows panting for breath.

"Sorry to wake you, Daisy dear. I reached for my medicine and the bottle dropped on the floor."

"Don't worry about waking me, let me plump your pillows and I'll spoon some into your mouth."

Daisy lifted Millie's frail body forward while she adjusted the pillows, dismayed at how thin her friend had become. Having given her the medicine, she sat by Millie's head and stroked her paper-thin hand.

"Thank you, Daisy," Millie gasped, exhausted at the effort of being made comfortable. "Stay here for a while. I want to talk to you."

"You mustn't waste your strength, Millie. You must save it for getting better."

Millie shook her head. "It's no use pretending, my dear. I'm not long for this world and I know it. I want to tell you something. I've left the shop to Simon 'cos he's me favourite. If I thought you'd run it with 'im, I'd die a happy woman. Why don't you marry him, Dais? Anyone can see he thinks a lot of you."

Daisy flushed and patted her old friend's shoulder.

"I'm sure you're wrong Millie but if it's what you want, I'll think about it."

Millie drifted into sleep and Daisy went back to bed thinking of the older woman's words, her mind in turmoil. She tossed and turned until the sky became a pale grey and she heard the lamplighter dimming the lights. You don't love Simon, an inner voice protested. He's very nice and you're fond of him, but is it enough? At last she fell asleep having reached no solution to her dilemma.

Millie clung to life for two more days and died on May sixth with the two people she loved best in the world at her bedside. The funeral took place on a bright spring day with fluffy clouds scudding across a blue sky. The pathway to the church was lined with daffodils, their yellow bonnets nodding in the breeze as a final salute to Simon's aunt.

It bought back memories of Polly whom Daisy had lost when she was only twelve years old. It seemed she was doomed to lose all those close to her, she thought, gloomily.

They were surprised by how many people attended the service held in the small Norman church. A notice had been put in the shop window telling of Millie's death and it seemed the whole local community came to show its respect. A shadow descended on the shop and Kate and Daisy were quiet after the funeral, each lost in their thoughts. In an attempt to hide his own distress, Simon declared a toast to Millie, before escaping to the inn.

The following week Simon and Daisy sat in the dusty office of Millie's solicitor, Mr Simpkins, at Lincoln's Inn Fields. The room was crammed with shelves holding yellowed papers tied with pink ribbon whilst old ledgers stood on the window sills. The mustiness made Daisy sneeze and she was startled when a parrot squawked. It was chained to a stand on the far side of the room and its black eyes followed Mr Simpkins as he took a faded file from a cupboard.

"This is the last Will and Testament of Miss Millicent Hargreaves. There's not a lot to tell. She leaves three hundred pounds to a Miss Daisy Smith and the rest of her estate to you, her nephew, Mr Simon Danbury. You, Sir," he nodded to Simon, "are now the owner of the sweetshop in Southwark Street, two small houses in Whitechapel, which are tenanted, bonds in railway stock, and other investments. Your aunt was a canny investor. Oh yes, there's some four thousand pounds in cash."

Daisy stared at Simon whose jaw seemed to drop to his chest. With his eyes opened wide, he gaped at Mr Simpkins, then said,

"Well, I never did. Are you sure? I had no idea she was so well off."

The solicitor tugged at his moustache and raised an eyebrow.

"You're a man of some means now, Sir. All funeral expenses are to be paid from the estate and I suggest you go away and think about your position. If I might make so bold, Sir, I think you should retain the tenanted houses to ensure an income, but you might want to dispose of the shop. A nice little business, that — it should fetch a good price."

He stood up and bowed to Daisy before shaking Simon's hand. "I look forward to receiving instructions, Sir."

The astonished recipients of Millie's wealth walked unsteadily down the rickety wooden staircase and out into the fresh air.

"What a surprise," gasped Daisy while Simon walked with slumped shoulders, deep in thought. They made their way back to the shop in silence. Kate made some cocoa and put the biscuit tin on the table, not speaking until they relayed the news.

"Upon my word," she said, not quite believing them.

Daisy put a mug of cocoa in front of Simon and asked gently,

"Have you any idea, what you'll do?"

He kept his eyes on the table, his face grim as he replied, "I need to sleep on it. I'll have an early night and perhaps I'll have come to a decision by the morning."

But his bags were packed when Daisy got up for work the next day. The coverlet was back on the couch, and Simon explained, I can't think down here in London. I'm going back to Thetford. I'll leave Kate to run the shop and I'll be back at the weekend."

He snapped the buckle on his case and was gone before Daisy could think of a suitable reply.

The two women, for Daisy now considered herself to be fully adult, shared some toast on which they spread mutton dripping. They ate slowly, each absorbed in their own thoughts. Kate didn't look surprised when Daisy told her she was expected to look after the shop.

"Mr.Danbury pays me wages, Duckie and it makes no difference to me where I am. I likes the shop anyhow. I enjoys the customers coming in and out. I see more people in London than I ever did in Thetford. I've got no family and there's only the maids up there to talk to."

"I suppose so," replied Daisy. "I don't mean to pry but I always wondered why you speak like a Londoner when you seem to have spent a lot of time in Norfolk."

"I was born in London, just like you, Daisy. But work was hard to find and when I was about eight, me Dad's brother suggested he worked on the land. I think he knew of a job going so we moved northwards. I s'pose I never lost me accent because me mum and dad were cockneys and I spoke like 'em. I was an only child and could have come back down here to live with an aunt when me parents went, but I decided not to."

"You poor thing."

"Not to worry — I had me reasons for staying in Norfolk. I had to work so started off as a maid in a doctor's house while I learned to cook, then worked my way up to being housekeeper for Mr Danbury, as you know. But, I'm enjoying the hustle and bustle of London again, so it's okay with me."

Daisy walked to St Paul's with a heavy heart. Besides losing Millie, Simon was away and there was every chance she'd have to find new lodgings. Vi Goodbody was sympathetic when she learned of the latest events in Daisy's life.

"All you can do is face it, whatever comes along. If I can help, let me know. You've got a job with me for as long as you need, so that's at least one worry you don't have."

"I thought maybe Simon would let me rent rooms in one of the houses he now owns but I'm a bit worried what the other tenants are like. Goodness knows Vi, nobody had a worse start in life than me but by the grace of God I managed to work my way out of it; I couldn't face living like that again."

"A little bit of deprivation builds character, in my opinion," said Vi sagely as she stooped to study a design on her drawing board. "But think carefully about what you want to do. Sometimes major upheavals in our lives prompt us to make changes we previously didn't have the courage for."

Daisy thought about Vi's words as she sewed. She kept her head down, not making conversation as she stitched the delicate seam of a gown. Once again her life was to be disrupted, but this time she was better armed to deal with it.

Vi spoke to her again when the pie man came at mid-day.

"I've been thinking, Daisy. If your friend gets rid of the shop you could stay with me for a few weeks, if you're pushed. As a last resort, of course. This might be a good time to let you know of my plans, too. I have a full order book at the moment and I've been thinking of opening up another shop for some time."

She looked out of the window while gathering her thoughts. "Perhaps I could put you in there as manageress. Shame you don't have any capital. We could have formed a partnership. Think over what I've said, Daisy, about another shop."

Daisy was flabbergasted at the suggestion. She hadn't told Vi about the three hundred pounds but had indicated some time ago that she saved as much of her meagre wages as was possible. Ever prudent, her savings were still kept in a little bag around her waist. She couldn't wait to get home to talk things over with Kate and felt her anger rise as she began talking.

"Oh, why did Simon have to go off like that?" she stormed, "he's left me up in the air as to what he's going to do with the shop."

"Calm down," said Kate as she patted the younger woman's hand. "I don't expect Mr Danbury's made any plans yet. That's why he's gone home — to have a think. He's a man of means now and might decide not to work for the Earl any more."

"But the estate's his life?"

"Yes," nodded Kate knowingly. "A life of long hours, too much responsibility and a low wage. The only perk is a big house, and he's got no family to fill it. No, I don't think the job'll be his big worry."

"But I thought he loved the countryside?" Daisy protested.

"He does love it. I can't see him living in a city. He'll be worrying about what's the best thing to do. Was that the shop bell?"

Kate hurried out to serve a customer, leaving Daisy to mull over what had been said. Would Simon continue to work for the Earl? It seemed silly to be an employed man, when he was rich enough to support himself. Would he sell the shop? Probably. Daisy couldn't imagine Simon as a shopkeeper in a dirty city. Should she take up the offer of a partnership with Vi? She went to bed that night worrying about her own future.

She'd come to no conclusion when she woke next morning, so walked to work determined to forget about Simon and concentrate on the work in hand. A few weeks previously Vi had suggested Daisy design a presentation dress for the daughter of one of their clients. She'd spent days thinking about the material to use and the cut of the skirt along with other details. When the design had been shown to Arabella, who was to wear the dress, she was enchanted with the fitted bodice that was modest but showed the young woman's curves to advantage.

Tiny bows adorned the sleeves and the dress was finished with a sash that swept into a bow at the back. The simple white voile was ideal for a young woman, not yet 'out' and looked both virginal, yet sophisticated.

Her design had been approved by Arabella's mother too, and Daisy cut the material under the watchful eye of Vi. The emotional debutante popped into the shop every few days to see how work was progressing, often accompanied by some equally excitable friends. They'd fidget and speak in loud whispers on the pretext of buying ribbons and peep through to the workroom where Daisy was intent on her work.

"I'm sorry about Arabella's friends," Daisy said to Vi one afternoon when the girls had been particularly irksome.

"It's hardly your fault, Daisy." Vi was a good business woman and could see the potential of Arabella's companions. "It's good publicity for us and who knows, they might bring in some business."

She was correct, within a couple of weeks two more designs had been commissioned for coming-out balls. Sometimes, after sharing an evening meal with Kate, Daisy sketched out rough pictures of dresses. She'd wash the dishes with a pencil in her mouth, stopping to change a frill here and adding some trimming there. She'd ask Kate what she thought about some of her designs and the older woman would laugh and reply ruefully.

"Don't ask me, duckie. Look at me. Hardly a fashion plate, am I?"

Debutantes always wore white, so it was quite a challenge to produce something different. Betsy and Maud did the main sewing under Daisy's instructions, with the finishers working on the delicate beading.

By the end of June, Daisy's back and eyes ached with the constant attention to detail.

Vi entered the sewing room as Daisy arched her back. "You know, Daisy," she said with a concerned look on her face, "I've been thinking of getting one of these new fangled sewing machines. Do you think it a good idea?"

"I'm not sure, Vi. I read about the Singer in a catalogue the other day and although it might take the hard work out of the seams, it seems wrong somehow — almost like mass production."

"I suspect you're right. We want to keep our reputation as a high class dressmaker, so we'll say no more about it."

There was still no word from Simon but Kate was happy in the shop and Daisy was too busy to worry about him. "He'll get in touch when he's ready," she told Kate.

Meanwhile a flood of orders had been received for new ball gowns and Vi announced one day in the middle of July she'd found some premises near Ludgate Circus.

Chapter 20

Vi took Daisy to see the proposed site one sunny morning. The shop was situated in the main road and set between a gentlemen's tailor and a tobacconist. The latter window displayed fine cigars and smoking pipes, all arranged in perfect order. There was a French milliner's in the small parade and when they unlocked the door to the empty shop, Daisy knew it was ideal. Light flooded from the large front window and the reception room would be perfect for a salon with cubicles around the perimeter.

There was ample space for workrooms at the rear also a small scullery with a sink. She opened the door to discover a tiny yard with a shed in the corner, which housed a privy and storage space. Daisy poked around the fireplace in the scullery which appeared to have been used quite recently, pleased that with a few embellishments there'd be somewhere to boil a kettle. She'd thought it a nice idea to offer clients hot chocolate while they were waiting.

"Not bad," observed Vi, as she inspected the rooms. "Apparently it used to be a gents' outfitters. I suppose it sold shirts and accessories which complemented the tailor's. Needs brightening up, of course."

"We could paint it white," declared Daisy." That would be quite revolutionary and give a feeling of space. What do you think?"

Violette laughed. "Slow down, slow down. We haven't talked yet. There's a coffee shop further along. It's patronised by men as a rule, but what the heck, women are more accepted in these places now, so let's go there for coffee and talk things over."

Daisy had told Vi about her inheritance some weeks earlier and they'd agreed to put up an equal amount each to enable them to open *Daisy's Designs*, as the shop was to be named. The money would be used to acquire the building and for buying an initial supply of materials and fitting out the shop.

Daisy would design and make a simple two-piece costume for day wear and a glamorous ball gown, both of which would be placed in the window to attract customers. A seamstress would be engaged and there was ample work from the combined shops to keep all the women busy for the foreseeable future. Vi, having had the necessary experience, would interview staff and pass her selection on to Daisy, who would have the final choice.

It was September before the shop was ready and a notice was put in

The Times announcing the opening date. On the prior evening, Daisy went home to find Simon in the back of the little sweet shop. She greeted him warmly and now being able to recognise good tailoring, complimented him on his new suit of clothes. Kate was busy dealing with a confectionary representative, so they had the room to themselves for a while.

"Tell me all your news," she urged as they sipped tea.

"Well," Simon began. "I don't work for the Earl any more. One of the first decisions I made was to resign but agreed to stay on until he found somebody to replace me."

"Was he surprised?"

"Shocked, more like it. He thought I was there until the end of my days. So did I, come to mention it."

"Did anybody we know get the job?"

"Sir Algernon recommended somebody from Foxlands. He seems to be a good man. I showed him the ropes and he's doing nicely. He has a little family, so at least the house is lived in properly now."

Daisy nodded, trying not to interrupt but was unable to stick to her resolve.

"Was I mentioned? Did he gossip about Foxlands?"

"No and I didn't encourage him. Might have brought up awkward questions."

"I see. It's a bit disappointing not to be missed. Any rate, what about you? Where are you living?"

Simon took another sip of his tea and urged Daisy to be patient.

"I'll tell you exactly what happened," he began, determined she should hear the whole story. "I took a bit of a holiday. Went up to the north coast of Norfolk and put up in a nice hotel in Cromer. Pretty part of the county. During the day I'd walk long the coast and think about what to do with my life."

"And what conclusions did you come to?"

Simon laughed at Daisy's impatience.

"Firstly, I decided if Kate would agree to run the sweet shop permanently I'd keep it. I found myself a solicitor in Norwich and he went over the figures with me and he confirmed it's a good little business. I've already spoken to Kate and she's agreed."

Daisy's eyes shone.

"Oh, goody, goody. Now I shan't have to move."

Simon's was disappointed at her excitement and his eyes clouded as he continued.

"No lass. You're okay here for the duration. As to the houses, I'm keeping them too, so I've no need to work if I don't want to."

154

Daisy was thoughtful. "True, but you'll need something to occupy you."

"Indeed. On my walks I saw a little cottage for sale, and bought it. Well, it's not all that small really, but pretty. It has roses round the door and wisteria growing up the walls. I fell in love with it at first sight. I can hear the owls at night and smell the perfume of the flowers when I sit outside of an evening. It's lovely."

Daisy wrung her hands with excitement. "Oh, I do wish I could see it. Where exactly is it?"

"Near a little town called Hunstanton, right up the north Norfolk coast. I can see the sea from my window, and watch fishing boats bobbing about. But that's only part of it. The house came with ten acres of land."

Daisy's eyes shone. "Oh Simon, I do envy you." Her voice wavered. "Perhaps I could visit, and you will still come to London to see us, won't you?"

Simon covered her hand with his own. "Of course I will. Now tell me what you've been up to."

Daisy told him of her and Vi's plans for the shop and he listened with dismay as he realised her heart was still set on making her life in London. Unaware of his feelings Daisy chattered on.

"I'm so grateful to Aunty Millie for leaving me that money," she said. "But I feel quite homesick now you've told me about your cottage."

Simon was solemn as he tried to articulate his emotions. "I've something to say to you but I don't think you're ready to hear it, but it has to be said."

Daisy tried to interrupt but he held up his hand and insisted in continuing. "I'm twenty one years older than you, Daisy Smith but I took to you the first time I saw you. I've been holding out the hope that one day you'd become my wife because I think I'd make a good husband for you. But, I see now that you're a Londoner and that London's in your heart, so we'll say no more."

Unaware of the depth of his distress Daisy looked into his eyes.

"The truth is, Simon, I don't really know *what* I want. Since my trouble that year, I've set myself against men. It seems to me a girl's better off on her own. What does a man do but give her babies year after year?"

She tossed her head in defiance. "I want to live. I'm not ready to settle down." She cast her eyes downwards and continued, "I look at women like Vi Goodbody and Aunty Millie, and realise women can look after themselves and I'd like to try to do it."

Simon looked downcast but she had to tell him the truth.

"You're one of the kindest people I know and a good friend, Simon. There's nobody I like better but for now, the answer's *no*."

She rose and leaned across the table in order to plant a kiss on his cheek. Daisy had never seen him express emotion before, and she felt a tear slide down her own cheek. Was she being a fool? *Probably*, she thought, answering her own question.

Simon was quiet for the rest of the evening and in the morning, left early to get the train back to King's Lynn. Daisy wept when the door closed behind him.

"Oh Kate," she cried to the older woman. "I've hurt Simon so much. I do love him, but only as a brother. Millie always said he wanted to marry me but I thought she was being silly. He's such a lovely man. What's the matter with me?"

"You're not fully growd up yet, Daisy Smith but when you are, maybe you'll change your mind. I only hope it's not too late then because my Mr Simon is one of the loveliest men on this earth, and I'd 'ave snapped a man like 'im up if he'd asked me."

Daisy said, "Please don't be cross with me. I know he's a treasure and I haven't forgotten the way you both looked after me when I was near to death, but I hope to be madly in love with the man I marry, and right now all I want is to open my shop."

"Don't get hard, Dais," Kate warned.

The opening of the shop caused passers-by to look curiously at the clothes in the large window. Two young women came in with their mother to ask the price of the two-piece costume. Daisy pointed out the cost depended on the materials used and gave advice as to what colours she thought would suit them. She mentioned casually that the shop was affiliated to Goodbody's Gowns in St Paul's, and much to her delight, the following day the girls came back to place an order.

"Mama said if the suits are well made, we may order a gown for our brother's wedding. Who made the lavender satin in the window?"

"I did," said Daisy proudly. "I designed it too. Do you like it?"

"It's beautiful," they nodded in unison.

By the end of October, the seamstresses were busy completing orders and Daisy tripped over London Bridge each morning with a light heart. It seemed that her clientele was to be the younger element of the middle classes, and it pleased her to design for these elegant young women who knew exactly what they wanted. One day the doorbell pinged to announce the arrival of a plump young woman who sought Daisy's advice.

"I have to attend my brother's graduation celebration," she said nervously. "I hate gatherings but Mama says that on this occasion I can't stay at home with a book. I'd welcome any suggestions and advice. I know I'm overweight. It runs in the family."

Daisy was diplomatic as she studied the girl's figure.

"I think you should try to achieve a sleek look. Your clothes should always be unfussy but well tailored. Here." She beckoned to the girl to stand in front of the cheval mirror which was placed in an alcove away from prying eyes. Taking a fold of material from the girl's skirt she tucked it behind her, making the dress appear less bulky.

"This is what you need. You make the familiar mistake of thinking that frills, furbelows and lots of material hide your full figure but in fact they only succeed in making you look plumper. You see, you may have a larger form than is average, but you're beautifully shaped."

Daisy stood to one side and studied the girl further.

"You're the sort of girl artists liked to paint, shapely and you've lovely skin. Men must find you very attractive. They don't all prefer sylph-like bodies, you know."

The girl blushed with pleasure. "I suppose you wouldn't sketch something for me to take home to Mama. Just a rough picture of something that would really suit me, I mean?"

Daisy took some measurements and stepped back to examine the girl's shape. "Do sit down, Miss....?"

"Henshaw. Avril Henshaw."

"What a pretty name. Take a seat for a few minutes, and I'll let you see what I have in mind."

With a few quick strokes, Daisy created a dress, which although still in the crinoline style of the period, took up much less material, and by cutting the bodice into a deep waist, formed a flattering shape. Miss Henshaw examined the finished sketch and said,

"Could I really look like that?"

"Of course," replied Daisy. "And I think ivory would suit you, it's subtle. Not satin, I think." She put her finger to her chin as she studied the girl. "Maybe taffeta," she thought, then decided, "a water-taffeta holds its shape well."

When she closed the shop that evening, she felt the satisfaction that comes with making a woman feel attractive, and was sure Avril Henshaw would return within the next few days. She did, this time with her mother, and between them they looked at materials and Daisy improved on her original ideas. Before leaving they placed an order for a day dress and an evening gown.

By the end of the year, Daisy's Designs had a book for orders well into the following year. Its popularity now rivalled Goodbody Gowns, and Vi invited Daisy to dine with her.

"Do you think we're a good advert for our shops," teased Daisy, as they sat at opposite ends of the table in their smartest gowns. They bought all the haberdashery magazines they could find in order to keep abreast of the latest fashions, and felt there should be no better advert for their shops than to be stylish themselves.

Vi's reply was cryptic. "More to the point, what on earth do you think our clientele would think if they saw us dining beyond our station? You know how the class system works; we're just shop girls to them, after all. They probably think we eat with our fingers and buy in everything from the cook shop. "

Daisy chewed happily on venison that had been roasting slowly in Vi's oven all day.

"I never think anybody's better than me, Vi. We all come into the same world the same way, don't we? And we go out the same way too."

"That's a comforting philosophy Daisy, but unfortunately the upper classes don't agree with it."

"I'd love to go to a big ball, to see people dancing. I can imagine the men, elegant in evening dress and the ladies in the gowns we make for them." Her eyes shone. "I can see them twirling and swaying as the band plays lovely tunes. I've seen some of the pictures artists have painted and it looks lovely. Oh, I'd love to be invited to something like that."

But Daisy wasn't really envious of the rich, her interest was purely professional.

After she and Vi had visited a wholesaler of materials a couple of days later, they thought a walk in the park was in order Although it was late in the year it was still quite mild and as Vi said, they should take the chance to get some fresh air. They walked into Regents Park and bought cups of chocolate and a gooseberry pie each from a stall.

They were sitting on a bench happily watching some children playing nearby, when Daisy glanced further along the path to spot a familiar face some distance away. Blushing furiously she tapped Vi on the shoulder.

"I've seen someone I know. What shall I do? She mustn't see me."

Vi looked round to see what had startled Daisy.

"Who on earth is it?"

"The woman in purple walking the little dog. It's the Countess — the one I told you about. The one I couldn't ask for a reference."

Vi acted with her usual common sense and said firmly.

"Calm down, Daisy, and don't draw attention to yourself. Don't you think it's time you told me what happened? We've known each other long enough surely, and I know all I need in that you are perfectly trustworthy."

Daisy cleared her throat and sipped her drink. "I left her Ladyship's service in a hurry," she said quietly, looking Vi straight in the eye. "I had to have an abortion." She felt a flush spread over her face as she waited for Vi's response.

"Oh that," replied the older woman casually. "I guessed it was something of the sort. What sort of a mess did you get into?"

"It was all very difficult. I made a fool of myself with one of the staff." She quickly told Vi about Vernon Fenn as she watched Lady Charlotte approaching.

"It was made worse when Lady Charlotte decided to marry Sir Algi because Vernon and I would have worked under the same roof. As it was, I discovered I was pregnant and when I told him, he wouldn't marry me."

"Had you really thought he would?" asked Vi gently.

Daisy nodded. "Oh yes. I had the romantic notion that love conquers all. It was inconceivable to me that he could only want me for my body. I really thought he loved me, you see."

"You poor little thing. How old were you?"

"Not quite sixteen. We only ever made love, if you can call it that, just once. At least it was love for me. But not him, just lust. I was five months pregnant when I went to an old woman on the moor."

Vi looked at her in horror. "That's far too late — very dangerous."

"I know that now but I was ignorant and had nobody to turn to. In the end my best friend's husband risked his job to take me to the abortionist, and he collected me later that day. The baby was a girl — I'll tell you all about it some day."

Vi was sympathetic. "You were very young to cope with all that. Do you still think about it much?"

"I think about the baby. Yes. Every day when I wake up. I imagine what she'd have looked like and it makes me very sad. I think if I ever married and had more children, I'd be betraying her and all that she could have been."

Daisy felt Vi's hand on her own, stroking it softly before she looked along the path again.

"Hold your head up, Daisy Smith. I do believe we've been spotted."

Chapter 21

Pretending to concentrate on her pie, Daisy took a deep breath and kept her eyes fixed on the ground. She felt a presence at her side and smelled familiar perfume.

"Well, upon my word, if it isn't the missing Daisy Smith. We thought you must be dead." It was a statement rather than a question.

Daisy placed her drink on the bench and stood up, facing the dowager Countess.

"Good evening, Lady Charlotte. Sorry to disappoint you but I'm very much alive — no thanks to your husband's secretary, Vernon Fenn." The words were out before she thought.

Lady Charlotte looked at her in surprise. "What on earth has young Vernon to do with your disappearance?"

Daisy drew a deep breath. "He made me pregnant, Your Ladyship. I had to have an abortion and came close to losing my life. Oh," she admitted, "I know it wasn't entirely his fault and that I should have known better. But I certainly do now, I assure you."

She lowered her voice. "I must apologise for running out on you but there was no other way. You wouldn't have wanted me back as a fallen woman, would you?"

Lady Charlotte dropped the dog's lead, looking visibly shaken.

"May I sit down?"

Vi Goodbody who'd remained silent, jumped up and helped lower the elderly woman on to the park bench whilst Daisy ran after the dog and retrieved the lead. She restored him to his mistress, who said vaguely,

"Have you been to the zoo? I hear they've a new arrival by way of an elephant called Jumbo. I understand he's come over from France and children are allowed to ride on him, so I want to look him over."

Daisy understood the woman was trying to make normal conversation to cover her confusion.

"No, Lady Charlotte, I've not heard about the elephant, and I must introduce you to my friend."

Having done So, Vi diplomatically offered to take the dog for a walk while Daisy and the Duchess renewed their acquaintance.

Daisy sat down next to the Dowager, who by now had gathered her composure, and spoke first.

"Vernon Fenn is no longer with us. Personally, I never liked him but Sir Algi says he did his job well enough. He got one of the maids into trouble at Foxlands. We dismissed him, and sent her home to her mother. It appears he's one of those fellows who can't keep control of his breeches."

She sighed. "How I wish you'd come to me with this, Daisy, but tell me, what are you doing now?"

Daisy apologised for not having introduced Vi earlier and explained about the shops.

"It was pure chance that I ran into Vi when I was desperate for work. She gave me a trial as a seamstress in her dressmaking business. I was unable to work for the big stores as I had no references but luckily for me, Vi gave me a chance."

"And, are you happy in your work."

"Oh yes," Daisy exclaimed. "And I've much to be grateful to you for. Although I knew I could sew a neat hem, I had no idea I'd take to cutting and designing, which I do now. I didn't realise how much I'd learned while working for you."

"Designing, no less, I'm impressed, Daisy Smith," smiled the Duchess.

"We've just been to the wholesalers," Daisy continued, "hence the walk in the park."

She spoke briefly about her recent experiences but omitted any reference to Jimmy Fawcett or Simon Danbury, or the part they played in her drama.

"I've always felt badly about the way I left you," she added. "I was very young and had no idea how ill I'd be. I stupidly assumed I'd be able to resume work the next day. You gave me a job when I needed it and it was one I enjoyed — I'm very sorry I let you down."

The Dowager rose, saying, "Apology accepted, but now I must get back to Algi. He'll be waiting for me. I'll tell him I met you and he'll be upset at the part Vernon Fenn played in your disappearance. I wish you well Daisy and just may pop into your shop with young Adelaide when she stays with us next. Ludgate Circus you say?" she added straightening her skirts, I'll find it. You'll be surprised at how's Adelaide's grown. And your secret will remain safe with me." She hesitated. "But you won't mind my husband knowing?"

"Not really, although I'd prefer he kept it to himself."

"He's a good man — he'll know it's between us. That damned Vernon Fenn."

Vi had now returned with the dog and handed the lead to Lady Charlotte who accepted it graciously and resumed her walk along the path.

"What a lovely lady," said Vi.

"Yes," said Daisy. "She is. I always liked her, she's not stuffy like some of the toffs. I suppose it's because she was a schoolmaster's daughter who married well."

Christmas Eve came and with it, Simon. The bell over the shop door tinkled as he burst through it, his arms filled with packets and parcels plus a goose purchased from a local farm.

On Christmas morning the goose turned slowly on the spit above the newly installed range, with the potatoes nestling underneath. The vegetables were prepared and Kate poured them each a glass of sherry to toast the occasion.

Simon dug into his pocket for a small box. "Happy Nineteenth," he said to Daisy, as he clasped a silver bangle around her wrist.

"Why, thank you." Daisy spun round the room with excitement. "Nobody's ever given me jewellery before."

Kate was presented with a package and when she opened it was delighted with her warm winceyette nightdress. Simon's Christmas present to Daisy was a winter bonnet in black felt trimmed with little feathers on the brim.

"It's lovely," she crowed and kissed him on the cheek. She was startled at the pleasure engendered by the contact with his skin and drew back hastily to make much fuss about trying on the hat.

"You look a treat," Kate declared. "Them feather's the colour of your eyes, I do declare."

She was excited and the sherry had made her talkative so Daisy's moment of embarrassment was covered by Kate's chatter.

"Upon my word, this is a good day. Me settled in this shop and Daisy with the dress-shop doing well and you Mr Danbury, happy in your cottage. I'll drink a toast to that any day."

Simon looked solemn but nodded and held up his glass. When the goose was browned, Daisy laid the table so that Kate could take it from the oven and place it on a large platter. The bird was then transferred to the table to be carved and Daisy watched Simon intently as he in turn concentrated on slicing the delicate flesh, manipulating the sharp knife with strong fingers. Daisy caught her breath. *What would it be like to feel those large hands on her own flesh?*

She immediately pushed the desire aside, angry that her body should seek to betray her once again.

"Shall I bring in the veg?" she called to Kate, determined to dismiss any affection she might feel for Simon.

That year Simon stayed for almost a week. He called for Daisy every evening after work, and on the way home, they sometimes stopped at a coffee house where they chatted amicably before returning to the warmth of the sweet shop. It was on one of these occasions that she told of her chance meeting with Lady Charlotte.

"And you told her who the father was? Why Daisy, you didn't ever tell *me*," Simon admonished.

"I'm sorry," she replied, seeing how dejected he was. "It was all too new when you took me into your house, and even when I was better I couldn't speak about it. Vi knows now, and of course the Dowager. I never told Aunty Millie either and as time went on I wanted to forget about it. I didn't mean to hurt your feelings."

Simon looked grim. "And it was?"

Daisy blurted out the words and reddened. "Vernon Fenn who worked for Sir Algi."

Simon's brow darkened. "That smooth little prig with the fancy waistcoats. I'd like to wring his neck."

"It's in the past, and he's left their service now."

She related the story leaving out no detail but assured him nobody knew of his own part in the debacle, adding, "I'd be dead if it wasn't for you,"

Simon was silent as he digested the news and ordered more coffee. When it arrived he stirred his cup slowly before saying,

"Daisy, I've something to say to you — something important." He looked serious and her heart sank. Was he going to tell her they could no longer be friends?

"What is it?" she asked, looking directly into his eyes.

"I'm going abroad — to America."

She gasped. "America but that's well. . . abroad. It's too far. Why are you going?"

"I need a new start. I've been toying with the idea for a long time."

"But when?"

"My ship sails from Southampton, tomorrow. It's one of these modern liners."

"How long will you stay? You're not going forever, are you?"

"I'm not sure. I'd like to start a new life. I have the money now and you don't need me any more." He looked into his coffee. "I'm not selling up entirely in case I don't like it over there. I'm keeping on the properties and I've let my house near Hunstanton, to a very nice couple with a child. They'll look after it, I'm sure."

They made desultory conversation after that, with Daisy feeling lower in spirit than she could remember.

Simon told Kate his news when they arrived home and the

atmosphere in the little dwelling was strained. Daisy said a short goodbye to him in the morning, and assured she'd write when given an address.

Simon's reply was resigned. "You can always find me care of my solicitor — you know where his chambers are."

With a heavy heart Daisy opened the shop and was uncharacteristically curt to her staff all day. As the weeks wore on her depression lifted and she became more interested in what was going on around her. Lady Charlotte called into the shop when Daisy was busily pinning a skirt on to a client.

"Shan't be a minute," she called when she heard the doorbell. She expressed her pleasure when she saw who it was and rose from the floor, excusing herself to the client. Lady Fox, as she remembered to address her, had a slim young girl in tow, whom Daisy recognised immediately.

"Why, Lady Adelaide! You've grown since I last saw you. How old are you now?"

"I'm ten, Daisy. I was ten last June." Adelaide who was incredibly pretty with her long fair hair and beautiful eyes, stared at the girl who had been her nursemaid.

"You're wearing a very nice outfit, Daisy. Grandmamma says this shop is yours. I remember how you used to mend my dresses when I was little."

"And I've never forgotten my little Adelaide, either."

Daisy bent to kiss the child's cheek. "Would you like me to make you a new dress?"

Adelaide opened her eyes wide. "Would you? Oh, yes please."

Lady Charlotte nodded her approval and the girls bent their heads over the design table while one of the seamstresses brought refreshments. More than an hour passed before Adelaide and her grandmother left.

Daisy designed the girl's dress in detail that same afternoon and ordered the delicate lemon voile they'd decided on. Two days later another unexpected visitor came into the shop in the form of Mildred. Daisy was astounded as the neatly dressed little woman tapped timidly on the door before entering.

"Mildred!" she exclaimed, hurrying to greet her. "What a lovely surprise. I suppose Lady Charlotte told you I was here?"

Mildred hadn't changed, either in appearance or attitude. She accepted a hot drink, taking off her soft leather gloves before holding the cup. She looked no older than the last time they met.

"I lost my mother, you know," she said looking round the shop.

Daisy nodded sympathetically. "Yes. Lady Charlotte mentioned it. I'm very sorry. Are you happy at Foxlands?"

"It's a job." She hesitated. "I shouldn't be ungrateful I suppose but it can be tedious. It's not like being at the Dower House where we always looked forward to having the children for the summer and Christmas holidays; It's quieter at King's Lynn although very pleasant."

Daisy commiserated. "I've been very lucky, Mildred." She told her about the inheritance that enabled her to open the shop.

"If ever you needed work, I'm sure either Vi or I could fit you in, but life runs at a different pace in London."

"That's very kind of you to offer and indeed I'll remember what you say, but for now, I'm better off with Lady Charlotte. She's promised me a cottage on the estate when I retire. I'd best get back, she'll be needing me." Mildred stayed for a few minutes longer then left as quietly as she came, and Daisy forgot all about her.

The material for Adelaide's dress arrived and she selected a pair of exceptionally sharp scissors before carefully cutting into the fragile material. She began sewing the seams in between dealing with clients, anxious that it be finished when Adelaide called in again. By the end of March it was completed and boxed, ready for collection.

That evening she breathed a sigh of relief as she closed the shop, realising she was tired. Her back ached from sitting in an awkward position and she hurried home to the warmth of the sweet shop.

"Is there a letter from Simon?" she asked as Kate weighed some brandy balls for a young customer.

"No. How long do you think it will be before we hear from him?"

"I've no idea. I do hope he's all right. I didn't realise how much I'd miss him."

"I expect he's busy, what with getting started all over again. Pity we don't 'ave an address or you could write to 'im."

Daisy shrugged. "I expect he's forgotten all about us."

"Why don't you go and see the solicitor? That's where he said we was to go if we 'ad any problems."

"I don't think so, Kate. We're managing well and he's obviously not thinking about us."

Life continued to be busy for Daisy. Sometimes something would happen that reminded her of Simon but she dismissed the memory with a toss of her head, and concentrated on the job in hand.

Mildred called in again on the day before she was due to accompany the Fox's to Paris. They were staying at the family's London house so she'd taken the opportunity to call on Daisy. She stayed to chat for a while and Daisy asked her to take Adelaide's dress with her.

She received a note a few days later written in the girl's childish handwriting. She thanked Daisy prettily saying it was a perfect fit.

Avril Henshaw had been back for a fitting and was due to pick up the ball gown she'd ordered but Daisy was surprised when she brought a gentleman with her. She wondered if it was her fiancé, although she didn't wear a ring.

"You wait outside, Larry," the girl called as she pulled the curtain over the cubicle rail. The young man smiled at Daisy as he lowered his large frame precariously on to a fragile gilt chair. Daisy watched him anxiously thinking he'd be a portly man once middle age set in. He grinned as he steadied himself and she noticed the way his eyes crinkled at the corners. They were bright blue and his brown hair was curly but Daisy considered he dressed rather foppishly, albeit in the latest mode. There was no doubt he had charm, and when he smiled, and he smiled often, a dimple appeared in his left cheek.

Altogether he was rather attractive and not arrogant as were some of the men who'd called at the shop to collect their wives.

Daisy went into the cubicle and helped her client into the finished dress. When she was satisfied and every fold was in place she stepped back and admired her handiwork. The deep blue-green taffeta bodice fitted firmly at the waist and hung smoothly over the young woman's hips. The colour complemented her eyes and the dress suited her. Miss Henshaw walked into the foyer and looked confidently at the young man who whistled admiringly.

"Gosh, Avril, old thing. You look a treat."

She swung round to face Daisy. "I really do look rather nice, don't I?"

Daisy was delighted and nodded. "Your fiancé seems to agree?"

The girl hooted with laughter. "Larry's not my fiancé. He's my brother. Let me introduce you. Laurence Henshaw, may I present Miss Daisy Smith."

Laurence took Daisy's hand and bowed. "Good day, Miss Smith. I must say you've done a wonderful job with my sister's gown. Congratulations."

"It was a pleasure, Mr Henshaw. She's a lovely client."

His sister interrupted. "For heaven's sake, his name's Larry and you must call me Avril as I'm sure we shall be seeing more of each other."

"Why, thank you. And I'd prefer to be called Daisy. Your brocade costume should be ready for a final fitting next week. Shall we agree an appointment?"

While Daisy bent over her diary she was aware of Larry Henshaw assessing her. Not many men called into the shop and she was pleased she was looking her best, despite feeling forlorn about Simon Danbury.

When Avril returned for her fitting, she hesitated before speaking Daisy, "My brother and I usually walk in the park on Sunday afternoon, to hear the band play. Would you care to accompany us?"

Daisy was rather surprised. An afternoon spent in the park would make a change from listening to Kate snoring as she took her afternoon nap. That brought another worry to the fore. Daisy could now afford her own rooms and the tiny flat above the shop was becoming vacant in a couple of months time. Vi thought Daisy should take advantage of the situation and move in, but there was the worry of telling Kate.

She realised Avril was waiting for an answer.

"That's very kind of you, Miss Henshaw. I'd like that very much.

"Avril," the girl corrected. "Where shall we meet?"

Daisy thought quickly. She didn't want the Henshaws to visit the London Bridge shop.

"I need to come into the salon on Sunday morning. Why don't you pick me up here?"

"Very well. Shall we say three o'clock?"

When she got home that evening she broached the subject of moving out.

"You see, Kate, if I don't take the rooms goodness knows who will, and they may be people who won't enhance the shop's reputation."

Kate grumbled as she pottered around the fireplace. "Who'll look after you? and goodness knows what'll happen with you living on your own. Then there's your rent here. What abut that?"

Daisy chided her gently.

"The rent is Simon's worry and I hardly think the little I pay will make any difference to his wealth. I'll write to the solicitor and tell him of my plans."

"When are you going?"

"A few weeks probably. I'll need to get the place cleaned and decorated. Will you come to see it with me?"

Kate was mollified. "Very well. I suppose it won't hurt to close the shop for an hour or two."

Daisy brought the ink and paper from the bureau and scratched a few lines to the solicitor and wondered how Simon would take the news. She didn't suppose he'd worry too much, he was too busy enjoying life in the United States.

Chapter 22

When Larry and Avril called for Daisy on the following Sunday she was busying herself with paperwork in the salon. She wore the hat Simon had bought for her a couple of years ago as she thought it particularly flattering. Her dress was of matching colours and she wore a mantle round her shoulders in case there was a chill wind. As they walked towards the park she enjoyed the banter between brother and sister and they had a wonderful afternoon.

Larry bought ices from the Penny-Ice Man and they sucked lazily on the various flavours, returning the tiny ice goblets to him when they'd finished.

As they listened to the brass band playing, they conversed in a desultory manner and watched families taking an afternoon stroll. It was very relaxing and all three agreed they must do it again when another fine Sunday presented itself.

Daisy took Kate to see her new rooms the following week. They were accessed by a staircase leading straight from the shop and they walked round the rooms, assessing what needed to be done. Kate grudgingly agreed the space could be transformed into a nice little home.

"It's a bit dingy, ain't it, though? It could do with a good clean if you ask me."

"You're right, Kate, but I can get somebody in to do that and they've some pretty wallpapers in the stores now. A lick of paint should brighten it up no end and I could get a carpenter to renew some of the wood, and we can buy one of those new stoves."

Together they discussed furnishings and eventually, men with paint and paper moved in. Daisy mollified Kate by insisting they chose some pieces of furniture together.

Before long her new little home was ready and Daisy moved in, with promises to call on Kate often.

She saw quite a lot of Laurence Henshaw that summer. The family lived close by in Fleet Street and since he was studying at the bar, he took her to see his rooms in Lincoln's Inn Fields, chaperoned by Avril. Before they went to the theatre one evening he took her to meet his parents. Laurence Henshaw Snr was a banker and Daisy was prepared for them to patronise her but they weren't as grand as Daisy expected. During their meeting she learned that his mother came from a somewhat unconventional background. She'd studied opera and wanted to go on to the stage but her father wouldn't allow it. Nevertheless, for all their informality, to them Daisy was a shop girl and even if she owned her own business was still 'in trade.'

She liked Larry enormously and would miss the outings should they cease but her conscience told her she must make up her mind whether she wanted the relationship to go any further. Although he hadn't declared his love she knew he'd grown fond of her and might propose. She needed to think carefully and have her answer ready.

As usual, she talked things over with Kate.

"Do you love this young man?" the older woman asked with a frown.

"I'm still not sure what love is. I like him very much and would have a comfortable life if we married."

"That's not love? Do you miss 'im when he's not there? Does he put joy in your heart?"

"I am lonely for him sometimes. I often feel quite abandoned in my rooms at night."

"There's many a woman has married for being lonely, and you mark my words, girl, you'll find more loneliness than you'd ever consider, if you marry without love. Best to marry a poor man if you think something of him, than marry rich and 'ave him in some whore's bed later 'cause you can't give 'im what he wants. Don't get hard, Dais. Don't let the past cast a shadow over the rest of your life."

Daisy was flabbergasted by Kate's outburst.

"Have you ever been in love?"

Kate's eyes grew misty as she spoke of the past. "Yes. Years ago now. He was one of them gypsies that used to set up camp in the squire's copse every year. Gideon was his name and he was handsome as could be. He had a ring in his ear and long black curls."

She was lost in time as she recalled her romance with the gypsy. "He kissed me once, down by the stream when he was poaching fish from the estate where me father worked." Her voice trembled. "His kiss went deep into me soul, shook my very being and I would have died for him there and then, I loved him that much. But when I spoke to me parents they locked me in the 'ouse and dared me ever to see him again. The gypsies broke camp that night and I never saw 'im from that day to this. But I never loved anyone since."

Daisy was silent as Kate remained deep in thought. The clock ticked loudly and when it chimed the hour, Daisy said it was time she went. She went over their conversation as the bus rolled over London Bridge and by the time she arrived home, she'd made up her mind. The following day she went to see Vi.

"What brings you here? Let's go over to the coffee shop," she said when Daisy walked through the door.

"It's obvious something's wrong," she said as they settled down with drinks.

"I need some time off," explained Daisy. "I've worked consistently for months and months, and I'm tired."

Vi spoke briskly. "We're all tired, Daisy. Come along, there's something else isn't there?"

"Yes." She told Vi about Larry and her uncertainty regarding her feelings. "I feel such a fool," she added "I think Laurence might be about to propose but I keep thinking of Simon. I had the chance to marry Simon and turned it down but now... I just don't know... I like Larry enormously. He's great fun."

"Do you want to share his bed?"

"He's kind. I expect I'd get used to it."

Vi patted her hand. "Is that good enough — getting used to it?" She looked straight into Daisy's eyes. "Getting used to it is good enough for some people, but for others it isn't, and I've a feeling you're one of the latter."

She signalled for the bill. "I agree you need a holiday. I can get one of the girls to cover for you. Daisy's Designs will be safe enough with Maud for a while. How long will you need — two, three weeks?"

It was agreed that Daisy would take three weeks off and she'd decided her destination long before she bought a ticket. She'd go to Hunstanton where Simon had his cottage and perhaps whilst there, she'd understand what he saw in the place and regain come peace of mind. Having packed a bag, she took a cab to Shoreditch Station and began the tedious journey to East Anglia. Mindful of Kate's warnings about marauding robbers who were said to plague the railways, she purchased a first class ticket and alerted the guard as to her whereabouts before sinking back into the well-upholstered seating.

She slept a little as the train laboriously wove its way through the countryside but became alert when she heard "Norwich – all alight," shouted by the ticket inspector. The railway company had recently opened a branch line to Hunstanton and as she sat in the waiting room for her connection, she overheard an elderly gentleman purchase tickets to Hunstanton for himself and his wife. She approached the lady and hesitantly asked if she could share their carriage. They proved to be a charming couple who chatted amiably throughout the journey.

Daisy was tired and hungry when the train eventually pulled into the station, so thanking her companions profusely, she left them and booked a room in a small hotel overlooking the sea where she fell into an exhausted sleep.

She woke quite early having slept well on a thick feather mattress and stretched luxuriously as studied the room. It was decorated in soft greens with muslin curtains fluttering at the window. A wonderful shimmering light filtered through the gauzy material, its effect being caused by waves as they lapped the shingle. She could hear the cry of gulls and became eager to venture abroad.

Her reverie was interrupted by a light tap on the door and when she called, "Come in," a maid entered carrying a large copper jug of hot water. She rested it carefully on the marble-topped washstand before pouring the water into a rose-patterned bowl.

"Morning, Miss," she said in a sing-song voice as she busied herself around the room. "Shall I plump your pillows? How about a nice cup of tea?"

"My pillows are fine thank you but I'd dearly love the tea."

"I'll be just five minutes so you'll have time to wash. And the missus says if you'd like breakfast she'll be finished serving downstairs in half an hour."

"I'll get dressed straight away."

The girl turned as she reached the door. "I'm Agnes, by the way."

Daisy was the last guest to have breakfast and ate quickly. Realising how hungry she'd become, she ate all the scrambled egg and rashers of luscious bacon followed by toast and marmalade. When she'd finished she went back upstairs to collect her hat before venturing onto the beach which lay below a towering cliff. A few children were making sandcastles on the pale gold sand whilst others ran to the edge of the sea, squealing with fright as waves rippled over their bare feet.

Mothers watched over them indulgently, making the most of the autumn sun. Daisy walked along the shore for about a mile before returning to the town where she bought a trade magazine. She spent the rest of the morning sitting on a wooden bench, reading and relaxing in the warmth of the sun.

After eating a light lunch she knew what she must do and made enquiries as to the whereabouts of Simon's cottage. A cart took her along the main track but she enjoyed walking the last mile along the dusty path that led inland. Leaves were beginning to turn orange and gold and it wouldn't be long before the coastal district saw foggy mornings. Aware she was following in Simon's footsteps she recognised the cottage immediately as she turned the corner of the path. Smoke curled from the chimney and there were the crows Simon had told her about, flying to and from their nests in the huge oak that flanked the outbuildings.

She opened the gate and noticed the hinges were well oiled so somebody was maintaining the property. Flagstones leading to the front door were lined with low box hedges that guarded blowsy geraniums from the cutting east winds, which she knew from experience were prevalent in this part of the country. The rest of the garden was neat and tidy, and Daisy nodded approvingly as she used the brass knocker to tap on the bright blue door.

A young woman carrying a baby on her hip answered and looked surprised at her visitor.

"Good afternoon," Daisy began. "I know this is an imposition but I wonder if I could see inside the house. I know the owner you see and I was in the area. . . and thought perhaps you wouldn't mind. . ." To her relief the young woman opened the door wide.

"Come in. I don't mind at all. In fact I'm glad of the company since my husband's away at work."

Daisy stepped into the hall and onto the polished floorboards scattered with rugs, then into the kitchen at the back of the house. It was bright and airy with an open range, on which stood a big copper kettle, steam gently hissing from its spout.

"I dare say you could do with some refreshment," said the young woman. "I'm Heather Dawes, by the way."

Daisy nodded and gave her own name. "Shall I hold the baby while you make tea?"

She held the toddler who gave her a gummy smile before turning its attention her necklace, cramming it into her mouth.

"She's obviously teething," she laughed as she handed the baby back to its mother. Cups of tea were served accompanied by delicious slabs of cake and Daisy could see the curiosity in Heather's eyes.

"Would you like to see upstairs?" she asked, "It seems Mr Danbury had the house prepared for the young woman he intended to marry but she refused him. He told my husband," she added. Daisy blushed as she followed Heather up the staircase which was carpeted in soft blue.

"This was to be her room." The young woman opened the door that led to a room on the left. Daisy stepped inside and was charmed with what she saw. The walls were decorated with rosebud patterned paper and the carpet and curtains were in matching pink. There was a desk in one corner and a seat had been built under the window, upholstered to match the curtains. The bed stood to one side with a washstand beside it, topped with pretty china. She looked out of the window at the wonderful view across the fens where geese were foraging for food.

"It's a lovely room," she said to Heather. "Thank you for showing it to me, but I mustn't keep you any longer. You've been very kind."

After dinner that evening Daisy sat in her room and composed a letter to Simon and sent it care of his solicitor. In it she wrote she knew now that she loved him, always had and always would. She was sorry it had taken her so long to come to her senses but that if he still wanted her, she was his.

She kissed the letter before putting it into the post box, and stayed at the hotel until the end of the week.

Then she journeyed to King's Lynn and on to the Foxlands estate where she called on Phoebe, who was delighted to see her.

She proudly introduced her three children, the latest of whom was still a toddler.

"You're so lucky, Phoeb," said Daisy. "Three children, two boys and a girl." The youngest boy looked shy and put his thumb in his mouth.

"Don't do that, Horace," said Phoebe as she put the baby into Daisy's arms. Young Ned looked on and Daisy immediately noticed his likeness to the Earl's family. Phoebe saw her looking at him and her brow creased.

"It's easy to see who his father is, isn't it," she whispered. Their conversation was stopped short by the appearance of Jimmy who came bounding in from the fields, and put his arm round Phoebe. It was obvious they were happy together and seeing them warmed Daisy's heart.

When Jimmy went back to work the children were put to rest and Daisy poured her heart out to her best friend.

"What a fool I've been. I loved him all along but just didn't see what was under my nose."

Phoebe smiled as she put the baby to her breast. "We'll expect to be invited to the wedding and then it'll be your turn, Dais. You can have a child to make up for the one you lost." She looked down at her own child as she fed. "This is the best feeling in the world. Even better than grunting with yer 'usband."

They both laughed and all too soon it was time for Daisy to return to her inn in King's Lynn. Curious glances came her way as it was unusual for a woman to travel on her own. She smiled to herself at the thought these regional folk would shrink in horror, should she tell them she'd walked the streets of London alone, at the age of five. But she held her head high and spent the next couple of days exploring the town.

Before she left for London she went into the old church to pray. She knelt down and asked God to bring Simon safely home to her so they could spend the rest of their lives together.

The following morning, and ever mindful of Kate's advice, she was looking along the platform for a likely person to share a carriage with, when the waiting room doors burst open. A young woman with three fractious children in tow looked around her anxiously as she tried to calm the youngest. Daisy could sense a friend in need and took the hands of the eldest two as the train approached.

"Do let me help," she offered, "I'm used to children."

"Oh dear," replied the young woman, "My husband's been held up on business and out nanny gave notice this morning — with immediate effect." She smiled apologetically, "I find the task of controlling three young children is quite a fete!"

"Don't worry," replied Daisy, "I assume you're going to London? Good. Then let's share a carriage so I can read to these two while you look after the baby."

Thus, having taken reasonable precautions to ensure her safety, Daisy returned to London with renewed vigour. She waited eagerly for the post to arrive each morning even though she knew it was too early to expect a reply to her letter from Simon.

Having been home for about a week she was surprised to find a letter on the floor when she went downstairs one morning. It was from America and must have passed hers in the post. Ripping open the envelope, her joy turned to despair as she read his words.

Dear Daisy

I've become engaged to Miss Kyle Chekov. You will see from my address I live in New Jersey and have done so for the past six months now. Kyle's father and I run a clothing business together, that's how we met. I'm sure you'd like her Daisy, she's clever and efficient and will make a wonderful wife. Perhaps I may bring her to England one day and you can meet. I'm sorry not to have written before but as you can guess I have been very busy. Do write soon with your news and I trust this letter finds you well.

Yours affectionately,
Simon

Biting her lip, Daisy hurried up the stairs to her rooms again, her eyes blurred with tears and her legs shaking. How could he marry somebody else? He was hers and always had been. She sobbed uncontrollably but when she heard her staff tapping on the door, made an extreme effort to composed herself. She managed to walk slowly down the stairs again with her head held high. How could he throw her lovely love away?

Later, anger took over from self-pity. If that was how he wanted it, she'd show she could do without him.

When Larry asked her to the theatre she said she'd be delighted to accompany him. They went to the Globe and he talked her through her first experience of a play by Shakespeare and when he presented his arm, she took it. Moreover, when he offered his lips on Christmas Eve she returned his kiss with a fervour she didn't feel.

She'd invited Kate for Christmas lunch and enjoyed preparing the meal. As she poured brandy over the plum pudding she remembered the Christmases Simon had shared with them and broke down.

Kate was horrified. "What on earth's the matter?" she asked.

The emotion Daisy had held back over the past weeks came to the fore and the dam burst. Daisy sobbed uncontrollably while Kate flustered around not knowing what to do. Bit by bit, Daisy told her about Simon and her feelings for him. She went to the dresser and took the letter out of the drawer, thrusting it in Kate's hand.

"Read this," she said bitterly.

"You know I ain't much good at reading. You'll have to do it for me."

Daisy stumbled tearfully over the words, ending triumphantly. "You see? You're wrong. He didn't love me after all."

"I'm sure as how he did, my love."

"But he's marrying *her* — this American girl. He couldn't do that if he loved me!"

"That's as maybe. I don't know I'm sure. What are you going to do?"

Daisy was defiant. "Marry Laurence Henshaw, if he asks me."

Kate shook her head. "That's silly, Daisy, and not fair to the young man. You don't love him."

"What does love matter? I thought the man who made me pregnant loved me. I thought Simon loved me, but none of it was real. I want nothing to do with what you call love. I'll marry for money and position, or not at all."

Kate looked at her sadly.

"Then best you don't marry at all, my girl."

She left soon after and Daisy tidied her rooms before bringing some sewing up from the workroom. She stitched as she thought. She thought as she stitched. It was her twentieth birthday and she reflected on her life. She had no family and the chance of her finding them was remote. She didn't even know their name and any attempt to seek them in the various workhouses around Mile End, was likely to fail. It was known the records they kept were sketchy. They could all have perished long ago. She wanted: no *needed*, her own family, and marrying Laurence would have been a way of achieving that. She longed to hold a baby in her arms and to give love to a man she loved.

After sewing for a little longer, she brewed some tea and tried to look at the positive things in her life. She had Kate, who was as near to a mother as she'd ever known, apart from Millie. Vi was a friend and a mentor, and of great help to her. She was a business woman now. She had her own rooms and was independent. Her staff admired and respected her and she was welcome to visit her best friend, Phoebe at any time. There was money in the bank and she could please herself.

She'd loosen her ties with Laurence and if that meant losing Avril's friendship so be it. Daisy knew she deserved it. She'd flirted with Laurence and led him to believe she was falling in love with him.

Her heart hardened as she fought to sever links with the past, at least those where Simon had played such a vital part. She's show the world she was an independent woman and need depend on no man!

Chapter 23

January was a quiet month in the shop. The rush to get orders out in time for the Christmas festivities was over, and now it was a matter of sending out the customer accounts. It was Sunday, and Daisy took her tea back to bed with her, pulling the feather eiderdown up to her shoulders. She snuggled back into the pillows and sipped her tea while curling her toes into the warmth of the bed. Once more she reflected on the past and admitted to herself that she was lonely but there was little she could do but get on with her life, because who could know what the future held?

It was a Sunday morning and there was snow on the ground, but a weak sun shone through the large window when Daisy eventually went downstairs to start working on the books.

She shivered and drew her shawl up to her neck, as she sat at the counter and began to look through the ledgers. Trying hard to concentrate, she was conscious of the change in her attitude and had begun to take life more seriously. Inside her dwelt a deep sadness which she hoped would recede in time. Lots of people loved and lost, she acknowledged, and they learned to live with it. So must she. There was much to be grateful for and at last she was growing up. Her pen scratched over the paper as she filled out invoices, unaware of the charming picture she made, poised over the books with a frown on her lovely face

But she paused, becoming suddenly aware of a shadow on the floor. She looked up and gave a short scream when she saw a figure silhouetted against the glass door. Fearfully, she shrunk back, thinking somebody was trying to break into the shop, but her alarm receded when she realised the figure was familiar. Choking back a shriek of joy she ran to the door and drew back the bolt. She stepped back and gave way to sobs of relief as Simon stepped softly onto the carpeted floor. She was rooted to the spot lest the spell be broken.

Suddenly, her love grew wings and she fell into his outstretched arms, not caring why he'd deserted her, neither was she angry any more, nor afraid lest he'd cast her aside. She stood on tip-toe and kissed his lips, his neck and ears, while she sobbed, and murmured endearments. He gathered her to him and cried with her, delighted at her response.

At last they broke apart, with Daisy wiping her eyes and laughing at the same time. The world had suddenly become a joyous place and she wanted to shout her happiness from the rooftops. Simon had come home.

Then, in a moment of horror, she remembered he was engaged, engaged to a young American woman. What *was* she thinking of?

She stepped back behind the counter, in an effort to put a barrier between them. "I'm sorry," she flustered, "I don't know what made me act like that."

He leaned across the flimsy counter and raised an eyebrow.

"I hope you do, Daisy Smith because I've sailed all the way across the ocean to marry you."

"Marry me? But your letter. Miss Whatshername — what about her?"

"She'll manage without me. She was never really serious and it doesn't honour me to say neither was I. I was on the rebound and she thought she could impress her friends with an English fiancé, but I'd left my heart in England although I tried to convince myself differently." His smile was apologetic, "I'm afraid it doesn't say much for me, does it?"

"I suppose not; but I'm very glad you found out in time. And what about your business partnership?"

"Her father had enough capital to buy me out — I think he was glad to do so under the circumstances. But it turned out well because she'd already met somebody else before I set sail, as a matter of fact."

"Was she upset when you broke off the engagement?"

"No. I'd already told her we weren't suited. She was a bit too bossy for me, so watch out, young lady!"

"You didn't answer my letter."

"It was delayed in the storms at sea and strikes at the docks. I came as soon as I read it, and don't fret — I'd already broken things off with Kyle."

Daisy blushed, still feeling somewhat embarrassed at her behaviour. "Oh. I can't remember exactly what I said."

He was enjoying her discomfiture. "I can. Every word."

She sat on the seat reserved for clients and twisted her handkerchief around her fingers, suddenly shy and overwhelmed at the depth of her feelings for this man who hadn't yet said her love was returned.

"Would you like to come up to my rooms? I could make you some tea." It seemed a good idea to be doing something when the atmosphere was charged with emotion.

"Sure," he said with a mock Yankee drawl. "I guess that'll be good."

She locked the front door again and he followed her upstairs where she set the kettle to boil and laid out cups and saucers. Still he said nothing but watched her every move.

"You're thinner than last time I saw you?" It was a question, not a comment.

"Yes," she replied. "I've been working rather hard."

"Business doing well?"

"Extremely."

"Still enjoying it?"

"Yes, but perhaps not quite so much."

"Why's that, do you think?"

She was becoming annoyed with him. "Why these constant questions? Have you nothing more important to say?"

"Nope! I think I said all there was to say before I left England. It's up to you now. I've already told you of my intention to marry you."

She poured the tea and they drank in silence, while she stared at the tablecloth trying to find the words that seemed to stick in her throat, but she knew they must be said or she might lose him.

"I've been very silly," she began, "I realised that when you'd gone. I took you for granted because you'd always been there, loving and supporting me. I likened you to a brother because I was too young to understand. I expected you to be like Vernon Fenn. I thought that was love."

Simon nodded sagely. "It wasn't a caring love, Daisy. Love gives, it doesn't take."

The tears fell again and she wiped her eyes. "I must look dreadful," she wailed.

"You're beautiful and no matter if you cry all day long, which I hope you never will, you'll be the most beautiful woman in the world to me."

She gulped then blurted out, "I love you, Simon. I love you with all my heart and I hope you still want me because I want you more than anything in the world." The words were out and she sat perfectly still, her eyes cast down at the table once more.

"Come here, my sweetest Daisy." She heard him whisper. "Come here."

She rose and went to him. He pulled her down onto his lap and their lips met in a long satisfying kiss. "We'll be married as soon as we can," he confirmed as he nuzzled into her neck.

Her stomach stirred and she longed for him to make love to her, to take her so that she could give him all her love, to show how much she cared; but he pushed her firmly aside.

"If this is love, Daisy Smith, it will wait. I'll not have my bride gossiped about because of a swollen stomach. We'll be married in Hunstanton, where we belong and we'll spend our wedding night away from the busybodies, safely tucked up in our own little nest by the coast."

Daisy stood away from him and poured more tea. "I'm very relieved you came back for me, I was dying inside. But this seems unreal, like a fairy story."

He smiled indulgently. "When we've finished this, I think we should make some plans and then go to see Kate, lest I go back on my word and ravish you, Daisy Smith."

His former housekeeper was astonished when Simon followed Daisy as they stepped into the sweet shop.

"Well, upon my word," she said. "I knewed you'd come back for 'er. I just knewed it. Now tell me what's going on?"

Simon began to explain about America and how things hadn't worked out.

"He's going up to Norfolk tomorrow to get the banns published," cut in Daisy excitedly, "And I'm going to see if Vi will buy me out of my half of the shop."

"Been making decisions, 'ave you. And where do I come in all this?" said a disgruntled Kate.

"You'll be expected at the wedding," said Simon, "I'll make all the arrangements for you. Furthermore, we'll need a housekeeper in Norfolk, if you can tear yourself away from London, that is."

They spent a few hours going over their plans with Kate and it was much as she'd said, like old times at Thetford. They stayed for what Kate called 'high tea' and she insisted on getting out the port so she could toast the happy couple.

The gas lamps had just been lit and hissed gently as Simon and Daisy walked back over London Bridge. Barges were still plying up and down the river, their mournful horns echoing downstream.

"The times we've walked over here," remarked Simon as he tucked Daisy's hand into his pocket, "When Aunty Millie was alive."

"Dear Millie," replied Daisy. "She'd be so happy to see us now. I truly miss her." She missed a step and did a little a skip so that she stood in front of Simon, barring his way.

"I've an idea," she said, her face aglow. "Let's call our first daughter Millicent — in Millie's memory, she'd have liked that."

Simon kissed her cheek. "That's why I love you, Daisy Smith. You have a wonderful disposition. You'll soon be Daisy Danbury, shall you mind changing your name?"

"Not at all, women do it all the time." Daisy Smith, she thought. I'll have to tell him how I got my name — I can't marry him unless he knows the complete truth about my past.

When they got back to her rooms she untied her bonnet and asked him to sit down. Her face was solemn so he looked at her quizzically as he took the seat opposite her.

"Simon," she hesitated, knowing she would hurt him but it had to be done. "You know I love you dearly but I have some things to tell you."

"Not more confessions," he joked as he pulled out a chair. His smile vanished when he saw she was serious.

"I'm afraid so." She started pulling at the fringe on the tablecloth, averting her eyes. "I haven't been entirely honest with you about my past. I hope when you know the whole truth about me, you'll accept my motives. If not, and you decide I'm not good enough for you, I'll understand. I don't want to lose you but I don't want my past to come between us either. I love you so much I could burst but you deserve the truth."

She plunged on. "When I was small, six years old in fact, I lived on the London streets."

"What?"

"That's right. My parents were very poor and we lived in a slum. We had hardly any food, our clothes were old and ragged and our rooms were in a hovel with rats running up and down the stairs. I used to sell watercress to help feed the family but when I went home one night our rooms were empty — my parents and the other children had gone into the workhouse."

Daisy could see she had Simon's attention as she told him about the girls in the cellar, and Rose. He learned of her spell in prison after Mr Tibbet's shop was raided and how she lived with Polly, and later about the house in Bloomsbury, and how she came to live in Norfolk.

The window from her room looked out across the rooftops and her eyes misted with tears as she recalled the past. "I'd never known such smells as were in that kitchen. I'd starved for as long as I could remember and thought it was normal. All I'd ever ask for my children is a home with enough food to eat and a clean bed to lie in at night."

She bowed her head the memories returned. She left out nothing, including stealing from Lady Charlotte, of which she was bitterly ashamed, and of course her part in Rose's tragic death.

Daisy looked Simon directly in the eye and smiled sadly. "If you don't want me now wouldn't blame you, I'll understand. So much deception. So many lies." Her eyes were bright with tears. "I should have been honest with you right from the start. But I didn't know I loved you then, and that it would matter. I'd lived with lies for so long I believed them to be true."

Her voice trailed off and she waited for his reply.

"Is that everything?"

Suddenly she was depressed. "Yes. You're disappointed." It was a statement, not a question.

"I'm just trying to understand how the good Lord would let one small child suffer so much?"

"I'm a liar and a thief."

"So would I have been, and worse, in your shoes."

"You mean you don't mind?"

He came over and took her in his arms, stroking her hair and burying his head in the abundance of curls.

"It'll be my life's desire to make it up to you. To give you the home you've never had, to ease the pain of losing your family but most of all, to love you with all my heart."

He tore himself away from her. "I must go before I forget my vow. It's time I got back to the hotel anyway. We have lots to do and I shan't see you again until I claim you as my bride. You sort things out from this end and I'll see you for the wedding, and don't forget — I love you."

He picked up his coat and left.

Daisy's heart was light as she went to Goodbody Gowns the next morning. Vi took her up to her rooms where they settled with the coffee pot between them.

"You look more cheerful than I've seen you for a long time," she said, offering a plate of biscuits.

Daisy took a ginger snap and nodded as she bit into it. "He's back," she said abruptly.

"Who's back?"

"Simon. The man who looked after me. The one from Norfolk. We're getting married."

She rose and began dancing round the floor twirling her hat while a flabbergasted Vi looked on.

"Well. There's a surprise," she said, then looked apprehensive. "This changes things. You'll want to live up there with him?"

"Yes. I need to talk to you about Daisy's Designs. Would you like to buy my half?"

"Oh, do sit down," snorted Vi, impatiently. "Sit down. I can't think with you prancing around. All this delirious happiness has a bad effect on me. I'm very pleased for you, of course, but do you realise we have a contract that can't be broken without six months notice on either side."

She held her hand up when she saw the dismay on Daisy's face.

"No matter. We're friends and will work something out. The truth is I can't afford to buy you out. I just don't have the capital. Both shops are doing well but I fear that when yours is valued, it will be beyond my financial capabilities. Let me visit my bank and give the subject more thought."

With that comment, Daisy had to be content. She also knew she must address the problem of Laurence and her brow was furrowed for the rest of the day. She couldn't put it off forever and must tell him as soon as possible

Laurence came to the shop later that week. Taking off his hat he waited until she finished with a client then said in a low voice,

"May I have a word, Daisy?"

"Would you like to come upstairs?" She'd never invited him to her rooms alone and was aware of the sly looks given by the other seamstresses.

Ignoring them, she called, "We shan't be long," and led Laurence up the stairway. Mustering her courage she turned to face to him, thinking there was only one way to deal with the problem.

"Larry," she began, but he cut her short.

"Daisy, sit down. I need to talk to you."

She dropped into an armchair and looked up at his face, nonplussed at the serious expression he wore.

He bit his lip as he rocked on his heels but said, almost defiantly, "It's like this, Daisy. I know we've been walking out quite a bit and I like you enormously but there's no other way to say it, I've met this girl. . ."

Daisy's heart leapt and she quickly rose from her chair to pump his hand. "You've met someone — but that's wonderful, Larry. Are you engaged?"

She couldn't stop smiling as the words were formed.

"That's what I came to tell you. Our fathers have spoken and it's agreed. We're to be married next year."

"Oh Larry, I'm so happy for you."

"You're not disappointed? I thought as we've been keeping company that you might think we. . ."

"Never. You're such a nice man and we flirted a bit I know but you were just a very good friend and I hope you always will be. As a matter of fact," she shrugged and felt elated as she told him *her* news. "I'm to be married myself, to a man I've loved for a long time. I just didn't know I loved him. I intended telling you the next time we met, I've been dreading it."

"That's wonderful news. So all's well that ends well."

Still holding Daisy's hand between his own he continued, "I do wish you well, Daisy. I must tell your news to Avril — she's been very cross with me."

"Please do and say I hope to see her soon."

He left and Daisy's elation grew. Things were working out.

But that evening Kate came to see her, supposedly, Daisy thought, to talk about moving to Norfolk but she was wrong.

"I've decided not to come," Kate said, with an anxious frown. "I don't like letting you down but you'll find somebody else easy enough. It's just that when I thought about it, I realised I'm 'appy 'ere in London. I don't fancy being stuck in the countryside again. Will you tell Mr Simon for me?"

Rather surprised at this outburst, Daisy assured her it didn't matter, and that they'd manage somehow.

"Of course, we'd rather have you with us but I dare say we can find some help locally. "

"Of course, you will."

"Personally, I'm disappointed because I'm used to having you around to share my problems and although Simon will wish you well, I'm sure he'll be a bit sad too."

"It'll be for the best all round. What would we do with the sweet shop with nobody to run it?

"I dare say Simon could put a manager in but he couldn't be trusted like you." Daisy patted Kate's hand and asked, "Are you sure there's no other reason?"

But Kate was not to be drawn and left, assured that she'd not upset anybody. Secretly Daisy looked forward to being mistress of her own house and could easily make do with day staff for the time being.

Her next visitor was Vi who threw her gloves on the table when Daisy led her upstairs. "I've been unable to raise the money," she said with a sigh. "I spent all morning with my bankers and they say I'd be too exposed financially."

Daisy put the kettle to boil and gathered the utensils for making coffee.

"Oh, Vi, what a shame — what can we do?"

"I've been mulling the situation over and even thought of approaching friends for a private loan but I don't really want to do that. However, I have thought of a solution which might suit us both. Do you actually *need* the capital you've invested?"

"No. Not really. It wasn't a question of the money, just convenience. I thought a clean break would be easier."

"Why not leave your money in the business? Another thought. Why not keep on the rooms above the shop for when you come to London? You'll need somewhere to stay when Simon comes down on business."

"We hadn't thought about that either. But who will manage Daisy's Designs?"

"We've known each other for some time and I've never told you much about my private life. I'm very close to a girl named Honesty. I met her at a business fair. She manages a shop near Hyde Park Gate and I'm sure I could bring her in to run Daisy's Designs."

"Can she design?"

"No, she doesn't have the flair but she's a high class seamstress and would be wonderful with clients. Plus, and this is important, she has a very good business sense and is also a book-keeper. I can flit between shops when necessary. After all, they're only a stone's throw away from each other."

Daisy thought carefully. Would the idea work? She certainly didn't need the money but at the same time Daisy's Designs was her baby and she wouldn't want the business to fail.

"Do you think you can trust this Honesty?"

"With my life. I know you've had a troubled past Daisy, but it was only because of your innocence. Honestly and I are. . . very close."

"I'm glad you have a close friend, Vi — I suppose Pheobe is the nearest I've ever come to a friend — and you, of course.

Vi toyed with her earring and tried to explain. "You must know that there can be love between men?"

"I've heard of poofs. Do you mean that?"

"Exactly. It can happen with women too. There's nothing wrong with it. Women like us simply aren't attracted to men." The implications dawned on Daisy who was horrified.

"Upon my word. I've never heard of that before. I'm surprised to say the least."

"You mustn't be narrow minded, Daisy. You've a lot of growing up to do. I'm the same person you've always known and trusted. I just have different feelings towards women than you."

"Do you really love this. . . Honesty?"

"Yes."

Daisy was remorseful. "Oh, Vi. Forgive me. I'm an ignorant person. Why should I deny you love when I have so much myself? It was a bit of a shock that's all. If you trust your Honesty, then why shouldn't I? I'd like to meet her," she added. "Tell me all about her."

Vi did, and took all of an hour. It was settled, Honesty would run Daisy's Designs and it was Vi's hope that she'd agree to share the flat above Goodbody Gowns. What a scandal that would create, thought Daisy secretly.

Chapter 24

Daisy began to sew her wedding dress. She'd decided to make a two-piece in pale blue silk and found a matching hat in Chapeaux de Celine, which was the shop a few doors away. She perched it on her head, turning this way and that until she was satisfied she'd make the correct choice. The milliner insisted in taking no payment, since Daisy often recommended her own clients visit the shop to purchase matching bonnets.

As she stitched she thought about Simon and wondered how things were in Norfolk, happy she'd be joining him at the end of the week. He'd written to say the wedding was booked for March 6th in the little church nearby and asked who she thought should be on the invitation list.

She'd replied that apart from people Simon would like to be there, invitations should be sent to Lord and Lady Fox, Mildred, and reminded him not to forget to include the Fawcetts. He left it to her to decide on bridesmaids, flowers, hymns etc. and said all he wanted was for her not to change her mind about marrying him.

Daisy visited Kate when she'd replied to Simon's letter.

"We thought you'd go up to Norfolk on the train with me, Kate. I'll have quite a lot to take, what with the wedding outfit and my trousseau. I thought of hiring a Hansom but the thought of the journey. . ."

Kate sat with her jaws clamped as Daisy prattled on.

"Did you and Simon decide to shut the shop for a few days, Kate?"

"No. I know of a man who'll take over for me for as long as I want. He's a customer and somebody I can rely on."

It was obvious Kate didn't want to be drawn so the decision was made that she and Daisy would travel by train together.

She was disappointed that she hadn't seen Avril Henshaw but wasn't really surprised. She was probably embarrassed at what she would see as her brother's betrayal, but Daisy couldn't be upset, as she was too happy. No doubt Avril would patronise the shop again once she realised Daisy was no longer there.

The weather was crisp on the morning Daisy and Kate left for Hunstanton with their wedding finery carefully packed in boxes. The journey was long and arduous with engines failing and connections delayed. They were exhausted when Simon met them at King's Lynn station in his new open cart and it was a relief to bowl along the lanes breathing in the fresh air. Before long they drew up at the cottage gate and it proved to be an emotional return for Daisy. Everything was the same except the door had a fresh lick of paint and bulbs were pushing their way through the earth. She'd last seen the cottage when nature was preparing for winter but now it was spring and everything held promise.

"Look," she cried, "Late snowdrops and crocuses. I remember them from Thetford — how lovely."

Simon took their bags inside and Daisy set about making a hot drink. She rummaged around finding the teapot and china, hardly believing she was in her own kitchen and that in a few weeks she'd be mistress of the house.

"I had some girls come in from the village to give the place a thorough clean," explained Simon. "But the tenants were very good and didn't do much damage considering there was a child in the house."

"Did they find somewhere else to live easily?" asked Daisy.

"Oh yes. I think the wife was glad they were able to move nearer to a town."

"That's good," she said as she bustled about, "I didn't much like the thought of turning them out so quickly, but if they're settled, I don't feel so guilty."

They all sat down for tea until Kate declared she couldn't stay awake for a moment longer.

Simon led the way to their sleeping quarters, taking the rest of the luggage with him. .

"I don't know why you wanted a place this big," grumbled Kate as she panted up the stairs.

"I'm used to plenty of room," Simon explained. "In any case, we plan to fill the house with children."

"Humph," came the short reply. "I suppose you'll insist on me coming back to 'elp you when the time comes."

"Why not?" joined in Daisy. "Perhaps you'll marry your mystery man and bring him back with you — we could find you a cottage."

Kate made no reply.

Daisy was to occupy the room Simon had decorated for her, with Simon in his own bedroom and Kate had one of the spare rooms. The house was quite large for what Simon called a cottage, there being six bedrooms in all.

That following day Simon told them of his plans. He intended turning his ten acres into a market garden. "I want to grow vegetables that I can sell at the markets."

"But surely, that'll be hard work," protested Daisy, and you've no need to wear yourself out any more."

Simon was reassuring. "I've always worked hard, darling. I can't sit around doing nothing and I'll hire staff to help me. What I make from the properties in London will pay their wages until the business gets under way. I hear there's more land for sale hereabouts and if anything suitable comes up, I'll expand."

"Will you only grow veg?" asked Kate.

"I thought about flowers but people hereabouts grow them in their gardens. What do you think?"

"Nothing to do with me, Mr Simon, but with the railways opening up all over the place, you could send them down to London."

Simon was impressed. "Now that's an excellent idea, Kate. What d'you reckon, Daisy?"

"I was thinking about fruit myself. We could have an orchard."

"We already have a few fruit trees but that's another good idea. I could plant some more."

He spent the rest of the afternoon and evening with a pencil and paper making notes.

At last Daisy's wedding day arrived and she threw the window open wide, breathing in the fresh sea air. Having washed her hair she rinsed it with lavender water, leaving it to dry and curl naturally. She donned her new underwear and wore a robe until she was ready to go to church. Although Daisy and Simon had spent the pre-nuptial period at the house chaperoned by Kate, Simon had spent the night before the wedding at the inn at Hunstanton.

The day proved to be bright with the full glory of the Norfolk skies enveloping the fens where reeds rippled in the breeze. Daisy inhaled deeply through the open window again, not quite believing she was to be married at last, and a little frightened her good fortune would disappear. For her the morning passed in a dream, bringing with it Phoebe, whose smallest child was to be Daisy's flower girl. Jimmy was taking the boys straight to church.

The friends embraced and although no words were spoken, they guessed each other's thoughts. They were like sisters who shared secrets and knew each other's minds, because they'd lived through so much together.

Kate looked after little Clarice whilst Phoebe helped Daisy dress, admiring the decorations in her pretty bedroom. Kate knocked on the door with a tot of brandy for each of them — "it'll help yer nerves," she assured them

The girls sat on the bed and sipped their brandy slowly and spoke of the past, each wondering that the years had passed so quickly.

"To think we both found a husband after all," said Pheobe with tears in her eyes. "Remember that dreadful day when we saw the Earl in the woods — no, let's not remember it," she giggled.

Daisy rested her glass against Pheobe's. "Thank you for being the best friend a girl could have," she sniffed, and they vowed never to lose touch.

Then the bride stood up and tied the ribbons of her new bonnet under her chin. She took her bouquet of spring flowers from Phoebe saying simply, "That's it. I'm ready."

They kissed, and went down to the waiting carriage where Kate chided Clarice for wriggling.

"You'll crease your lovely dress," she said, moving her aside so as not to mark the bride's gown. The drive to the church seemed endless but at last the carriage stopped and Daisy stepped down to walk along the flag-stoned path to the entrance. Her heart fluttered at the sound of the organ and her legs began to tremble at the enormity of the step she was taking.

Then, waiting for her at the front of the church, she saw Simon and her tremors ceased. He had his back to her and looked so fine in his new clothes, she wanted to cry. He stood proudly before the altar waiting to claim her as his bride, this man to whom she owed her life and would never cease to love.

She walked slowly down the aisle on Jimmy Fawcett's arm and when Simon turned to greet her, she held out her hand. They were married in the name of God and Daisy Smith became Daisy Danbury, wife of Simon.

After the ceremony the congregation repaired to the church hall where the wedding feast was spread over several tables. The guests congratulated them and were invited to eat from the vast selection of food on offer. There was cider and porter to drink, with wine for the more discerning, and the atmosphere became lively as people relaxed.

Daisy moved among her guests, making sure Mildred and the Foxes were fed and included in the jollity. When the three-piece band arrived people began to dance and Daisy felt a tap on the shoulder. It was Simon who'd come for the first dance and they jigged around the floor as they had done at Lord and Lady Fox's wedding.

"We seem to have been here before," laughed Simon as he brought Daisy to rest. "It was when I fell in love with you."

"Really," said his bride. "Sadly, I didn't realise I loved you until a lot later."

"So long as you'll love me forever, I really don't mind."

He looked into her eyes. "How soon do you think we can slip

away?"

"I think we should stay for at least an hour but I'll have a word with Phoebe. The Foxes won't stay for long."

"I dare say the children will become fractious soon, but at least they'll have Kate to help them."

Daisy smiled coquettishly, "It was kind of them to put her up so we can have the cottage to ourselves."

Simon squeezed her hand. "Very well, we'll be off as soon as we can. I'm leaving one of my men in charge of the clearing up."

True to her word, just an hour later Daisy threw her bouquet into the crowd of well-wishers and she and Simon drove back to the cottage in his new pony and trap. As the horse clip-clopped along the lanes, Daisy's smile became broader. She was now a married woman and at last Simon could claim her body. He took his time tethering and stabling the horse, before he picked her up and carried her over the threshold. Untying her bonnet, he kissed her thoroughly before carrying her upstairs to his room.

"You'll always have your own bedroom but I shall expect to be invited in often," he laughed as he laid her on the eiderdown.

The wine had made Daisy light-headed and the touch of Simon's hands on her naked flesh as he unbuttoned her bodice encouraged her to melt into his arms. At last she knew what love was, realising it was the giving of the soul.

She wanted nothing more than to be united with her husband, so without pretentious modesty, helped him remove her clothes. Words were superfluous as she was overwhelmed by desire and gave herself to him completely.

It was still early evening when they sat on the settle before the kitchen fire wrapped in blankets. Lamps flickered on the mantle-piece, their pink shades throwing a rosy glow where the light fell. Even the blue and white china on the dresser took on a different hue in the artificial light. Daisy looked with pride at the new range Simon had installed especially for her homecoming. She was indeed a lucky young woman and wanted nothing but to show her gratitude and love.

She turned, putting her arms round Simon's waist before laying her head on his chest. The blankets dropped to the floor as Simon gently lowered her onto the lamb's-wool rug, its softness inviting, as if made solely for the purpose of lovemaking. She would never forget the scent of pine logs as their naked bodies entwined, silhouetted against the blue and orange flames.

They marvelled at the depth of their feelings and laughing with joy, made cups of cocoa to take up to Daisy's room.

In bed, they huddled together like children, eating large slabs of cake while they planned their future. At last, tired from the day's events, they needed to sleep, but not before they confirmed their love one more time.

As Daisy watched Simon dress in the morning she was overwhelmed by her feelings for her husband who was twenty-one years her senior. His age didn't matter to her; she remembered his wisdom and his generosity when she needed help, so how could she fail to be devoted to him. She loved his slight Norfolk burr, she loved his strength, but most of all she loved the tenderness he'd shown her on their bridal night.

They didn't leave the cottage for a week, loving and laughing, happy just to be together. They walked in the garden holding hands, and made love whenever overcome by desire, be it by the stream or under the massive oak trees that bordered their land.

Such happiness had to end, and on Saturday the postman brought the mail. There was a letter from Vi confirming Honesty had agreed to run Daisy's Dresses but her present employers were unwilling to let her go until the end of May — two months away.

"Oh dear, what shall I do?" wailed Daisy as she handed the letter to Simon.

His expression grew grim as he read it. "I don't see as there's much you can do, darling, but go back to London and meet your obligations."

"But I don't want to go. I prefer to stay with you. We've only just been married and I'll miss you. "

"Spoken like a child, Daisy Danbury. I feel the same way but let me ponder on it a bit, to see if I can find another solution."

Daisy's mood darkened as she swept and dusted her house. She took much pleasure in keeping it bright and clean and couldn't bear to leave. She still found it hard to believe her good fortune and feared it might vanish should she go back to London. She was taking a pie from the oven when Simon came home. While he washed his hands she dished up their evening meal.

"Well," he said, cutting into the pastry before sniffing appreciatively. "I've been talking with some of the men I had in mind to work for me. There's one chap in particular, Robin Oakley, who I'm making my manager and he says we need to get the fields ploughed right away if we're to start growing crops this year."

"You'll be busy then?"

"I will, and a sight too busy to miss you." He laughed. "I'm only teasing. But it's true I shall be busy for the next few weeks. I need to get some stabling built for the horses, and we'll be hiring animals and implements for the present, but I want to have my own equipment by next year. I intend looking into this new steam powered apparatus; they say it makes work much lighter. And poor old Clip deserves better quarters than that old shed."

"You spoil that horse, Simon. I think you're more fond of it than me."

Simon sensed her mood and put his fork down.

"You must grow up, Daisy. You have obligations in London — I know you don't want to go back alone but you can't let Vi down when she's been so good to you. I've thought and worried because I don't want to be parted from *you*, either.

"But, I can see no other way than you must return for a couple of months. I shall miss you every bit as much as you'll miss me, but I'd be out of the house a lot anyway. Cheer up. I'll come to London as often as I can, we've still got the flat."

Daisy brightened at this. "You'll come down to see me? That makes me feel a bit better. I was thinking I'd have to come up here and since the shop only closes on Sundays, I'd never make it."

He beckoned to her to sit on his lap and stroked her hair. "You'll see. It'll work out all right. I'm not tied to a rigid routine. As soon as I see Robin Oakley's got things under control, I'll be free to visit, and it's only for a couple of months."

"When I think of poor old Phoebe, she got married in June and had to stay in London for six whole months before being properly married. I'm being silly, of course. The time will soon pass."

So it was resolved. Simon would drive Daisy to Hunstanton Station the next morning. She spent the rest of the day packing and baking, determined to leave plenty of food in the pantry. As she lay in his arms that night, she wondered how she'd manage when she was away from him, before realising she'd coped perfectly well in the past.

The following day, Simon saw her comfortably settled in a first class carriage and having made their tender farewells, Daisy's spirits lifted as the train approached London.

No matter how much she loved the countryside, the place where she was born would always hold a special place in her heart.

Much later, it seemed strange to be back in the little flat above the shop, the rooms appearing neglected and lifeless. She soon improved on that by lighting a fire in the grate and flicking over the furniture with a duster. Later, she collected the books from downstairs and went through the accounts, checking them in detail. It appeared Maud had done an admirable job with the ledgers and she must remember to congratulate her in the morning, but it was worrying that the order book looked so sparse.

Daisy thought about this as she made a sandwich before going to bed. Maud was an excellent seamstress and had done well with the figures but lacked the presence needed to maintain custom. She'd have a word with Vi the next day.

Tired out by the day's events, she went to bed early and missed Simon being close to her but she was exhausted from the journey, and soon fell asleep.

Having welcomed Maud the following day, Daisy went to Goodbody Gowns. "You're back," said a delighted Vi when she saw her. "Come along upstairs, I'll make us some coffee."

Having got the preliminaries out of the way, Daisy came to the point.

"I came down from Hunstanton yesterday," she began. "I went over the books last night and am a bit concerned about the lack of orders."

Vi was pensive. "I'm finding it quite hard to supervise both shops. Goodbody is doing as well as ever, but Daisy's Designs seems to have hit the doldrums a bit. I'm not sure why but I've a feeling that, good as Maud is, she doesn't appeal to the young."

"I get that impression too. She's very nice but rather dowdy and we need somebody with a better appearance and more personality. I'd like to keep her in the shop but I'll watch her over the next few days to see how she reacts to customers."

"I think that's a good idea. Things will change when Honesty takes over, obviously. By the way I'm cooking dinner for her on Wednesday, why don't you join us?"

It was agreed, and Daisy left to return to her own shop, anxious to get back to work. She stayed downstairs and re-arranged the window where the same two outfits were still on display as when she'd left. She explained to Maud they must keep the window interesting and set about sketching a ball gown to be made up in peach satin. Looking through the latest fashion magazines she created a simple cotton day dress with a narrow collar and a three-quarter length hooded cloak to be made of fine wool. Lastly she sketched a child's party dress, hoping the latter would catch the attention of young mothers.

The following morning she closed the shop so that she and Maud could catch the bus to Petticoat Lane where they were immediately caught up in the flamboyant atmosphere of the market. In contrast to the dirt and rubbish beneath their feet, glamorous materials were for sale almost everywhere, some from stalls and some from shops. Roll upon roll of satins and silks were inside the shops owned by canny merchants and

Daisy, having conferred with Maud, was able to purchase what she needed.

When they got back to the shop she chatted with Maud. "I intend making patterns tonight, and if I can start cutting tomorrow, we can all begin stitching. I plan to use the same child's pattern as I used for my little Lady Adelaide. You wouldn't have seen her, but this is the dress."

Daisy referred to her sketch book and showed Maud how she planned to drape the material, hoping to engender some enthusiasm, but met with little response.

When she went to dine with Vi on Wednesday, she was able to report progress. The child's dress should be in the window by tomorrow and the others would follow later.

"The shop lacks inspiration, that's the problem," she explained to Vi as they waited for Honesty. "Maud hasn't been able to bring her personality to the business but perhaps that's unfair since she's not been in charge for long."

She was worried about meeting Honesty, fearing she'd be very masculine but in the event she found her charming. She was pale as a lily with fair skin and light blonde hair drawn into a chignon. Daisy was fascinated by her china blue eyes that shone with candour when she spoke.

"I'm looking forward to working in your shop. I only wish I was able to start sooner."

Daisy took the opportunity to explain her views. "Although I've only been away for a few weeks I've seen it through fresh eyes. The presentation has become dowdy and I expect Vi's explained about Maud. She's a very good worker but I've been watching her and she can't cope with upper-class arrogance."

Honesty grinned. "We get very aristocratic customers at Hyde Park and it's fatal to let them intimidate you. I always offer gentle advice when I think they're choosing the wrong cut or colour. It's a matter of handling them properly."

At the end of the evening Daisy was satisfied her shop would be in safe hands.

Chapter 25

When she went up to her rooms Daisy put the kettle on, and while she waited for the water to boil, pondered about Vi and Honesty. Had she not known about their relationship, she'd never have noticed anything untoward in their behaviour. But now she'd been made aware of lesbianism, the subject intrigued her. Why wasn't a beautiful woman such as Honesty interested in men? She didn't understand. Did they kiss like she and Simon kissed? How odd. Although she still liked Vi and considered her a friend, she was aware of a subtle change in her feelings towards her, and she couldn't understand why. She made a mental note to discuss the subject with Phoebe at the next opportunity.

The next day Daisy lined the floor of the shop window with a length of green brocade bought during the excursion to Petticoat Lane. It was the perfect foil for the newly stitched confection of white voile that would enchant any child. She spent the rest of the day working with Maud on the other new designs, with the finisher stitching the trimmings.

Daisy knew her instinct had been right in changing the display. Nannies taking their charges out for a walk idled as they looked into the window, as did young mothers. Enquiries were made and orders received so when the last of the new designs went on show Daisy felt more optimistic. After the rush and when she was in her rooms during the evening, she felt very lonely, her thoughts being constantly with Simon. She longed to be with him and began to make excuses to go back to Hunstanton, hating the time they were forced to spend apart.

However, he walked into the shop a few days later and, delighted, Daisy ran into his arms. Proudly she introduced him to her staff before he whisked her upstairs to be thoroughly kissed and cuddled. Things were going well in Norfolk, he told her, the fields were being ploughed that very minute and work had begun on the stables. He'd brought plans and documents with him so that he'd be occupied when Daisy was working. Her busy schedule didn't prevent her from frequently running up the stairs to make him drinks and confirm he *really* was back with her.

After they made love that night he held her from him.

"You've changed, Daisy Danbury. You're softer. You've become a woman — my lovely little woman."

"In what way have I changed?" asked Daisy coquettishly.

"Oh, I don't know — you've matured, I suppose. The change is subtle but whatever it is, I like it." She snuggled into his arms and fell asleep in the certain knowledge she was loved.

Thus the pattern of their life was established whilst Daisy was in London, with Simon visiting as often as he was able. Daisy missed him dreadfully when he went home and sometimes cried when the shop was closed. She was lonely for him and welcomed the occasional visit from Kate.

"When do you plan to bring your man to see me?" Daisy chided as they shared supper one evening.

Kate had brought in fish and chips and the delicious smell permeated throughout the rooms. Having liberally applied vinegar and salt they tackled the food with relish. Kate emphasised her words with her knife as she spoke.

"He's not my man, nor ever will be."

"Why's that?"

The older woman had the grace to blush. "He's already spoken for."

Daisy raised her eyebrows and admonished Kate.

"That can't be right, Kate. You mustn't steal somebody's husband. I'm surprised at you."

"It's not 'is wife, Daisy. It's his mother. Right old termagant she is by all accounts. He 'as to do everything she tells him or she acts up very nasty."

"She sounds awful but why does he put up with it – can't he leave?"

"He's too nice, that's his problem and I think she *is* quite poorly, even though she makes the most of it."

"How on earth did you come to meet him, if she's that possessive?"

"Comes into the shop, 'e does. Buys her snuff for 'er and a bit o' baccy for 'imself. Poor devil."

"This is the man who looked after the shop for you when you came to our wedding?"

"That's him." She chewed on her food, deep in thought, and added, "She let him do that on account of me paying him to do it, and he bought her a new scrubbing board with the wages I gave him."

Daisy nodded approvingly although she didn't really understand why a grown man couldn't stand up to his mother.

"If you married, couldn't you go to live with them?"

Kate was horrified. "No indeed I couldn't. I've been me own boss all these years and I'm not kowtowing to the likes of her. There's nothing in it. No physical relations, like. We're only friends."

"Sometimes that's the best way to be. Simon and I were friends long before we fell in love."

But Kate wasn't to be mollified. "But, we're not young. I'd like him to leave the old trout but he won't."

"Then he must be a good man," Daisy replied as she began clearing the dishes. "You can't expect him to leave her when she's so old and I've heard tell you should judge a man by the way he treats his mother."

"I suppose," sniffed Kate. "I'll just have to 'ope she turns up 'er toes sooner than later."

"Whatever you decide, don't forget you can always come to us at Hunstanton. Simon said he'll find a cottage for you. What's his name, this man you think so much of?"

"Ernest. Ernest Billings."

"You'll think about what I've said, wont you?."

It wasn't long after Kate's visit that Daisy and Maud made another excursion to Petticoat Lane and Whitechapel. Whereas they normally ordered cloth from the wholesaler, Daisy had started buying in speciality material from the Jews as they had a fine eye for exotic fabrics; the girls spent a happy morning selecting unusual cloths.

Today, having finished their shopping they were going to catch the bus home when suddenly Daisy felt sick. She groaned as her legs weakened and her head began to spin. Sinking to the cobblestones, her last thought before losing consciousness, was of her money purse which was tucked safely around her waist.

When she felt less dizzy, she allowed herself to be helped up by Maud and a girl who'd been passing by.

"Thank you," said Daisy feebly as she rose to her feet. "I can't think what happened, I never faint."

"Well, Mrs," interjected the girl. "P'raps it'll be a boy. Me mum, always said if you faint, it's a boy."

Daisy was puzzled. "I don't understand."

The girl grinned. "The baby! You're in the family way, ain't yer?"

In a flash Daisy realised she was probably right. The depression, her breasts were tender and yes, she hadn't paid much attention to her missed monthly flow, thinking it was due to the excitement of getting married. A smile began to form at the corners of her mouth, she was going to have a baby! A child of her very own to hold and kiss and to nurture, but best of all, Simon was its father. The infant would know security and be loved by both parents. Simon would be thrilled. She gathered her thoughts and looked around her.

She looked at Maud who stood with the packages in her arms, embarrassed at the turn the conversation had taken. But Daisy ignored her and said to the girl, "I think you're right and that I *am* expecting a child. You've been very kind. Is there somewhere we can buy a cup of tea? I'd like to sit down for a while."

"Course," said the girl, taking Daisy's arm and leading her to a coffee stall. "Me name's Lily. I'll see you're okay."

The girls sat down on a makeshift bench provided by the vendor and although the heat from his open fire didn't help with her nausea, Daisy asked Maud to order coffee and Banbury cakes which Lily bit into hungrily. Daisy pretended to nibble at a cake while she looked Lily over, taking note of the shabby boots and clothes.

"I can't thank you enough," she began, "Is there any way I can repay you?"

"Nah, you added some excitement to me day. What was you two doing down this way?" asked Lily. "I never seen you 'ere before."

"We were looking for material," explained Daisy. "We're dressmakers and discovered the joys of Petticoat Lane a long time ago."

Lily was a chatty little thing. "Did you find what you wanted?"

"Oh yes. Several lengths in fact. They're being delivered tomorrow. Do take another cake?"

Lily didn't hesitate and took another one that she stuffed into her mouth, and ate with gusto. Poor little thing, she's obviously hungry, thought Daisy.

"Do you live near here?" she asked.

"Just up the alley. I live with Mrs Brady, she's not me mother, but she took me in."

"Took you in? I see. Have you no family of your own?"

"Nah. Me mum and dad died in the work'ouse along with me sisters and brothers. They got this sickness. Swept through the work'ouse like an 'ouse on fire so it seems. I was lucky 'cos being older I was strong."

Maud pretended to sip her coffee but Daisy could see she didn't approve of Lily. She had no such pretensions though, and said, "I thought it was difficult to get out of the workhouse. How did you manage it?"

"The City Mission lady what used to come in to visit, said she'd try to get me put out with someone who needed a bit of 'elp and some company. I got put with Mrs Brady, she's a kind woman wiv no kids of her own She's nice. I like 'er. I went to school for a bit in the work'ouse but not reg'lar, like."

"Do you work?"

"Nah. I'm trying to get into the sweatshops 'cos I'm good at sewing but it's 'ard to find work and Mrs Brady's against it 'cos she says I'll get all twisted up in there. It's sitting down all day long, see, with yer legs crossed."

Daisy took off her bonnet so she could straighten her hair.

"I see you got red 'air, an' all," remarked Lily as she looked at Daisy's freshly washed curls. "Mine's curly when it's been washed. Nuisance ain't it?"

Daisy commiserated. "It certainly is. Mine flies all over the place and I hate the colour."

"I know," said Lily, helping herself to yet another cake. "I'm always getting called Ginger Nut or Carrot Top but Mrs Brady says I'm lucky, she'd likes red hair and wishes hers was curly."

When she felt better, Daisy stood up and Maud picked up the packages, making her distaste for Lily obvious by ignoring her.

Daisy held out her hand. "Thank you for helping me, Lily. I'll look out for you when I'm this way again and perhaps we can have more coffee together."

"Thanks, Mrs," the girl answered and she looked about her wistfully. "I don't usually use the coffee stalls."

Daisy thanked her once more then she and Maud went to catch the bus, with thoughts of Lily receding as Daisy hugged her secret to her bosom. So she was with child, she was sure of it. As the bus rocked to and fro she felt like retching but extracted a promise from Maud not to reveal her condition to anybody.

She waited each day for her stomach to swell, disappointed when her figure appeared to remain the same. Perhaps she was wrong; but she *felt* different, she *knew* she had a baby growing inside her. Her thoughts went to her first baby — the one that never knew life, but she assured herself it lived happily in heaven, and she would have better luck this time.

She longed for Simon but he didn't appear the following week although later a letter arrived, telling her he was very busy with the smallholding. He'd make it to London as soon as he possibly could.

When Daisy went to bed she thought about Lily and the coincidence that she had red hair. How wonderful it would be if she were her long lost sister. She could be, she seemed about the right age, but she dismissed the idea as a romantic notion. That night, she tossed and turned worrying about Kate and her man friend, wondering how their situation could be resolved. Then there was Vi with her lady friend, life could become very complicated.

She woke up the next morning feeling nauseous again and weak. When she eventually felt strong enough to creep downstairs, the girls commented on it, and enquired if she was unwell. Unable to stand at her easel since she felt a little giddy, she sat at the counter with a drawing book on her lap. She was relieved when the bell tinkled, heralding Avril Henshaw.

200

"Daisy," she said tentatively, "I thought you were in Norfolk. I went next door to buy a hat and Celine mentioned it. You got married, didn't you?"

"I did. It's so good to see you. I married Simon who's been a friend for years."

"What are you doing back here?"

"Come upstairs," said Daisy. "It's a long story."

She was glad of Avril's company and they chatted about old times.

"Dad's going to retire soon and we're moving to a suburb. I don't know where yet, but the good news is that I have a job!"

Daisy was surprised, Avril's parents didn't approve of working women, she remembered. "How on earth did you get your parents to agree?"

"It was down to Veronica, really. She told us about this old uncle of hers who's opening a bookshop in the Charing Cross Road." Her brown eyes shone. "The parents thought I'd be safe with somebody they knew, however vaguely, so I'm going to become a bookseller."

Daisy poured more tea and told her how delighted she was.

"But where will you live?"

"I shall be able to come into town on the train now the railways are improving. Papa says he'll take a house in an area where there's a station. But I haven't told you the rest and you're to promise not to breathe a word."

"Of course not, silly."

"Well, I met the uncle and it transpired he's not as old as Veronica described him. He's in his forties and we've fallen in love!"

Daisy kissed her friend. "Why that's wonderful news. My Simon is twenty-one years older than me but I wouldn't change him for the world. "And guess what?" she broke her vow that Simon would be the first to know.

"I'm sure I'm expecting a baby." She described her symptoms.

"Oh, it sounds as if you are to me. You seem to have all the signs. How do you feel?"

"A little better now but I've been sick in the mornings and I get giddy sometimes."

"Your husband will be thrilled. When do you expect to see him?"

"I'm not sure. He wrote that he's very busy." She explained about the smallholding. "But he'll be here very soon, I'm sure. I can't wait to tell him."

Before Avril rose, Daisy asked," Did you come in for anything in particular?"

"Yes. I wanted a couple of outfits to start work in, and who knows, I may need something special for my wedding."

They giggled as they went downstairs but when they entered the salon, Daisy became professional and offered advice on style and fabrics.

Custom grew again and she was busy for the next couple of weeks. Having put the new designs in the window she offered the original ones at a reduced price.

Then one day Simon arrived with a huge bunch of flowers and a dozen eggs from home. He had, he told her, installed some hens at the far side of the yard.

"That's wonderful, Darling," she said as she hugged him. "I hoped we could keep a couple of ducks too. I do like ducks."

"You can have anything you want as long as you come home soon," he murmured into her hair. That evening they ate in a small pie shop that had recently opened just round the corner. Simon had hot eels in a parsley sauce with mashed potatoes, and Daisy picked at a pie. They didn't linger, anxious to get back to the flat and bed.

"I don't know if I can stand this separation for much longer," groaned Simon as he took her into his arms."

Daisy snuggled up to him. "I miss you so much. I hate being away from you but it's only for a few more weeks."

Having made love they slept soundly and Daisy was reluctant to get up the following morning.

Simon tried to hold her back. "You're surely not going down to the shop, are you?"

"I certainly don't want to, but I must. You know that. You must have brought some bookwork with you?"

He kissed her hand. "Come up to see me often then," he conceded, "like a dutiful wife."

"I shall. I'll not be downstairs a moment longer than necessary and I've been thinking. I'll pop out for some faggots and peas pudding tonight. You like saveloys, don't you? I want dinner to be special because I've something to tell you."

The day passed slowly with Simon working on plans and figures and Daisy working in the shop but at last she was able to run to the cook shop.

Anxious to look pretty when she broke the news, she changed her dress and piled her hair on top of her head, leaving a few tendrils escaping to frame her face. Simon caught his breath when she came out of the bedroom.

"You look ravishing, my sweet," he said as he kissed her on the cheek.

"And you, Sir," she replied, "Always look very handsome."

She laid the plates on the table and poured Simon a sherry and at last they sat down to eat.

"Go along then," said Simon, prodding his fork into peas pudding. "What's all this news?"

Daisy didn't know which piece of news to tell Simon first. She wanted to share her excitement about the baby but decided to leave it until last. She couldn't wait for him to take her in his arms and tell her what a clever girl she was, and how a child would make their lives complete. Although the temptation to talk about the baby was great, she told him first about her trips to Petticoat Lane.

"I've two things to tell, as a matter of fact. Firstly, a strange thing happened to me a couple of weeks ago. I've taken to going to a market called Petticoat Lane. It's near Aldgate and there are some wonderful shops selling all sorts of materials — I rummage around and find some unusual cloths for the shops. I pick up lengths of material I think might be useful for Vi while I'm there."

"I've heard a bit about London markets, darling — are you sure it's a safe place for you to go?"

"It's certainly seedy, with its run-down buildings and dirty streets. Being a market it's littered with rubbish from the stalls and they say pick-pockets abound. . ."

Simon was alarmed. "Oh dear — it hardly sounds a suitable place for a young woman?"

Daisy brushed his fears away with a smile. "I take Maud with me, she helps to carry the parcels, and we're very aware of the dangers. We never, ever go into the side streets although some of the stalls look tempting."

"Perhaps you've just been lucky, my dear and I'd really prefer it if you'd find somewhere else to shop."

"I'll think about it. Anyway, when we were there a couple of months ago, I felt a little faint and a girl helped Maud get me to a coffee stall. The girl was, well, badly spoken and certainly, poorly educated but very sweet to me and while I was recovering she commented on the colour of my hair. It was the same as hers, you see."

"Go on," said Simon as he poured some more sherry into his glass. "This is very tasty," he interrupted as Daisy continued to speak. She waited until she had his attention again before continuing.

"I didn't think much about it at the time because I felt unwell, but since being in my rooms on my own, I've had time to go over our conversation. Her name was Lily and my smallest sister was called

Lily." She looked over at Simon to see if he was listening. "Don't you think that's strange?"

"Not really, there must be lots of red haired girls with that name, it's very popular. But do go on."

"Then she told me her family had died in the workhouse."

"I see what you're implying — you think she might be your sister?"

"I did wonder. I understand most families perish in the workhouse. It just seems a strange coincidence, that's all."

"I agree. And I don't know how you'd ever prove she *is* your sister, even if you think she might be."

"But would I need to prove it, if it felt right?"

Simon shrugged and a doubtful expression crossed his face. "Didn't you question her further? Perhaps ask how many brothers and sisters she had and their names. That might have proved it one way or another."

'If only I'd had the foresight to do that. The trouble is I was feeling a little faint and couldn't collect my thoughts."

"Perhaps you'll run into her again. Then you'll be prepared. Do you think you might?"

Daisy was delighted he seemed to be encouraging her. "I think so."

There was a lull in the conversation as they concentrated on their food for a while until Simon broke the silence.

"I didn't realise I was so hungry. These faggots are nice, very tasty indeed — and the other piece of news?"

Daisy couldn't suppress a smile. "Guess what?"

"Really, Daisy, I can't guess. You look like the cat that got the cream. What's happened? Has Queen Victoria herself asked you to make her a gown?"

"Don't be silly." Her smile grew wider as she put down her fork and looked into his eyes. "*You*. . . are going to be a father?"

His reaction wasn't what she expected as he replied sharply, "A father. Are you sure?"

Chapter 26

Daisy's smile became hesitant as his brow creased but she replied, "Pretty certain. Yes."

"I see."

"Well, aren't you going to say something?"

He didn't reply but picked at his food. It was as if she hadn't spoken and he certainly didn't want to listen.

Nonplussed, she ventured, "Simon, you and I have made a child, did you hear me?"

"Of course, I heard you. I'm sorry if I'm not getting excited but the news is unexpected."

Daisy shook her head with disappointment and said miserably, "I can't see why you're surprised."

"I know I said I wanted a family but the timing is inconvenient, what with the new business and all. It's a lot to take in but I expect I'll come to terms with it."

"Inconvenient? Babies come when they're ready and you haven't even asked how I'm feeling!"

Simon was immediately contrite. "I'm so sorry — I'm being selfish. Are you keeping well?"

"I suppose so," she replied miserably. "Excepting for feeling sick in the morning."

"Poor you, you must take care of yourself."

He refused the current pie she'd bought for dessert, although it was a favourite, and spent the rest of the evening making forced conversation. No tears of joy, no plans for the nursery, nothing.

News of a baby obviously hadn't been good news to him and Daisy fretted as she cleared away the remains of their meal. She didn't understand but knew from the sombre look on his face, he didn't want to discuss the subject. What could be wrong?

Simon had always made a great fuss of Phoebe's brood and although they'd never discussed the subject of children specifically, he'd made references to having a family. There must be something else. Perhaps she'd been wrong to assume he wanted a son. He was too kind to hurt her like this deliberately — didn't he realise?

The evening wore on with Simon burying his head in his books and Daisy trying to cover her hurt feelings, but he slept with his back to her that night. She put her arms around him in the hope he'd turn to her, but he didn't, so she cried herself to sleep not knowing what she'd said to upset him. She'd never seen him like this before and was bewildered at his withdrawal.

At last she fell asleep and woke soon after dawn to find him dressed. He handed her a cup of tea and announced his intention of going back to Norfolk. He looked very handsome in his county dress with fashionable peg top trousers, and Daisy yearned for him to take her in his arms. She needed to know what was amiss, indeed, what she'd done wrong.

But he'd countenance no more conversation and with an aggrieved look on his face, said, "There's much to be done, and I'd best get on with it."

Daisy was near to tears again. "But you've only been down here for two nights?" she stammered.

"That may be so. But now I need to return."

His eyes were pained and his voice cold. Daisy didn't understand. Surely he should be happy that she was with child? The baby was the result of their lovemaking, created by them in the depths of passion.

Her voice was accusing as she retaliated. "You don't want the child. You don't want *my* child. You don't want *our* child. You're a monster, Simon Danbury. I hate you." She threw herself into the pillows and sobbed, to no avail. She heard the catch on the door click, and he was gone.

She stayed in bed fretting and turning their conversation over in her mind, seeking clues as to his behaviour. Still confused, eventually she dressed and opened up the shop, advising the staff that she hadn't slept well and would remain upstairs for the day. She tried to recall every word that had been said, those that were harsh, some loving, coupled with every nuance, each smile and tender touch. Having reached no conclusion, bitterness filled her heart. Her husband was no better than the hapless Vernon Fenn, having abandoned her in the same manner. But this time there'd be no visit to a crone in a hovel. This time her child wouldn't perish, she'd bring it up, on her own, if necessary, and it would be loved.

Later she went down to the shop in order to take her mind away from the events of the previous evening. The girls looked at her curiously and spoke in muted tones, aware that something was wrong, but reluctant to ask. Mr Danbury had only stayed for two nights which was unusual, and their employer's step wasn't light as was customary when he came to London. Instead she seemed preoccupied.

By the next day Daisy's heart had hardened and she dressed in her prettiest gown and bonnet, summoned Maud to accompany her, and ventured out, making another trip to Petticoat Lane. With heavy heart, she helped Maud choose some fabrics and looked around for the girl with red hair but didn't see her again. They even loitered around the coffee stall but Lily wasn't there. It had been a coincidence, she thought, she'd been chasing a dream that would never come true. Resigned, she bought white flannel to begin making a layette in preparation for the arrival of the child.

Throughout the excursion Maud hardly spoke, except to give an opinion when they looked at what was for sale. Daisy sensed her resentment but failed to understand it, not understanding she had everything Maud wanted for herself — a husband, a business and now a baby. She reminded Daisy of Mildred in Norfolk, an embittered woman.

Daisy spent the following evenings making tiny garments for the baby, wondering whether it would be a boy like Simon, or a girl like her with red hair. The morning sickness had eased now, so having seen all was well with the shop, she took the bus to the West End and window shopped for a bassinette. Some of them were very large and she realised they'd be difficult to wheel through the shop door. The area was crowded with vendors and shoppers who had fractious children in tow, all jostling for space. She realised she was becoming fatigued but found a drapery that stocked cradles and other baby paraphernalia. Browsing at the most expensive on show, Daisy became determined her baby would have the best on offer. There would be no hand-me-downs and second hand articles as in the past.

It began to rain as she wandered through the thoroughfare, telling herself her child would want for nothing, before becoming aware it would have everything but a father. Tears mingled with the rain that dripped from the rim of her bonnet as she struggled to find the bus stop. Finally she hailed a passing cab and went home, to the rooms where she'd experienced so much joy; but now felt empty.

Each morning she waited for the post but Simon didn't write and neither did she. After a couple of weeks she drew a veil over the past, and wondered what to do about Honesty taking over management of the shop. She thought it through and came to the conclusion that she should still employ Honesty as manager, but carry on designing and with some of the stitching, which she enjoyed. She'd need help in the shop as she'd have a baby to look after, moreover a baby to support.

Her life wasn't easy. When she was alone she'd think of the cottage and all she'd planned to do when the weather improved, such as wash cushion covers and curtains, even sew seeds in a patch of the garden. She wondered if Simon had added ducks to their little menagerie as she'd asked, but concluded he wouldn't want to please her now, so dismissed him from her mind.

One evening, Daisy was about to make herself some supper when the doorbell rang. She held tightly on to the banister as she went downstairs, careful not to put her child in danger should she slip. The caller was Kate who'd brought a pie she'd baked.

"Daisy — thank goodness you're in! I haven't seen you for ages so I thought I'd best pop round. Is everything okay?"

"Yes," replied Daisy, her voice flat.

"Oh," said Kate a she slammed the door closed. "You sound a bit fed up, what's up?"

Daisy climbed the stairs with Kate panting after her. "I'm feeling a bit run down, that's all," she replied, as she put the kettle on to boil. She was aware of Kate's sharp eyes assessing her.

"Run down? That's not like you."

There was silence as Daisy retrieved the biscuit tin from the dresser. She put it on the table where it lay between them, an object on which to fix their attention.

"Seen Simon?" came the next question.

"He was down a couple of weeks ago."

"You're due to go back home at the beginning of June, aren't you? That's why I thought I'd better come round. That what's 'er name, Honesty starts then. Nothing wrong there? She's still comin'?"

Daisy sighed. "Yes. She'll be here," adding sharply, "why all these questions?"

Daisy flinched as Kate drew in her not inconsiderable chest and thrust her jaw forward.

"Are you going to tell me what's wrong, or do I have to guess, young woman."

Tears stung Daisy's eyes as she tried to say the words. "It's Simon — he doesn't love me any more."

Kate's mouth opened in astonishment. "Doesn't love you? Why, he adores you, child. And always has."

"No," wailed Daisy, her face creased in unhappiness, "not any more."

She began to cry and Kate led her to the couch, stroking and petting her until the sobs subsided.

"Now, now. Tell Kate all about it. You can trust me — you know that."

Daisy blew her nose but began wailing again, her voice reaching a crescendo as she blurted out, "I'm having a baby and he doesn't want it."

Kate rose and went to the sink to fill the kettle again, her expression nonplussed. "I find that hard to believe. You'd better tell me exactly what's 'appened while I make some fresh tea."

Daisy began by telling her about buying his favourite meal and making her special announcement, and Simon's reaction.

"He was so cold, Kate. He couldn't even look at me. What did he expect? We're married for heaven's sake and people have babies."

Kate nodded sympathetically but suddenly the worry lifted from her face.

"Oh, you poor girl. Don't you understand? He's afraid. He lost his first wife in childbirth and doesn't know how to cope. I might not be married Daisy Danbury but I know a lot more about men than you it seems."

"You mean he's afraid I'll die?"

"Of course. You don't stop loving somebody because they're having a baby. He'll be up there on that farm of his now, worrying and wondering what to say, having upset you. I know him. Soft as butter, is my Mr Simon. I always told you that."

"I'm not sure. He seemed so distant."

"If I was you, I'd try to feel better about him. Give it a day or two then write him a letter, perhaps. Tell him as how you don't intend to die and you understand his worries. But get in touch with 'im you must."

"I'm due to go up there for good in ten days time. I don't really want to go before then, it's a bit of a trek, what with the baby and everything."

"Are you keeping well?"

"I get a bit tired."

"Then write as if nothing's happened. Tell him how much you're looking forward to coming home again and — another good idea. Go to see a doctor and get yourself looked over. Then you can reassure him in the letter."

Suddenly, Daisy's mood lifted and she kissed Kate on the cheek.

"I do hope you eventually decide to settle in Hunstanton. I shall miss you."

Daisy felt much better after the visit from Kate. She regained much of her enthusiasm and began to update the books, making sure everything was in order for when Honesty took over. She made a final trip to Petticoat Lane with the vague hope of seeing Lily again but was unlucky, so decided there was not enough evidence to suggest the girl was long lost sister, and she must put the dream behind her.

Her final ten days in London passed quickly. She wanted to take Kate's advice and get looked over by a doctor but wasn't sure if there was one in the area, so she visited Vi who was able to recommend somebody.

"Honesty had some inside trouble and went to a good man in the West End, he deals with women's problems so he's the one you want. Honesty is coming to supper tonight — I'll get his name for you."

Three days later Daisy rang the bell of an address in Harley Street. The house was similar to the one in Bloomsbury but this time, she went in through the front door. The hallway was covered in black and white tiles so the nurse's footsteps rang out as she showed Daisy to the waiting room. She was nervous as she'd begun to worry lately that she'd been damaged during the abortion.

Daisy's heartbeat was listened to and she was examined internally. The doctor looked down her throat and after another few tests, she was declared fit and healthy plus three months pregnant.

She was confident that the assurance given to her by the doctor would set Simon's mind at rest and she hugged her secret to herself as she left Harley Street. She was perfectly well and the baby was due at the end of December. It would arrive some time near her twenty-first birthday, and all should be well.

Once more she put pen to paper.

"My darling Simon,
I hope everything is well at the cottage. I visited the doctor today. Everything is fine and the birth should be perfectly normal. I'd forgotten about Kirsty when I broke the news to you last time you were in London, which was a bit careless of me. I'm sorry. I was so happy and wanted you to be happy too. I've talked to Kate and she made me realise you might be worrying about me. Anyway, things are going to plan here and I shall be home very soon now, as promised. I can't wait to see you.
With all my love
Daisy

On her last Saturday in London, she had a long talk with Honesty and was happy to hand over the keys to the shop. Daisy left copious notes and lists and when she'd snapped the last lock on her suitcase, fell into bed and a dreamless sleep.

Sunday dawned bright when she took a cab to Shoreditch. She hired a porter to help with her bags, determined nothing should go wrong with her pregnancy. Fortunately, she was able to find a carriage which had a single female occupant who offered a smile of welcome and helped Daisy put her bags on the rack above the seats. Daisy's smile grew broader as she blew a kiss to London from the train as it steamed out of the station. She was going home, home to her Simon.

She hadn't warned him of the exact day of her arrival as she wanted to surprise him. The train was slow and her impatience grew as it stopped and started again, seemingly never to arrive. She ate from coffee stalls when making connections and was weary when she arrived at Hunstanton.

Fortunately there were a couple of cabs waiting to ferry passengers to their destinations and she was able to share with a married couple who were going in the same direction as she.

It was late afternoon and as the cab bowled through the countryside, Daisy was reminded of how fresh the air was, and how beautiful the scenery.

At last, she put her key in the lock and leaving her luggage under the porch, went inside the silent cottage. A cat, obviously a new addition to the household, was curled up on the hearthrug and she smiled, realising her child might have been conceived on that very spot. Humming to herself, she filled the kettle wondering where her husband was. Probably busying himself in the fields, she decided. Gazing through the window she smiled at the scene before her. Hens were strutting up and down on the far side of the yard, their heads bob-bobbing as they pecked at the ground. She looked beyond and saw there were ducks, four of them, clucking at a barking dog. In an instant, she knew it would be all right.

Then Simon came in view, and she watched as he threw a stick into the pond encouraging the dog to plunge into the water and retrieve it. The tea made, Daisy put the cosy on the teapot and went outside. She called, and when Simon looked up she could contain herself no longer. She ran into his outstretched arms, sobbing with relief. In turn, he kissed and hugged her, begging her forgiveness for his behaviour and vowing never to treat her badly again.

"It's all right," she whispered. "I understand. I really do — but nothing's going to happen to me Simon. I'll be okay — all three of us will."

That evening they talked and Simon told her of his misgivings.

"It was as if it was happening all over again when you told me you were expecting. I was completely taken by surprise, though goodness knows why." He laughed as he recalled their passionate lovemaking.

He grimaced suddenly. "I had visions of that long night with Kirsty screaming; and the doctor telling me there was nothing to be done. In the morning it was all over. I'd lost them both, and I'd want to die myself if I lost you too."

Daisy threw him a sympathetic smile. "I know. Kate told me." She took his hand. "That's all over Simon, and I'm sure that Kirsty would want you to make the most of the rest of your life. I'm another person. We must have faith."

"Oh, Daisy. Will you ever be convinced of how much I love you?"

"I have an idea and tonight you can prove it to me. And, I won't take no for an answer this time."

The rest of the summer proved to be golden. The orchard was thriving and young trees stretched their branches to the sun. Simon's business was developing and all was well. They now had two dogs as well as the cat and Daisy spent her days resting and sewing more clothes for the expected child.

Phoebe and Jimmy visited in October. They arrived with their children and stayed for three days, bringing more joy to Daisy's heart. When they left she wandered in the orchard with Simon. Her body was more rounded but in his eyes she'd gained in beauty, her eyes clear and bright, and her skin like peach blossom.

"I didn't know I could be this happy," she said, taking his hand.

"And neither did I," he said simply as they walked between the apple trees.

It was their first Christmas in the cottage and they spent it alone — making excuses not to accept invitations because of the imminent birth. Daisy was very heavy now but lumbered around the kitchen cooking Christmas lunch, with Simon preparing vegetables, just as he had in Aunty Millie's sweet shop. They toasted their absent friends while they ate, and then sat together quietly watching snow fall on the distant fields.

"I have a twenty-first birthday gift for you, I'll bring it down," Simon said, rising from his armchair.

He returned from upstairs with a velvet case containing a gold pendant on a chain. A circle of diamonds with a splendid sapphire at their centre, sparkled in the firelight.

"To match your eyes, darling" he said as he closed its clasp around Daisy's neck. She was overwhelmed by Simon's generosity and smiled sheepishly as she retrieved her gift to him from underneath a cushion — it was a night shirt she'd stitched for him herself. They laughed together as Simon reminded her she'd soon be giving him the most precious gift of all, a child. Then he gave his Christmas gift to her — a cape made from fox fur. Daisy wondered at her luck in meeting this lovely, generous man.

By evening, the snow was falling heavily and as Simon drew the curtains he became worried lest the cottage became isolated. His feet crunched over the crisp snow as he made his way to the woodshed to gather more logs, making sure of an adequate supply in an emergency. Daisy looked on anxiously, careful not to exert herself, praying for the weather to improve before they had to summon the midwife.

Luckily, it wasn't until January 3rd that Daisy felt her first labour pains. Simon hovered as each contraction rose and subsided, fretting for the safety of both his wife and child. He wiped Daisy's brow and held her as she cried out in pain, then when the time was right, he saddled Clip and galloped into town for the midwife.

There was nothing dramatic about Millicent Danbury's entry into the world. The birth was easy and within an hour of the arrival of the midwife, Daisy was sitting up in bed with an adoring husband beside her. She felt her heart would burst as she gazed at the healthy child asleep in the cradle her father had lovingly carved. Under the window stood a rattan rocking chair which he'd insisted was necessary for when Daisy nursed her daughter.

And when she was alone she wondered at her good luck, no shortage of money, a beautiful cottage, and a loving husband. From such humble beginnings, she now had so much, and smiled wryly at the thought of the modern coach-built perambulator that even The Countess wouldn't be ashamed of. It seemed greedy to hope for healthy sons, but wish it she did: for her husband.

Her reverie was broken by a shrill cry. Little Millie had strong lungs and was hungry, so like all mothers Daisy bent to her child's will. As the child fed contentedly Daisy recalled the past. She remembered how as a forlorn five-year-old she'd walked the streets of London with unshod feet, unaware of the danger and without realising there could be a better life. She was now entirely without ambition, and filled with sadness as she thought of her own mother trying to rear children under such terrible conditions.

Tears filled her eyes as Daisy remembered her first baby — gone on that terrible day on the moors. And finally she recalled her youngest sister, who could possibly be living in Aldgate. *She would discover the truth one day.*

How lucky she'd been with most of the people in her life as she'd developed from the child spurred on by the quest for survival, to the girl embittered by rejection from the man she thought she loved. She smiled wryly to herself as she recalled the young woman who became fiercely ambitious but eventually found happiness as a wife and mother. But she realised fate had smiled most kindly when she'd met the man she would spend the rest of her life with.

The End